JULIET THE MANIAC

JULIET
THE MANIAC
A NOVEL

JULIET ESCORIA

MELVILLE HOUSE
BROOKLYN · LONDON

Juliet the Maniac

Melville House Publishing
46 John Street
Brooklyn, NY 11201
and
Suite 2000
16/18 Woodford Road
London E7 0HA

mhpbooks.com
@melvillehouse

ISBN: 978-1-61219-759-3
ISBN: 978-1-61219-760-9 (eBook)

Designed by Richard Oriolo

Library of Congress Cataloging-in-Publication Data

Names: Escoria, Juliet, author.
Title: Juliet the maniac : a novel / Juliet Escoria.
Description: Brooklyn : Melville House, [2019].
Identifiers: LCCN 2018055371 (print) | LCCN 2018055784 (ebook) | ISBN
    9781612197609 (reflowable) | ISBN 9781612197593 (paperback)
Subjects: | BISAC: FICTION / Coming of Age. | FICTION / Literary.
Classification: LCC PS3605.S36 (ebook) | LCC PS3605.S36 J85 2019 (print) |
    DDC 813/.6--dc23
LC record available at https://lccn.loc.gov/2018055371

Printed in the United States of America

1 3 5 7 9 10 8 6 4 2

For Scott

"It is, in short, pointless to attempt to see into the heart of another while affecting to conceal one's own."

—JEAN-JACQUES ROUSSEAU, *CONFESSIONS*

"And I was a hand grenade that never stopped exploding."

—MARILYN MANSON, "MECHANICAL ANIMALS"

CONTENTS

PROLOGUE

It is hard to tease out the beginning. When I was living it, my dis-
integration seemed sudden, like I had once been whole but then my
reality swiftly slipped apart into sand. Not even sand, but slime,
something desperate and oozing and sick. But looking back—I was
a slow burn that eventually imploded.

My school was at the top of a hill, at the dead end of a street in a
quiet neighborhood full of million-dollar homes. The playground
overlooked the ocean. I was in sixth grade, and it was early spring,
after an El Niño winter, unusually cold and rainy. The first clear day
in weeks, the sunlight an odd metallic citrine from the moisture,
shifting in strange shadows. We'd just had P.E., capture the flag,
and we were young enough that I was still the fastest in the class,
faster than the boys, and I'd managed to slip out of Matt Irwin's

fingers to victory. I couldn't catch my breath. I turned away from my classmates to look out at the ocean, shimmering in the yellow light, and it was so beautiful I couldn't stand it. I felt a shift in my tectonics, a sensation like I might burst out of myself, a rupture in my chest leaking something hot and dirty like lava. My first awareness of the foreign thing. It felt electric and thrilling but I also knew it was something to hide.

So I swallowed it down. I willed myself silent and still. There was not something mutating inside of me. There was no growing evil. Everything is normal, I whispered to myself, over and over again until my breathing slowed and the sunlight smoothed into its usual ordinary color.

Maybe that was it. The first moment I felt the dark thing, acknowledged there was something invading my brain and body. That there was something sick inside of me. That soon would come a plague of bad thoughts, a chant in my brain saying: *I want to die. I want to die. I want to kill myself. I want to die.*

But that was also the year the rock star shot himself, so suicide was on everyone's mind. Heroin still seemed glamorous, celebrities still smoked, and the radio played songs filled with angst. At that point, maybe I was still a normal adolescent, with the normal pangs and problems that come with that age. Maybe there was not yet something actually wrong with me. I know for sure, though, that things had turned dark by the summer after eighth grade, so I will start there.

BOOK ONE

TWIN ETCHINGS

Nicole bought the switchblade when she went down to Tijuana with her mom and dad. They'd let her go off by herself as long as she was back when she'd promised. She pretended to go shopping for dresses but instead went to the nightclubs, where Mexican girls not much older than us blew whistles loud in her face, dumping cheap tequila down her throat. She pretended to swim but instead bought things you couldn't here, pills that made us sleepy but not high, and, of course, that switchblade. It looked exactly like a joke switchblade I'd had as a kid, one that was actually a comb. Same black and silver handle, same plastic switch, just as flimsy and cheap looking. But the blade was heavy, pale and cold like the moon.

She kept the switchblade in her makeup case, alongside the bright lipsticks she often put on but never wore. This was something we did a lot at her house—put on makeup. Everything Nicole owned was expensive: MAC eyeshadow, Clinique foundation, Dior powder, all purchased from Nordstrom or Saks. Nicole was a pro, blending powders on her eyelids and cheeks with gold-handled brushes until she looked like a doll. She plucked my eyebrows high and thin, drew an X across my cupid's bow before slicking on lipstick, lines smooth and everything perfectly symmetrical. When she finished, I looked just like Drew Barrymore or Clara Bow.

I didn't think anything when she took the switchblade out of her makeup case. We were listening to the Sex Pistols in her new room in her new house, big and empty because they'd just moved in. The music was as loud as it would go, fuzzing the speakers of her gigantic stereo, the wild and quick beat of my heart. She flicked the knife out, held it close to my throat and laughed. Her eyes flickered and she made a face like a crazy killer and I laughed too, nervous, feeling as though for a second she had turned from my best friend into a stranger.

"God, I'm so fat," she said, releasing me, looking at herself in the full-length mirror. She wasn't fat. Her arms were thin and her legs were lean but she did have just the smallest ripple of fat on her stomach. "I wish I could just cut this off," she said, switchblade hovering over her belly button. Her voice went soft, like she was saying it only to herself. "It makes me fucking hate myself."

I had told her she wasn't fat enough times before, so I said nothing. "Does it hurt?" she asked, pointing to my hip. A few days earlier, we'd gone swimming in her new pool, and as we were changing she saw the scabs, a triangle I'd cut there with a pocketknife, one night secretly in my bedroom. I'd started cutting myself years ago, before I even knew what it was, just this thing to relieve the pressure when I felt too mad or too happy, a letting out of the air. She was the first to notice, and it made me feel naked and embarrassed, the way her eyes had splayed wide. But I realized now that she wasn't disgusted, didn't think I was a freak, the way I had thought that day. To her, the cuts made me cool.

"No," I said. "Not if you do it right. If you do it too light, it stings, but if you go just a bit deeper, it feels good." I didn't tell her you had to be in the right mood, or that it always hurt the next day. She could think I was tougher than that, even though I wasn't, even though the whole reason I did it was because I was weak in the first place, a person who couldn't stand the simple act of being herself.

She took the point of the knife into her arm, and I watched her carve a line straight down. I didn't tell her to stop. I didn't tell her not to do it on her arm, not ever, but especially not during the summer, especially not a couple weeks before school began, this place on her body where anyone could see. So she drew two more lines, turning the first into an F. I watched her the whole time as she carefully carved each line, perfectly straight and even, like she had written it on paper.

The album ended and neither of us got up. She was almost done with the second T. She acted like it didn't hurt, didn't make any noises or faces, and with each line I felt something in myself softening, as though our secret thoughts were creeping out and curling together. This action done for me, to show me she was tough, to show me there was no difference between the two of us. When she was done, she held it up, an art project for me to admire, and I took my finger and smeared the blood in a straight line through the word, crossing it out. FATTY. The one and only thing she hated about herself—her body. I felt a heavy pull to lick her blood, taste its metallic hotness. Instead, I just wiped it on my pants, and later, I couldn't get it out in the laundry, this copper patch belonging to Nicole, staining my favorite jeans.

IN MY ROOM AT NIGHT

I liked to listen to the radio. Talk shows, the oldies. The voices made me feel less empty. Sometimes everything settled inside me too still. I would turn off the lights and burn candles instead, drawing for hours or painting my nails. Often I lay on my back, staring at the popcorn ceiling, looking for shapes the way people do with clouds. As my parents went to sleep and the night wore on, a thick smoke curled in from the corners. The smoke became faces, people, worlds. I looked at the crystal ball, and in it I saw the future. What I saw frightened me.

OTHER BAD THINGS WE LIKED TO DO

Nicole's neighborhood was construction sites and dirt lots, a new development for rich people who wanted custom houses and lots of land. Theirs was one of the first finished. We would tell her mom we'd be out riding bikes. I'd take Nicole's brother's, too small and neon orange, and we rode them to the construction sites. Once we got there, we hid the bikes, just in case her mom tried to find us.

The houses were in all stages of construction. Some were nothing more than beams, which were useless. Others were further along, encircled in catwalks and ladders. Those we climbed. The more the houses were finished, the better. Sometimes we scratched things on the walls with nails, started little fires with wood scraps.

One day Nicole's parents told us they were going to Orange County, to buy antique furniture and go to a party. They wouldn't be home until late. The only problem was we didn't have any alcohol or pot, not even cigarettes. In the liquor cabinet, there was just one bottle of expensive-looking whiskey and a few bottles of wine, all unopened. In the garage, there was a big 24-pack of Zima, mostly full. We figured we could drink two each.

Nicole filled her backpack with the Zimas, and we rode down to our new favorite house, which had everything finished except for the carpet and paint. The sun was pouring in the floor-to-ceiling windows, greenhouse hot. We could only stand it long enough for one Zima. We took the rest back home.

"Maybe we should look in your parents' closet," I suggested. Nicole didn't understand why I wanted to look in there, but she got excited as soon as we opened the doors. Even though they'd just moved in, the closet was perfect already—big fancy organizers holding all of Nicole's mom's shoes, her dad's ties and cuff links, tiny lights hidden throughout that switched on when you opened the door. There was a step stool that matched the shelves, the kind you might find in some rich person's private library. Nicole stood on it, grabbing a big leather bin on the top shelf, which she handed to me. I sat it on the ground. There were some scarves and a wooden box inside it. Inside the wooden box was a gun.

It looked fancy, cushioned by black velvet. Nicole told me it was an old police revolver. It was loaded. We decided to go behind her house and shoot at birds.

The whole time I was expecting the gun to go off by accident. Nothing happened. Nicole held the gun gingerly, her finger away from the trigger, the nozzle pointed away from us.

We got to a clearing in the brush. It was late afternoon and the shadows of the sagebrushes were long, fuzzy nests of spiderwebs in the branches. There were a couple birds out there, little brown sparrows, pecking the dirt. I thought we would talk about it first, that Nicole would show me how to shoot the gun. But she just cocked it, aimed, and pulled the trigger.

The shot rang out over the emptiness, so loud it made the brush quiver and my ears ring. She missed. The birds flew off. But it didn't matter. She looked so cool with it in her hand, feet spread wide, arms out, just like they do in the movies.

She handed me the gun, but told me I had to wait until some birds flew back because there were only six rounds in the chamber. I hadn't shot a gun before. It was heavy and cold. I held it in front of me like Nicole, in order to get the feel of it. I put my finger on the trigger. I felt dangerous, like Charlie's Angels.

We waited for the birds to come back. In between we sat on the sand and drank another Zima. When we finished, there were still no birds so we decided to move somewhere else. We walked around until we heard cooing in the bushes. "Shhh!" Nicole said, and we crept toward them. In a clearing, there were two doves with big bellies, and soft brown feathers and eyes.

They seemed so sweet and stupid, but I spread my feet apart, cocked the barrel, squinted until one of them was square in the middle of my sight. It seemed silly to aim at something so helpless. I pulled the trigger. The noise of the shot was so loud it throbbed in my skull.

I assumed I would miss.

I was wrong.

I could tell Nicole was saying something because her mouth was moving, but my ears were ringing too loud to hear, her face smudged into an inky thumbprint. I felt something sick creep through my bones, dark and thick and making me nauseous. It was growing.

I didn't want to look but it seemed like I had to, so I walked over to the bird. I kneeled over it, silently, like I was saying a prayer. It didn't even look like a bird anymore, just a splat of feathers and blood and squishy guts. I touched the mess with my fingers. It was slippery and warm. I brought my finger to my forehead and anointed myself with the blood. I told myself this was why the bird had died, to save me. It would erase the malignance swelling in my brain. It would make me good now.

FIRST DAY OF HIGH SCHOOL

Nicole and I had picked out our clothes months ago from a catalog. For weeks we discussed how we'd do our nails, our makeup, and our hair. That morning I left the house assuming I would be sorted with the right people first thing—popular, cool. People who deserved both respect and fear. Instead, I met no new people. Nicole wasn't in any of my Honors classes, so I didn't say anything all day but *Here!* By fourth period it reverberated around in my skull like a pinball, echoing and distorting until it sounded almost demonic. *Here, here, here.*

It was weird to be so silent around that many people. Their voices were mostly a drone, with only the occasional phrase slipping through—*Oh my god. Did you see her? What's up? Where were you?* The hallways were filled with dizzying movement, and I held tight onto my notebook in an attempt to anchor myself, but it was too late. I couldn't get back into my body. I couldn't stop seeing myself as a stranger. All the people around me seemed to know each other, and they were all in the same world, one different than mine, one where everyone knew what they were doing and what they wanted.

The warning bell rang and I snapped out of it enough to walk into the classroom and find a seat at a desk in the back. But then I heard someone calling my name.

It was a girl who'd been my friend in elementary school—her name was Blair. In third and fourth grade, we'd hung out at the Boys & Girls Club every day after school. We made Cup O' Noodles soup in the microwave and sang "Under the Bridge" by the Red Hot Chili Peppers on the baseball field. Back then, she'd lived in the rural part of Santa Bonita, on a property surrounded by horse ranches that had since been paved over and turned into a strip mall. I didn't know where her family lived now. On the weekends, I had gone to her house, and we jumped on her big rusty trampoline, stuffed her baby goats into doll clothes. In the summer, I went camping with her family, and she went to Catalina with mine. In fifth grade, she'd switched schools and we'd tried to stay friends but eventually we'd just lost touch.

She was sitting closer to the front of the classroom, at a table with some guy, wearing a purple T-shirt with a peace sign on it and khaki cargo pants. There was a thick hemp choker on her neck, dark brown lipstick on her mouth. The boy was real small, kind of ugly, wearing a skateboard shirt, with a bright shock of temporary blue color in his dingy brown hair. She told me to come sit with them and smiled at me real big, like there was no question that I would.

I thought about it for a moment. I remembered a sleepover we'd had one night in a tent in her backyard. Her dad had built us a campfire and we'd used it to make s'mores, and it felt like ghosts might creep out any moment from the empty hills. I'd been too afraid to sleep. Blair wasn't scared, but she stayed up with me anyway, telling me jokes and stories until it was light out. It had been a simple night, before there was room for trouble, and it stood out in my memory. The eerie stillness of the air, the brightness of the moon, and the dark shadows, the way that staying up all night laughing made me crackle with electricity the next day. When we were little, we'd been mistaken for sisters. We'd both had big bright eyes and little mouths. She would have been beautiful now, prettier than me, if you took off those ugly clothes and that lipstick.

This was Honors English, where nobody was cool. But quickly I imagined what my compliance could turn into. Her and the little guy following me to lunch. Me introducing them to Nicole; the look she'd give me afterward. Blair calling me. Blair wanting to do homework together. Blair tagging along to parties, becoming a burden. I imagined a chain on my neck signaling NOT COOL, me eventually yelling at her when it became too much, her crying, the look of disgust and pain she would wear.

So I ignored her. I became what I wanted. I became a bitch. I became cool.

GIFTED AND TALENTED

Everyone said Ms. Novak's Honors English class was the hardest in the school. If you did well there, you'd be fine at the toughest college— good practice because I wanted to go to UC Berkeley, maybe Columbia. Our first major project was making magazines that showcased different aspects of life from the time of *Madame Bovary*. I paired off with Kelly Parish, who was funny and in all my Honors classes, and we decided to make a fashion magazine. Her mom dropped us off at the library, the big one downtown, which smelled like dusty books and piss. I read about women improving their complexion through arsenic and belladonna, while Kelly read about death by corset, each of us leaving with a giant stack of books. I held them in my arms, sniffing their old-book smell the whole drive home.

That weekend, I didn't go to Nicole's house on Friday like usual, and I didn't go to any parties, or even answer the phone, because I was locked in my room. I barely slept. Instead, I spent the weekend taking notes on the books, then rewriting them in my neatest hand- writing until they were alphabetized by subject. I painted water- color illustrations, measuring precisely with a ruler to ensure they were perfectly to scale. I borrowed my father's neon-bubbled level, making sure my printed-out text was perfectly aligned. It felt some- thing like fate as I worked, a divine guidance enveloping my hand, zapping everything into place, as cleanly and neatly as Tetris. I saw the magazine in the future, when I was famous for whatever type of art I'd be famous for, spotlighted behind glass in a museum, proof of my early genius.

I had nightmares about Ms. Novak hating it, making fun of my writing and illustrations, smashing my future of prestige and ge- nius. But when we got it back, her handwriting looped across the pages, spelling out words like *Wonderful!*, words like *Brilliant!* She gave us an A+. She never gave anyone an A+. I walked out of the classroom that day, blanketed in gold: perfect, shining, chosen.

BUT THEN I STARTED HAVING PROBLEMS SLEEPING

My eyes were always red, like I had pink eye or dust in them. My bones ached hot, a feeling of perpetual fever. I was desperate for sleep, devoting hours to just staring at the ceiling, but was never able to drift off until one or three or five. After a couple hours, my heart woke me up, beating against my chest too fast and insistent, and I'd be left feeling cursed by this change to my body.

One morning, very early. My room was still mostly dark, but there were little trails of light beaming from the cracks in the curtains. They shot through the air in pale rainbows, and it was like being trapped in a prism.

I sat up in bed. I caught a glimpse of myself in the mirror. There was something wrong with my face. My eyes, my mouth, my nose—they were gone. In their place, there was now a bird. Its wings shuddered, in a way that seemed like it was dying. I raised my hand to my face. I touched where the bird was and I felt no feathers, just my nose. In the mirror I didn't see my hand or that finger, just the sooty mark of a claw.

I WAS AT A PARTY

I didn't want to be there but I also didn't want to leave. I was sitting in a corner of the backyard, drinking beer that had gone flat and warm from a plastic cup. I lit and smoked cigarette after cigarette. I had gone to the party with Nicole and a couple other girls she'd made friends with in her classes. We'd done coke together as soon as we got there, and then I left to smoke and hadn't seen them since. But I hadn't bothered to look for them either.

There were some guys out in the backyard too, guys I didn't know but had seen before. They were doing dumb shit and laughing too loud. Either too drunk or pretending to be. Every once in a while they'd give me a look. I didn't know what they were thinking. I didn't know if they thought I was cute or crazy. At one point, I thought one of them said something to me, it sounded vaguely like "Hey you." I didn't want them to come over so I just glared. I didn't care if they thought I was crazy. I didn't have feelings anymore. It was like something metal had replaced my insides. Everything was steely and flat.

Eventually, the boys left me alone. I guess they'd given up, either trying to talk to me or talk shit about me. I felt safe enough to stare at them now. I didn't want anything from them, they were just something for me to look at that wasn't the backyard or a plant and I was bored. Now that I was looking at them full on, I could see something coming out of their chests, from their hearts, like glow-in-the-dark string. At first I thought it was just a special effect. They were tied up in each other, going back and forth, twisting thicker and then thinner and then they'd get thick again. A girl came out onto the patio. She ran to the side and vomited in the bushes. She had the strings too, hers pale and flimsy, but they reached into the boys' and when the ends met up each strand grew stronger. The boys were laughing. She finished puking and went back inside, the strings trailing and knotted behind her.

After a while Nicole came out to find me, and she had the glowing strings too. Hers were greenish and especially beautiful. I watched them tangle up with the dumb boys' as she walked past them, as she walked toward me. I looked down to see if mine would come out, but nothing happened. There was only darkness in front of my chest. Someone had severed the wires.

THIRD PERIOD WAS THE WORST

In school, during Biology class, the shadows came together and glued themselves into shapes. An army of shadows pressing against my chest, jabbing their fingers into my throat. The noises they made, not like humans or even demons but like shuffling paper, something ambivalent and clinical. I watched as skulls erupted from the walls, wild in psychedelic rainbows. I tried to shut the shapes out by closing my eyes, but the colors flickered brighter across my eyelids. The shuffling rumbled into thunder, laughter filling in the gaps. I tried to slow my breaths, imagining myself as a tree with solid roots sinking into the floor, but the chaos just swelled into violence. I felt blood, wet and sticky. It poured down my arms. It was horrible.

I forced myself silent and still. I tried to zoom out to a wider angle, see the girl wearing jeans and a white shirt, normal. *Be normal.* There was no blood on my arms. But I lost the illusion when I started making choking sounds, the fingers jabbing too sharp. Mrs. Jernigan stopped class to ask if I was OK. I tried to say I was fine but couldn't make the words. I watched the jeans-wearing girl's face turn red. She wasn't normal. She was choking over fingers that weren't even there.

Mrs. Jernigan asked another student, this quiet girl I'd never spoken to before, to take me down to the nurse. Everything went away as soon we got into the hall.

The first thing the nurse asked was if I had asthma. I didn't. I told her my heart was beating really fast and I felt dizzy. She made me sit in a chair with my head between my knees, and when I felt better, she handed me the card of a psychiatrist. It was probably an anxiety attack, she said. I threw the card away. I figured it wouldn't happen again. I would try harder to be normal in the future.

But a couple of weeks later, it did. Same closed-in feeling, same noises, same skulls. That time I didn't even try; I just got up and left. At first I figured I'd go to the bathroom, chill out for a couple minutes, then head back. But as I was sitting there on the toilet, it occurred to me that this only ever happened in that one class, and it all went away as soon as I exited the room. The shadows never followed me. I didn't want to go back in that shit.

I sat on the floor of the bathroom until class was over. At one point a girl came in to pee. I pretended sitting on the floor of the bathroom for no apparent reason was a perfectly logical thing to do. It seemed to work.

It was embarrassing to have to go back and get my bag. Mrs. Jernigan was still in there, the classroom empty, her head bent over the pile of papers on her desk. I told her it was an anxiety attack because I didn't know what else to say. Except then I started crying, the frustration of failing to be someone else. Mrs. Jernigan came over and hugged me and I wanted her to stop but I knew it was the wrong way to act so I just stood. I kept telling her I was sorry, and she kept saying it was OK. She didn't seem to mind, but it was always difficult to look her in the eye after that. Instead, on the days I was able to come to class, I kept my head down, listening carefully to her lectures, taking orderly notes, making sure the evil couldn't slip in the gaps.

I STARTED SPENDING A LOT
OF TIME BY MYSELF

Nicole got a boyfriend. He was this idiot senior with a criminal record, a BMW, and spiky hair. Like, he really was an idiot—he could barely read, and a conversation with him wasn't even a conversation so much as a string of observations:

"It's Thursday already."

"The sun is hot."

"Jake's party was gnarly."

"Chemistry is hard."

I couldn't understand why Nicole liked him, other than his body and the car, which he made sure you were always aware of by wearing wifebeaters and carrying his keys around in his hand. I couldn't understand what they did together, what they said, what they had in common. Mostly all they seemed to care about was getting fucked up at parties and making out.

She tried to set me up with one of his friends, inviting me to the parties, which were always terrible and boring, revolving around doing drugs and games like Quarters and Beer Pong and not much else. It seemed like a good idea to date one of them—they were good-looking and popular—but I couldn't stand the thought of someone whose idea of high humor involved blumpkins. (Blumpkin: when a guy gets a blow job while he's taking a shit.)

A couple weeks into their relationship, we went over to some older guy's house, maybe twenty-five, who lived in a run-down apartment by the beach papered in peeling seventies wallpaper and surf posters. Everyone was hyped-up due to a big bag of coke and a handle of 151. Their shit music, some sort of rap-metal, was so loud everyone had to yell. I did four lines and two shots and got an instant headache.

Some guy tried to talk to me. He had long greasy hair, zits all over his chin, wore a Padres hat flipped backwards and a football jersey. I pretended I couldn't hear him, hoping he'd go away, but he only squished in closer, placing his fat hand on my thigh.

"Get the fuck off me," I said. I had made a vow before I'd gotten in the car that I would try to be nice. I would try to have fun and be open-minded. But that music and those drugs and that disgusting hand. I stood up. I knocked over a cup sitting on the table, the contents spilling onto some magazines.

"Whoa whoa whoa," someone yelled. "Party foul!"

"Fuck all of you," I said and left, fucked up but not high. I walked down a few blocks to the ritzy shopping center for the rich tourists and spent all my allowance money on a cab ride back home.

After that, Nicole stopped inviting me out on weekends. I was supposed to grovel back into her good graces, but I couldn't make myself do it. Instead I gave up, didn't even try to make other friends, just spent the weekends by myself, weird and alone.

EXTRACURRICULARS

I wasn't sure if the problem was me or the school, but I couldn't handle it at Carmel Heights anymore. Like something magnetic—trying to go because it was normal, but as soon as I got there the poles flipped, pushing me away. So I pretended to be sick all the time. I had a stomachache, or a migraine, or I hadn't been able to sleep the night before (often true). Most of the time, my excuses worked. On the days they didn't, I got out of Mom's car with my backpack and headed to the school doors, but as soon as she drove away I walked back home. I spent a lot of the time in the canyons behind our house, smoking pot and listening to my Discman, reading or writing poems.

One day I went up there in the afternoon and I stayed too long. The sun was starting to set and the air was getting darker and colder. I hadn't brought a jacket and I was probably missing dinner. I was sitting in the bushes where nobody could see me. I was busy watching the plants grow. The branches twisted up to the stars. The leaves stretched and spiraled, weaving themselves into nooses and snakes. The flowers disintegrated into lace, and I put my face under it, a mourning veil. I was ready to die. I was ready for the people to cry for me.

DUNCE

We were reading *The Odyssey* in English class. The goal was to categorize everything: when Homer mentioned a color, the role of Odysseus as hero, the way women were treated. When I finally went to class, I saw everyone else's notes, little colored Post-its like flags, long trails of highlighted text, invented codes of letters and symbols, definitively marking each item as clearly as roads on a map. My book was unblemished, the spine barely cracked, pages still crisp and new.

Even though I hadn't been in class, I'd tried to keep up with the work. But I hadn't seen any of the right things. Instead, I'd only noticed the violence. It was hard to miss: *blood, stabbed, wounded, beheaded, dead.* The words had stood out like they were the only ones in the book, this feeling that it had been written thousands of years ago simply to attack me, now, here, in the future. I leaned over my desk, shielding my book with my body, hoping no one would notice my obvious absence of work.

I went straight home after school. I would catch up. I would notice the things everyone else had. I read all of Book 1 and most of Book 2 before realizing I hadn't highlighted anything at all.

I thought about the time I'd just wasted doing nothing. I still had all the math homework and the science and it crumbled down on me until my lungs felt void of air. I closed my eyes and tried to think. I just needed to slow down, break it apart, page by page, paragraph by paragraph. If I could understand what each sentence said, then I could piece it all together and everything would become clear. I read a paragraph. It seemed like gibberish. I read it again. I read it again. The letters looked like random objects, fluttery and weightless as confetti.

I decided to switch to my science textbook, biology, the orderliness of chromosomes and Punnett squares. But that book seemed meaningless too, written in cuneiform rather than letters. I tried to make sense of the pictures but they appeared diced up, the white pages surrounding them too luminous, as though I was viewing them through a kaleidoscope. There was something wrong with my head, with my vision. I looked at my hands and I could see the individual molecules that made up my flesh, the air between them, neon pulsating veins. I was dissolving, slipping from the human world into an angel, a demon.

I ran to the bathroom and threw up straight bile, the same neon yellow as my unused highlighter. The act shocked me back into my body. I rinsed out my mouth and lay down on the bed and cried. The dreams I had of going away and being smart and cool in Berkeley or New York felt like discarded photographs, something I was watching get wadded into a ball, inevitable garbage. My future. It was trashed.

MY LAST TIME AT NICOLE'S HOUSE

I hadn't been over there in a couple months. The whole house had changed. They'd furnished the place. There was a collage of photos on Nicole's wall, showing her and her boyfriend and her new friends doing things like going to the beach, making silly faces, at Splash Mountain at Disneyland, their mouths matching O's. I wasn't in them. I wasn't friends with these people. There was only one photo of me, from last summer when we went to church camp. The girl in the photo was blond and smiling, indistinguishable from the rest of the glossy teens on the wall.

I sat there on her bed and she put on a CD, not punk but Rage Against the Machine, and she talked at me, not with me, telling me things about her stupid boyfriend and stupid parties and stupid people. I tried to interrupt a few times, saying I was having a hard time just making it to school, but she barely looked at me before going back to her original train of thought. That weekend, she was supposedly going on a mission trip, but really she and her boyfriend were going to Cabo. She'd bought a new swimsuit, did I want to see? These were the kind of things we were supposed to be talking about; she was instructing me. Every time I failed to respond correctly, ask the right questions in the right voice, her face flickered in annoyance at what she clearly saw as my choice to be abnormal. I watched her body, the tenseness of her arms as they crossed against her chest, as her chin tilted away from me, as her legs edged together until we turned into strangers.

I wasn't too upset when her phone rang and it was my mother. The thing that did make me upset was what she said, and how she sounded. She told me to come home right away. Her voice was clipped, like she was mad. I figured maybe the school had called. Usually I was the first one home and I just erased the message. I was trying to think of excuses for why I'd been absent. I got my period; I felt sick.

Nicole's mom drove me home, saying she had to go to the grocery store anyway, and surprisingly Nicole came with us, even getting out of the car to hug me before I went in, her arms light around my shoulders in a way that felt condescending.

Inside, my mom had some of my things out on the kitchen table—a razor, a lighter, a used pipe I'd made out of aluminum foil. My face went hot as soon as she'd called, and it got hotter when I saw she'd gone through my stuff.

She started screaming right away, about my grades, my truancies, my sullen demeanor, the pot and the cutting: "I don't even know who you are anymore. You're not my daughter. You're a disappointment." She got right up in my face, and I couldn't stand the noise for another second. I couldn't really see anymore; everything had gotten fuzzy and dark on the edges.

I took the candlesticks on the table and threw them against the wall.

Then I grabbed the table itself and threw it on the ground.

I went into the bathroom and locked the door. I started crying, the gasping ugly kind impossible to stop. My hands were shaking and I wanted to puke.

She opened the door somehow. I was sitting on the bathroom mat when she came in, sobbing. She grabbed me by the arms. She was yelling. I didn't even know what she was saying. Her mouth was blanked out. I didn't mean to but it felt like I was choking and I hit her, not knowing if it was her face or body, just that my hand had connected with something softer than the wall. She left me alone after that. The air in the room settled, and I was breathing hard but my vision and hearing slid back into place. My face blotchy in the mirror, eyes glassy and hysterical. A little beast.

My dad came home shortly thereafter. A floor tile had cracked when I'd thrown the table, so he was furious because they'd just had it put down. He told me I had to pay for it. I didn't know how I was supposed to do that because nobody would hire a fifteen-year-old fuckup to do anything, and my allowance had been cut off to just lunch money until my grades improved, but I didn't say that.

My dad wasn't like my mom and me when he got angry. He didn't yell. But that day, the anger sprung out of him in pointed black daggers I could see stabbing the air, and his words seethed as he asked what was wrong with me, why was I acting this way, a look of disgust on his face before he sent me to my room. But he didn't have to tell me. I already knew.

HALLUCINATION #43

I swallowed a handful of Benadryl to try and make myself pass out. It didn't work. Instead of sleeping, I just read and read. I was down to teen horror novels, the only thing I could focus on. After a while I felt tired but still I kept the light on and kept reading. I fell asleep. When I woke up, a couple hours had passed. I noticed what looked like writing on my arms, but it turned out they were chains. There was blood on them.

I looked closer, and I saw bones under the chains, torn skin, the bubbly tissues of fat, sinewy grains of muscle. I would have been alarmed but everything was glistening and pulsing and alive. Which made it beautiful. I shook my arms and the chains jangled. I expected it to hurt but it didn't. I fell asleep again and when I woke up an hour later the chains were gone. In their place, my skin was coated in a thick scrim of glitter. I had burned hot into golden.

I DIDN'T KNOW WHAT TO DO ANYMORE

I no longer slept. It was so loud all the time. Each day I was assaulted by ringings and whispers, my heart pounding out the center of the chaos like a metronome, the order of the days splintering, popping apart, the ropes that once tethered me to the rest of the world had snapped and I had floated too far to find my way back. Each morning I was sick to my stomach, a feeling that only increased as the day wore on. The world falling away like bombs, leaving only me, the darkest war in it. There was nothing I could do. I was scared.

I was only able to go to school one day that week. I sat in class, completely silent—no one talking to me, the teacher's voice making noises but not words—unable to move because it felt like my bones might break from my body. I watched the normalcy around me, the students and their textbooks and their notes, the easy things I was supposed to do that had now become impossible. I was a freak.

I ditched second period to go to the library. I wandered around the shelves until I found the books on psychiatry. It took a while because I didn't want to get caught skipping class, so I kept on having to duck in different aisles where the librarian couldn't see me. I picked out a book that was red and fat like a dictionary. It looked very official. I flipped through awkwardly, my fingers feeling stiff and plastic.

I found the chapter on schizophrenia. It was the only thing I knew of that made sense.

This is what it said:

DIAGNOSTIC CRITERIA FOR SCHIZOPHRENIA

A. *Characteristic symptoms*: Two (or more) of the following, each present for a significant portion of time during a 1-month period (or less if successfully treated):

1. delusions
2. hallucinations

3. disorganized speech (e.g., frequent derailment or incoherence)
4. grossly disorganized or catatonic behavior
5. negative symptoms, i.e., affective flattening, alogia, or avolition*

All I could think was: *Fuck.*

Fuck.

Fuck.

Fuck.

Fuck.

I am so fucked.

The anger gurgled up inside me hot and quick. I clapped the book together, put it back on the shelf, pretending I hadn't touched it. I walked out of the library. Then I just kept going. I saw the school narc's yellow truck as I left the parking lot. He was sitting in it. I didn't care. If he tried to stop me, I'd tell him to back the fuck up because I was a schizophrenic bitch.

But he didn't try. I didn't have to tell him anything.

I wanted to go somewhere, I wanted to get away. But I couldn't think of anywhere to go. I couldn't think of anything to do, anything that would take this away or make it better. There was no way to fix it. I just walked home.

Crazy. Frequent derailment. Going to die. Fucked. Shit ass. The thoughts gathered in gray spiderwebs, tying together my limbs, caught in my hair.

The problem had ruptured into something I could no longer ignore or keep to myself. I didn't want to; I had to. I tried to plan out what I'd say to my parents but I didn't really get anywhere.

---

* *Diagnostic and Statistical Manual (DSM)*, fourth edition, ed. Thomas A. Widiger, Allen J. Frances, Harold Alan Pincus, Michael B. First, Ruth, Ross, and Wendy Davis (Washington, DC: American Psychiatric Association, 1994), 285.

When I got home, I found some paper. I told myself I was describing somebody else so I wouldn't cry. I was relaying the plot of a movie. I was merely transcribing the troubles of a friend. It wasn't me who was experiencing this. Nope, not me. Not me. Just a girl.

And soon it became true. I floated out of my body, somewhere above my head. I watched the girl with the sun-bleached hair and the skinny arms, as she sat at a desk covered in papers and books and trash, writing a letter. Her name was Juliet. She was fifteen years old. She was the daughter of Helen and Robert. She was no genius. She was just crazy.

She wrote all of it down.

Dear Mom + Dad,

I have been having a hard time lately. Maybe you have noticed. I have tried to deal with things the best I can but it seems that things are quickly becoming unmanageable. Here a some things that have been going on lately that I am having trouble with.

1) SLEEP: As you know it is very hard for me. I slept one hour last night. I slept two hours the night before. It is very hard to go to school with only one hour sleep.

2) Concentration. I dont know whats is happening but nothing I read makes sense anymore.

3) Heartbeat: My heart is beating too fast and hard for no reason I don't know why.

4) Appetite: I do not feel hungry anymore.

5) Dark thoughts: Sometimes I cant get thoughts of death out of my head. Dont worry I don't plan to do anything. Its just sometimes something I cant get out of my head

6) Noise: I keep hearing noises that I know aren't really there. Mostly it is phones and alarms

7) Speech: sometimes I have problems talking. It is hard for me to get the words out because my head is going faster than my mouth can. I am not accustomed to this.

8) Sight: I keep seeing things that aren't really there. Mostly they are shapes like shadows but thinner. It is very distracting when this happens at school.

As you can see, I have been struggling. I am hoping you have some ideas of what to do.

Love,

Juliet

Note to parents, November 1998.

35

SPECIAL DELIVERY

I left the letter under their bedroom door. My mom came home shortly after. I heard her footsteps as she went up the stairs. Several minutes later, she knocked on my door. The look on her face was soft and concerned and I wanted to tell her everything, the way I used to when I was little, but I couldn't make myself say anything at all. I just cried and pointed to the letter I'd written, which she'd placed next to me on the bedspread, like if she didn't touch it any longer than she had to it wouldn't be true. When my dad came home, I heard the two of them go in their bedroom, their muffled voices going back and forth for a long while.

THAT NIGHT

They decided we should go to a family therapist. My dad got the name of a lady from someone he knew at work. "It'll be good to get some outside help," Mom said to me, more than once, in a way that made me think she was mostly saying it to herself.

Between the letter and the appointment, I went into my parents' bedroom to look for something, a pen or a pair of scissors, and I found a stack of my books on their desk.

I picked them up, flipped through the titles, trying to figure out why they were there. *The Bell Jar*, *Go Ask Alice*. This book about a girl who has a breakdown and likes to talk to goldfish. A book about a boy in foster care.

The dots connected. To my parents, this was a stack of explanations. They must have thought I was bored, crafting something to fit my teenage melodrama. Wasn't that hilarious. Super funny.

THE THERAPIST

Her office was in a business complex behind a bank, this building we'd driven by dozens of times on the way to my junior high but I'd never noticed before. It was real ugly, designed to look like some sort of historic mission but failing miserably. We took the boring brown elevator up to the second floor, walked down a boring brown hall into a boring brown office, where my dad went up to the counter to check us in. My mom and I sat down in the boring brown chairs. She seemed nervous. She didn't pick up any of the magazines they had laying around, just stared straight ahead, her back perfectly straight in the chair, like some sort of zombie. When my dad finished the paperwork, he did the exact same thing. It was creepy.

I hated the therapist right away. She had frosted blond hair, short and sprayed with too much hairspray, and was wearing this ugly maroon business suit, with a big, stupid-looking silver brooch on her lapel.

She asked us how we were and we said we were fine. My parents talked about how smart and talented I was, while I just sat there. Then they started describing my anger and my bad grades and the drugs and my yelling. They were talking like I wasn't even there, looking only at each other and the therapist. Then they handed over the letter I had written, folded into quarters so you couldn't see the writing until you opened it. The therapist read it with a look on her face like she was a bad actress pretending to be concerned:

Things are quickly becoming unmanageable.

Concern.

Slept one hour last night.

Concern.

When she was done, she folded it back up. She wanted to speak to my parents for a while. I went back to the waiting room.

I tried to look at the magazines. To my parents, I had become an abstract problem, a plumbing leak or a lingering cough.

The therapist called me in, to talk to her alone. When I passed my parents in the hall, I couldn't even look at them. I tried to pretend I wasn't angry when I sat down in the chair, but immediately she said, "You seem upset."

I said nothing. She asked what was on my mind. My first reaction was to ask her if she was reading off a script, the one they had for angry teen girls, except I started crying. She pushed over a box of Kleenex and told me it was OK, like she was still following the script.

"I don't know what to say," was what I settled on.

She sat there, looking at me in a way that I tried to tell myself wasn't judgmental, just interested. After a long while, she finally said, "I think you've said it all in this note."

"I guess I did."

"So what about your parents," she said. "How do they feel about all of this?"

I had stopped crying, mostly. "I'm not sure. We haven't talked about it," I said. "My parents read the note and then my dad made this appointment." He'd looked upset afterward, but I couldn't tell if he was mad or sad or just nervous. My mom hadn't said much either.

"Well, they love you very much," she said.

"I know. That isn't the problem."

"So what's the problem?"

Where to start when everything was wrong. I'd already explained it the best I could. I had an urge to grab the note, now sitting on her desk, crumple it up, burn it, as though by doing so it'd turn me into a different person. "I just don't think they take it seriously," I said, and then I told her about the books.

She smiled. "I heard about the books. I understand. That seems like it would be very upsetting, to tell them all that and have them think you're making it up. But try to imagine where they're coming from. They have a beautiful, smart daughter who is suddenly not doing well at all. It's the kind of thing that's hard to believe."

Imagine where they were coming from? It seemed absurd, but I stuck to the script. I asked, "So what do you think is wrong with me?"

"To be honest, I'm not fully equipped to make a diagnosis. My specialty is in family dynamics. But I've written you a prescription, and given your parents the name of a doctor who's better qualified to work with this kind of thing."

And then our time was up. I joined my parents back in the waiting room. They both smiled at me, tiny grim little robotic smiles. It made me wonder if the therapist coached them on how to act. My dad went to pay the bill. The receptionist said the price quietly but I still heard what she said. Two hundred fucking dollars. The insane thing seemed to be paying that much just for a prescription.

I still didn't even know what was wrong.

We went across the street to the shopping center. My mom dropped off my prescription at the pharmacy. My dad and I waited in the car. We didn't say anything because talking was pointless. My mom came back and we went to McDonald's to get hamburgers while we waited for the prescriptions. We never ate McDonald's. My dad was always making fun of the fat people who ate there, called them fat piggies eating from a fat piggy trough.

I didn't know what to order so I got a Big Mac because that was on the commercials. My mom and dad ordered the same.

We sat there eating our hamburgers, still not saying anything. My mom said the therapist was nice, but all my dad and I could do was nod. The cheese was rubbery and slimy and everything tasted vaguely like plastic. It made me want to vomit, but I continued chewing and swallowing anyway, watching my parents as they chewed and swallowed, the thoughts buzzing separately inside all of our heads, and it felt like we were insects, biting off nutrients with our mandibles. We chewed. We swallowed.

DOCTOR'S ORDERS

The prescription was for Tegretol, a mood stabilizer, and Well-butrin, an antidepressant. They were supposed to take up to a month to work. I was just supposed to wait.

So I waited.

SIDE EFFECTS

All the medicine seemed to do was make me dizzy in the mornings.
I kind of liked it. It was a little bit like being drunk. It made it easier
to go to school, this doctor-prescribed slurry haze.

TAKE TWO

I went to the new-new psychiatrist a few days later. He was skinny and silver haired, kind of reminded me of Mister Rogers. I liked him better than the lady immediately. The shelves behind his desk were filled with books, not just psychiatric books but novels—*Jane Eyre* and *Madame Bovary*. He was easy to talk to and nothing I said made me cry. He did things in a way that made me feel calm because his script seemed scientific. I took a quiz, like at school where you fill in the bubbles, but these were all about how I'd been feeling.

Did I ever think of harming myself?

Why yes I did.

Did I find it difficult to concentrate?

Yep, all the time, thanks for asking.

Then he had me go across the hall, where a nurse in an old-fashioned nurse cap took my blood. Three vials, each with a different-colored top.

Afterward, I went back into his office. There, he told me that I was bipolar, type I, rapid cycling. I liked the specificity in those phrases. I liked that the thing wrong with me had a name now.

The thing that hadn't changed was my medication. The medications and doses were kept the same. The psychiatrist said I would get used to the dizziness, and, eventually, they would start to work.

"That seems impossible," I said. "It seems impossible to just sit around and wait."

He seemed to get it, but in the end, he said there wasn't anything else he could do. "I know it's hard," he said. He smiled at me. It was a sad smile.

AT SOME POINT

I thought there were cameras hidden in my room. I thought there were people watching me from the bushes also. I kept the curtains closed, but I was concerned they could still see through the cracks.

I started to change in the closet. I didn't want them seeing me naked. The closet was so narrow, I smashed my knee into the wall when I was putting on jeans.

It occurred to me that this was completely insane. I couldn't come up with a good reason why anyone would want to spy on me. But I kept changing in the closet anyway.

Then I started thinking there were cameras in the closet too. If I held very still, I could hear the whirring of a tape. I got a chair from the kitchen so I could look in all the corners but I didn't see anything. The whirring continued. They were smarter than me.

I heard God a few times too. I thought it was God, at least. She had a female voice, and never had a lot to say. Mostly it was stuff about me having been chosen. I always wanted to respond, *Chosen for what?* But it was like having an argument, where you only think of the good comeback once it's too late.

If I was a different person, I might have tried harder to listen. But holiness is supposed to be something you work for. Something you pay for by sitting and praying and trying very hard to be quiet for a long time. I hadn't done those things. I didn't want to be special, I didn't want to be chosen, I didn't ask for anything holy to enter my heart.

I started to pray. I prayed over and over. I prayed for the opposite of salvation. I prayed for abandonment. I prayed for God to forget me.

But still I heard the voice:

You are chosen.

SUPERFREAK

I had been on the medicine for a few weeks, still dizzy in the mornings but there weren't as many noises or shadows. Maybe it was starting to work. It wasn't enough.

It was Friday, early December. I hadn't talked to anyone all day. I didn't see Nicole or anybody else during lunch because I had to take a make-up test for Math. I hadn't studied and I couldn't make sense of the questions, so I just started filling in bubbles. I made sure each one was very dark.

When I finished, there were only ten minutes left until the period was over. I spent it walking around campus very fast, pretending I had somewhere important to be. When the bell rang I couldn't imagine going to class. I went out to the parking lot, laid right down on the blacktop in a shadowy spot between two cars. I watched the sky. It was very blue. All day long I'd had this roaring in my ears, like I was surrounded by bugs.

A couple hours must have passed but it didn't feel that long at all. People were coming into the parking lot. School was over.

I walked down to the pickup circle. In the very beginning of the school year, when it still seemed like I would be cool and popular, Nicole's mom pulled up every day in her big Mercedes, and on Fridays I went home with them. We'd hang out in Nicole's room until it was late enough to go to a show or a party. She'd dress me in her outfits, do my makeup, fix my hair, and I felt like her little sister—irritating because I was older and smarter than her, but nice because it made me feel safe and cared for.

Now, Nicole was not my best friend but my best acquaintance. She had broken up with her boyfriend a couple weeks ago, and I thought that'd mean we'd get close again but instead she replaced me with this girl Ariana. It made things seem so slippery and interchangeable. Because I'd behaved the wrong way, I'd been traded for someone more compliant.

I only went to the pickup circle because I knew I'd just keep slipping if I went home alone. Nicole had recently dyed her hair maroon so I found her right away, standing next to Ariana, gleaming like a flame in the sea of pastels.

"Hi," I said to them. "Hi," they said to me. I asked them what they were doing. They said they were going to Nicole's. I figured they'd invite me along. They didn't. I stood there anyway because it seemed wrong to just walk off. My hands were shaking very badly and I couldn't figure out if it was because I had forgotten to eat that day or something else.

"Do you see that?" I asked them. I held my arm in front of me, my hand limp. It looked like it was vibrating. There were colors pulsing off it, purple and orange.

Nicole looked at it and said nothing.

"Damn," Ariana said. "Are you OK?"

Nicole stepped off the curb, away from me. She looked at Ariana.

Before I could say anything else, Nicole's mom pulled up. They both slid into the leather seats, the heater so high I felt it on the curb. "Bye," they said. They smiled. They shut the door. They drove off.

The roaring made everything else sound too quiet. It was a weird day. It looked like it might rain. The sky was darkening fast, the blue dissolving into a dirty kind of yellow. It felt like a bad sign.

I walked down Bonita Valley Road. People went past me in big SUVs and expensive bicycles. The air grew colder and the wind began to blow. I got this strange feeling in my chest, cold and heavy like a part of me was dying. Brown leaves swirled from the gutter as I walked. I saw shadows in my peripheral vision. My hands shook.

WHY I'M SCARED OF BIRDS

I always took a shortcut through a vacant field. It had been undeveloped for years, a blank square behind the mall at the top of the hill, before you got to the stucco apartments. Once the plants in it had been green and pretty, tall grass with bushes and wildflowers. It didn't look like that anymore. Everything had turned chalky and gray. The dead grass crinkled when I stepped on it. At the far end of the field, there was a whole flock of crows, dozens of black marks like a pox.

I expected them to fly away as I got closer, but they didn't move. They were black, black, black all over, claws to beak, and I felt their black-bead eyes following me.

I decided to sit down in the dirt, try to get the shadows to go away by willing myself solid and impassive like a tree. But the shadows caught up with me, and there were more of them now, shifting from shapes into pieces of people. Disembodied limbs, screeching mouths, long rotted hair. Ghosts. Wanting something from me, for me to do something, as if I could break their suffering and deliver them to heaven. They were saying something but all talking at once, and I couldn't make out what they said. The crows were still watching me. They began to caw. They were all trying to tell me something. They were all trying to tell me what to do. The sun shone through the thick clouds, a yellow blob in the sky.

My heart beat faster, faster until it was just one long thrum. The molecules around my head buzzed, the crows cackled, the shadows clung at me, and all of it was cloaked in doom. The poison in me was spreading, burning like bile in my veins, dismantling cells and becoming contagious. It would spread into my parents, into Nicole. The only way to get the evil out, to exorcise the ghosts, was to choke it. To choke myself. It was the only way. I stood up and it began pouring rain.

When I got home, I was soaked. My parents were getting ready to leave for dinner. They seemed surprised to see me, surprised that I was soaking wet. "I didn't know it was raining," my dad said.

A new Mexican restaurant had opened up near the gas station. "Do you want to come?" my mom asked. I told her no. "Are you OK? You look sick," she said. I said I was fine. I was just tired, I was just cold and wet. I said I would take a hot shower. They left.

The Other Thing took over, pushing me into the bathroom. I watched my hand take out my medicine—Tegretol, Wellbutrin. The pills poured onto the counter in a neat pile. It didn't seem like enough. I walked into the kitchen, the tiny cupboard where my mom kept the vitamins and headache medicine. There was a big bottle of Tylenol from Costco. There was a smaller bottle of Benadryl too. I set both of them down on the counter. I grabbed one of the kitchen chairs. I dragged it in front of the fridge. There was a bunch of liquor bottles on top. I grabbed the gin. I stepped down, got a tall glass. I poured the gin into it until it was full. I didn't put the bottle back. I took the glass and the pill bottles and went into the bathroom. I poured the Tylenol and Benadryl out next to the other pills, threw all of the bottles in the trash. They looked pretty—the white of the Tylenol and Tegretol mixed with the bright pink and red of the other pills. I grabbed a handful, shoved them in my mouth, swallowed them with the gin, until it was all gone. They went down my throat so easy it was like they belonged there.

I went into my bedroom. The lights were off and the room was very dark. I lay down on the bed. My eyelids grew heavy and I closed them. Everything felt thick and dumb. I think I fell asleep. I dreamt I was tied, my hands behind my back, my feet together. Someone had lit me on fire. The flame that burned me was very white and very hot, but it didn't hurt. I couldn't see anything else but flames. I lost place of my body. I became the fire.

And then my dad was shaking me. I opened my eyes and the fire was gone. He was sitting on the bed, over me. It looked like there were three of him. My mother was over his shoulder. There were three of her too. Her face glistened, I think she was crying, and the tears glowed, brilliant as stars.

The next thing I knew, I was in the car. My mother was in the backseat with me. My face was against the window, the glass cool on my cheek. She kept on saying my name over and over, her hand grabbing my arm. It seemed too difficult to answer her and so I didn't. We were on the freeway and the other car lights went by in streaks and blurs, like lines of fire.

EMERGENCY

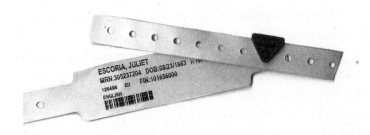

Hospital bracelet, December 1998.

There are so many things to learn after an attempted suicide.

Here is one: the most embarrassing feeling in the world is waking up in the hospital after a botched attempt.

A burning mortification. I'd fucked up on the ultimate fuck-up.

Next in its vividness: there were things stuck into what seemed like every last place on my body. Needles and tubes in both arms and both hands, monitors and wires attached to my chest and back and one finger. I even had a catheter.

The catheter was the thing that was most shocking.

Somehow less surprising:
    I had been intubated
    because I had stopped breathing.

Also memorable: an intense and overwhelming pain in my throat. However, this was not something I could mention because the intubation made it so I couldn't speak. It seemed a fitting punishment, an important right that had been revoked.

Or rather, that I had given up.

I had rendered myself speechless.

The embarrassment was for the obvious reasons, but it was also because I knew strangers had inserted all these things into me without my consent or knowledge, in the most mortifying possible conditions to be seen naked.

I felt like:
    disembodied teenage breasts,
    disembodied teenage pussy.

In that way—a typical teenager.

The embarrassment made me desperate to reverse time, so I could either undo the whole mess, or try harder so it would stick.

The funny thing: I wasn't sure which I preferred.

The embarrassment made me want to go back to sleep, go back to being parts of a body. A physical object, in need of care, but not attention.

The embarrassment made me want to rip out all the wires and tubes and needles, kick all the nurses and doctors in the face, smear their blood on the walls and floors, and burn down the flimsy curtains that surrounded me in a pathetic attempt at privacy.

But the embarrassment paled in comparison to the guilt that rolled over me when my parents walked into the room. I had never seen them look so old or so tired. Eyes completely bloodshot, lips thin and gray. The expression on their faces displayed not anger or frustration or even concern, the way I might have thought. There was one word for the look on their faces, one measly syllable that encapsulated it all:

Pain.

The mundane became strange. The nurses fed me a stream of drugs through the IV. I fell asleep and woke up again. I fell asleep and woke up. Time was marked not by hours but by hospital trays, and it was impossible to tell how long they'd been beside me, because the food was not really food at all. Instead, broth and jello. Food they feed the very sick and the dying. Over those three days I had been classified as both.

Sometimes God slipped in, but not in the way I would have thought. He put rats on the ceiling, rainbow rats, rats that were iridescent and glowing, rats that ran over each other, caught up in the tiles by a seemingly endless coil of rainbow iridescent string. Their beauty was so majestic I could have looked at them for hours. But I didn't, because once again I fell helpless into a drugged, dreamless sleep. When I woke up, God reminded me of one thing:

You have been chosen.

Sometimes the Other Thing slipped in too, equally as unexpected. Gurneys passed in the hallway, urgent beeping and the hushed noises of rushed movement from a few doors down. Shadows crept in. Almost comically, I wanted to tell them, "Next room."

When I felt a little bit better than totally out of it, they removed the breathing tube and catheter. They told me the catheter removal would hurt, but the tube, they claimed, would cause me to feel "a tickle." This was a lie. It felt like they were pulling a long rubber hose out of my gut, one that happened to be covered in needles and barbs. It turned out this was because I now had pneumonia. Sometimes this happens with intubation, I learned. The nurse who gave me this information shrugged, like it was no big deal.

And I guess, in the scheme of things, it really wasn't.

Then there are the math problems.

Q. A fifteen-year-old girl weighing 100 pounds consumes approximately 300 pills and 12 ounces of 40-proof gin. 60 minutes pass before she receives medical attention. How long will she remain unconscious?

A. 3 days

Q. How many cards and visits and flowers would a girl like me receive from her friends after a suicide attempt if she went to a school like Carmel Heights?

A: Zero.

Some trivia:

Q: How much time does the State of California require a person to involuntarily spend in a mental hospital after attempting suicide?

A: 3 days.

Q: What is the State of California's term for this involuntary hold?

A: 5150

(It doesn't matter if you already spent three days in the regular hospital. Those days don't count. If you don't remember them, the State of California doesn't either.)

Because of the pneumonia, I still couldn't talk. This is what I wrote on a notepad to my parents while waiting to be well enough to be admitted to the mental hospital:

It is the kind of thing meant to be said when you accidentally bump into a stranger at the grocery store.

It is the kind of thing meant to be said when you forgot to call somebody back.

It is a completely and totally inadequate thing to say when you've brought an unfathomable amount of pain to the two people who love you more than anything in the world. When you have mutated from their daughter into a monster.

Years later, the logical part of my brain reminds myself that it wasn't necessarily my fault. I was sick. I was suffering. Poor girl. A victim of her own brain.

Still, here is the thing. I am thirty-two years old now. The suicide attempt was over half my life ago. I have apologized for it, and all the things before and after, dozens of times, both explicitly and abstractly. I never had to be forgiven; to my mother and father, it wasn't even something they felt they needed an apology for. But the guilt is seemingly endless, remorseless. Therapy of all kinds, doing the twelve steps, "writing as a form of catharsis"—this type of work can heal so many things—and it has—but I don't know if this specific source of pain will ever go away, or even fade. Maybe it will if I write this. If someone reads this.

If the usual methods don't work, do you think forgiveness can be granted by a passive act from a stranger?

Does it work like that? And if it doesn't, do you know what does?

I've only been trying to find an answer to this question for half my life.

Are you a liar? Have you ever told a lie so many times that it started to feel like the truth? This is the opposite of that. These are truths I have told myself so many times they feel like a lie. My memory isn't remembered. It is a movie, with all the scenes out of order, not of myself but of some random girl, a stranger. Who is that girl in that story? That is some other girl. I do not own her, or know her, but she both owns and knows me.

NOTES FROM ALTURA MENTAL HOSPITAL: THE DOCTOR

Patient Evaluation, December 1998.

The psychiatrist I was assigned seemed like a creep when I met him. His desk was filthy, covered in files and papers and pens from pharmaceutical companies, five empty coffee cups. When I sat down, he leaned back and put his feet up on the desk, folded his arms behind his head. He kicked over an empty paper coffee cup, but didn't seem to notice. Then he asked me what was "shaking." I think he was attempting to "bro down" with me. It didn't work. He just looked like an idiot, an old fat guy wearing an ugly tie with a fucking guitar on it.

I answered his questions as briefly as I could while still being polite. The questions seemed insane. Like it seemed insane to not be able to pass his test. It seemed insane to answer "Do you feel suicidal?" with a yes. It seemed insane to answer his questions about drugs with the truth. It seemed insane to be asked "Are you experiencing any hallucinations?" If I was hallucinating, wouldn't I not know I was hallucinating?

I didn't feel suicidal when I was sitting there in that chair, but I didn't not feel suicidal either. Truthfully, I still wished I were dead, but I was now too lazy to do anything about it. Turns out killing yourself is hard.

And I suppose technically I wasn't hallucinating because I didn't see any skulls or hear any ringing phones. But the hallways in that hospital were hideous, covered in these thick gray spiderweb things. I kept my mouth shut about that.

NOTES FROM ALTURA MENTAL HOSPITAL: WARDROBE

My clothes were all wrong. They took away my sandals because they said we had to wear closed-toe shoes. My mom had packed boots for me, but they wouldn't let me wear those either because of the heels. She'd also packed my Converses, but shoelaces weren't allowed because you might hang yourself with them. The shoes slipped off my feet without them, and they told me that was dangerous. I had to wear creepy hospital socks until the next day during visiting hours, when my mom could bring me some cheap slip-on sneakers she bought at the drugstore. I didn't understand how the socks were any more protective than my sandals, but when I pointed that out the lady just rolled her eyes.

My pants were bad too—they were too big without a belt because I'd lost weight in the hospital, and they didn't allow belts, so I had to pull them up all the time. My sweatshirt had a drawstring around the hood, which they cut out. They took away my books and journal without even telling me why.

The belt made enough sense, but the shoelaces and drawstring seemed absurd. They weren't long enough to hang from, and they'd probably break with the weight of a body. All around me were things that would make better nooses. The curtains, the sheets, the towels.

NOTES FROM ALTURA MENTAL HOSPITAL: PNEUMONIC DEVICE

Spirometer.

In the hospital, I was given this plastic device that I was supposed to use twice a day for a month to increase the strength of my lungs. It had a tube, and I was supposed to put my mouth over it and blow just right until a yellow ball rose up to the smiley face. So basically it was the same as sucking a dick.

NOTES FROM ALTURA MENTAL HOSPITAL: HORMONES

"Everyone in here just wants to fuck."

That was the first thing another patient said to me. I was waiting at a table in the recreation room while they decided where to put me. I don't know why he was in there. Everyone else was in group.

He wanted me to be sick like him. Fucking seemed like something you would do only if you gave up on getting well, if you didn't care how many days they tacked on for acting crazy, if you were trying to replicate life in here like life on the outside.

He sat next to me in every group for the rest of the day, sometimes touching his foot to mine, staring at me until I noticed. He wasn't unattractive. His eyes were bright blue, and his teeth were all crooked but in a way that seemed cute. I didn't know why he was in there; he hadn't attempted suicide, which meant it was probably something worse. I didn't need anyone's crazy dick inside of me.

By free time that night, he'd given up. He was sitting next to this girl on the couch with stringy hair and sunken cheeks. I watched him put his hand under her shirt. She just sat there, no trace of emotion, no movement of accommodation or refusal, as though nothing was happening to her at all.

NOTES FROM ALTURA MENTAL HOSPITAL: MEDICINAL SERVICES

The medicine came in little paper cups on a tray, just before bedtime. There were other paper cups filled with water for us to swallow the pills. I had more pills in my cup than normal. When I asked about them, the nurse didn't seem to care. She just checked back over my name on her clipboard and pushed the little cup toward me. "Doctor's orders," she said, like she was a robot, like she'd said that line hundreds of times before. Which she probably had.

She checked my mouth to make sure I swallowed everything, but really she just made me open my mouth and gave it a perfunctory glance. I could have hidden the pill under my tongue, or on the side of my tooth. If you think about it, there are so many places to hide a pill.

NOTES FROM ALTURA MENTAL HOSPITAL: ROOMIES

My roommate's name was Sam. She said she'd been in here three times, the last time for a whole month, and if I had any questions I could just ask her. I didn't know you could get stuck in here for a whole month. I wondered what you would have to do to be locked up that long. I asked her how long she was staying this time and she said she didn't know. Maybe a week. She said she had new insurance and that's when it ran out.

Her face was pretty, with these big brown cow eyes, but a pretty cow, soft and sad. Unfortunate legs though—tree trunk thighs pocked with cellulite. I saw this when we were changing into our pajamas. It was weird to get almost naked in front of someone you knew nothing about. She had big bandages on her arms, which I hadn't seen before because she was wearing a sweater. Now she was wearing a sports bra and white Hanes underwear.

"Oh," I said. "Did you try and kill yourself too?" I wasn't sure if this was appropriate to ask. I didn't know the etiquette of talking to someone you barely knew while standing together in your underwear in a mental hospital.

"No," she said, like it was a normal question. She looked at the bandages, like they weren't a part of her. "But no one believes me. I cut so deep I almost bled out. It was an accident. If I was trying to kill myself, I would have cut on the bottom, not the top. I'm not an idiot."

I stepped closer to look, even though there was nothing to see because the bandages wrapped all around her arms. I could see the scars on her thighs, though, white and scaly and thick as ropes. Next to her scars, the ones on my own thighs seemed so tiny and normal.

"What did you do that with?" I asked her.

"A knife," she said.

"What kind of knife? Like a pocket knife? I did that once."

"No, a kitchen knife. One of those big ones." She didn't say it like she was bragging. She was saying it because it was true.

When I got in bed, which was more a cot than a bed, I couldn't stop thinking about her scars. I couldn't stop thinking about her taking a big kitchen knife and carving into herself like she was nothing more than food. I thought about doing it myself and I couldn't. I couldn't turn myself into food. I couldn't stop being a body.

NOTES FROM ALTURA MENTAL HOSPITAL: WAKE-UP CALL

In the morning, someone flipped on the overhead lights. Sam groaned, and I didn't move, thinking they would go away if they thought I was sleeping. But whoever it was started shaking me. I looked up and it was some guy, wearing scrubs, which was confusing because everyone I had seen so far wore regular clothes, even the nurse who passed out the medication. He told me to follow him, so I got up.

Whatever they'd given me the night before made me so dizzy it was hard to walk. He led me to the end of the hallway, where there was a nasty-ass chair. He stabbed a needle into my arm. The needle looked thicker than the ones in the regular hospital. He collected four tubes of blood, jiggling the needle a bunch each time he hooked up a new vial. Then he put a Band-Aid on it, told me to apply pressure for five minutes. I bled through the Band-Aid immediately.

Everyone else had been woken up. Sam said they did that to everyone the first three days—took blood. She didn't know why, and neither did anyone else. My veins were already sore from the hospital, and by the time the three days were over, they were covered in thick scabs and bruises, yellow ones from the IVs in the hospital, fresh blues and purples from the morning blood tests.

NOTES FROM ALTURA MENTAL HOSPITAL: NUTRITION

The food was disgusting. Everything was either full of starch or grease or both—blobs that resembled scrambled eggs, biscuits and gravy, spaghetti with unidentifiable chunks of meat in a runny sauce. The milk came in bags and tasted like chemicals and glue. The juice was served warm, in these pitchers that sat out all day. There was no soda or coffee.

Nothing had a brand name—the ketchup came in packets that said KETCHUP on the side, the cereal in big industrial boxes labeled CORN FLAKES. We weren't allowed knives, which made no sense because the utensils were plastic. How much damage can you possibly do with a plastic knife?

NOTES FROM ALTURA MENTAL HOSPITAL: HEALING TECHNIQUES

The days were broken up by different types of therapy. CBT involved worksheets and diagrams that explained how the way we acted and thought was wrong. Group therapy involved a counselor asking us all the same question on topics designed to make us cry, about mothers and fathers and abuse. It worked, sometimes, on the others. They had boxes of industrial-sized Kleenex (labeled FACIAL TISSUE) around the room, wherever they could fit them.

My favorite was art therapy. The art therapist was young, in her twenties, and unlike everyone else, seemed to actually enjoy her job. I couldn't draw because my hands shook too much from the new medication, so she brought me paints. I figured out a way to do it so the shaking didn't matter. All I had to do was limit myself to fat lines.

I tried to make the art therapist my friend. She looked more like me than everyone else did, her hair blond and straight and shaggy, pretty eyes, good bone structure. Her clothes were like mine too. I tried to talk to her, asked her about the job and what degrees she had. She had an engagement ring on her finger, so I asked about her fiancé. She told me they both liked to go hiking. I told her about a plan I had for when I got out, how I would go deep in the canyon and camp by myself and not eat anything. I thought she would think my idea was interesting, but instead she looked hard at my eyes like she was assessing me. My pupils had been dilated for weeks by then. I wasn't sure if it was the psych drugs or the mania, but either way I always looked high, even when I wasn't.

"I don't think that's a good idea," she said. I think she noticed how upset I was so then she added, "Or at least you shouldn't for a while."

I was so stupid. There was no way she would be my friend. We had nothing in common.

NOTES FROM ALTURA MENTAL HOSPITAL: STEREOTYPES

On the afternoon of my first full day, I heard someone screaming like they were being killed. Sam said it was somebody in solitary. I asked what solitary was and she said it was the padded room down the hall. I thought she was joking, but later I saw a nurse go inside with a needle, and when the door opened I saw the white pads, like gym mats tacked all around the walls.

I walked by later, and peeked in the window real quick. The person who had been screaming was now asleep. I couldn't tell if they were a boy or a girl. Their hair was too short and their body was too fat.

They showed up at group the next day. It was a girl. She'd tried to kill herself by stabbing a pencil into her neck. The stab hole was covered by just a Band-Aid, so it mustn't have been very deep.

NOTES FROM ALTURA MENTAL HOSPITAL: THE OUTSIDE WORLD

Visiting hour came every day, after dinner in the recreation room, with the couches and the TV and the old board games and the terrible books, at a bunch of small tables there for that very purpose. My parents didn't miss it once. It made me feel guilty because some people never had visitors. Sam's grandfather, who raised her because she had no parents, only came once. Sam said he was mad at her because he was religious. She explained that she wasn't trying to die, but that just made him angrier. It was a sin to treat a perfectly healthy body like that.

My parents still looked heartbroken and tired. You could tell it was an effort for them to come, that they felt responsible for cheering me up. They seemed to always have something saved for me, like they had lived the whole day waiting for something to report. Something that would give me a reason to live. My father told me about the dolphins he saw playing that morning when he was surfing, how they got in the waves to surf too. My mother told me about her six-year-old student who had started saying, "Oh hell!" during class. They told me about the sunsets, the brightness of Venus, and it did make me want to get out. The only bit of sky we got were slivers through the narrow shatterproof windows, so filthy that everything outside was just a smear.

The first three days were nice. I still had enough guilt to be remorseful. But I assumed I would get out on the fourth, after the involuntary hold was up. I was wrong. "It has been decided it is best to keep you longer," a nurse told me that morning.

I was furious with my parents. The first three days were on me, but that day, and the ones that came after, were their fault. I sat down with them like normal, but they didn't apologize or anything, so I got up to leave, angry, so fast that the chair sprang back and hit the table. I went back to my room and cried. I don't know what happened to my parents.

On the fifth day, they brought Nicole. You could tell they didn't want to, that they somehow blamed her. Two days before, they'd said I needed to get some new friends. They must have brought her as a peace offering.

She didn't have much to say, just relayed the plot of some dumb show she watched. She told me about her diet. There was a lot of silence in between. She'd already lost seven pounds. She didn't once look me in the eye.

Instead, she stared at the other people. I tried to see them through her eyes: pasty skin, bloated faces, dirty hair. Nobody wearing a belt or shoelaces. I pulled my baggy pants up. I touched the ends of my dirty hair. I was becoming less and less like her, more and more like them. A chasm.

NOTES FROM ALTURA MENTAL HOSPITAL: DREAMS

The new pill was Zyprexa. It was an antipsychotic, just temporary until I got better. "It's like gently putting your feet on the brakes," the psychiatrist said. He told me if I took it long term, I would get fat.

It made it so all I wanted to do was sleep. After breakfast we were supposed to get dressed and shower, but my eyes and feet felt so heavy that I just went back to sleep. We had ten free minutes in between each therapy, thirty for lunch, so for all of those I returned to bed. Head on the pillow and I was out, sucked into the shitty mattress. Sleep more than sleep; an overpowering force.

During the naps I had realistic dreams. Things like being at school and trying to avoid talking to people, oversleeping because I'd forgotten to set my alarm. Mom mad at me—why did I slam the door, why was my hair in the sink, could I please answer the phone. Each time I woke up it was so confusing to find myself on the too-thin mattress in the ugly room with the smeary windows and heavy door. Outside the world. Inside the world. Plucked from it.

A FACT SHEET FROM THE FUTURE

In 1990, a group of researchers at Harvard conducting studies on Prozac found that six of their subjects became suicidal after being placed on the drug. The patients previously showed little or no evidence of suicidality.[1] This research was largely ignored, most likely due to the limited scope of the study.

Prozac became available to patients in the United States in 1987, the first of a new class of antidepressants called SSRIs (Selective Serotonin Reuptake Inhibitors). Other medications that fall under this category include Paxil, Celexa, and Zoloft. They work by, as the name suggests, limiting the reabsorption of serotonin in the brain.[2]

Wellbutrin, on the other hand, is an atypical antidepressant that works by limiting the reabsorption of dopamine. It also releases additional norepinephrine and dopamine.[3]

At the time of my diagnosis in 1998, Wellbutrin was considered the best, safest option for someone with a diagnosis of Bipolar I.[4, 5]

In 2003, Prozac became the first and only antidepressant that was FDA approved for treating depression in adolescents and children. Previously, any prescription of an antidepressant was done so "off-label." As of 2013, Lexapro, Effexor, and Wellbutrin "may be considered" for adolescent use off-label.[6]

[1] Teicher, Martin H., Carol Glod, and Jonathan O. Cole. "Emergence of Intense Suicidal Preoccupation During Fluoxetine Treatment." *American Journal of Psychiatry* 147:2 (1990), 207–210. PDF.

[2] "Selective Serotonin Reuptake Inhibitor." *Wikipedia*, April 24, 2016.

[3] "Buproprion." *Wikipedia*, April 19, 2016.

[4] Fogelson, D. L., A. Bystritsky, and R. Pasnau. "Bubroprion in the Treatment of Bipolar Disorders." *Journal of Clinical Psychiatry* 53:12 (Dec. 1992), 443–446. NCBI.

[5] Hartmann, P. M. "Strategies for Managing Depression Complicated by Bipolar Disorder." *Journal of American Board of Family Medicine* 9:4 (July–Aug. 1996), 261–269. NCBI.

[6] Rappaport, Nancy, Deborah Kulick, and LeAdelle Phelps. "Psychotropic Medications: An Update for School Psychologists." *Psychology in the Schools* 50:6 (2013), 589–600. PDF.

In 2012, a study showed that only 9.2% of antidepressant prescriptions given to juveniles were associated with FDA-approved indications.[7]

As of the time of this writing, there is no antidepressant that is FDA approved for the treatment of bipolar depression, for patients of any age. Moreover, studies have shown that there is no research backing up the efficacy of antidepressants in bipolar disorder.[8]

Although research has shown a correlation between antidepressants and increased suicidality since 1990 (particularly in children and adolescents), this evidence was continually dismissed by the FDA, saying it was "anecdotal."[9]

However, after "a blue-ribbon scientific advisory panel" in September 2004, the FDA placed a black-box warning on antidepressants, due to the "increased risk of suicidal behaviour among pediatric users. Black-box warnings are typically reserved for lethal drugs." They concluded that suicidality was nearly twice as likely when pediatric patients were placed on antidepressants versus a placebo.[10]

The black box warning states that it is especially important to monitor the patient for suicidality during "initial treatment (generally the first one to two months)."[11]

This suicide attempt occurred approximately three weeks after I was placed on Wellbutrin.

[7] Lee, E. et al. "Off-Label Prescribing Patterns of Antidepressants in Children and Adolescents." *Pharmacoepidemiology and Drug Safety* 21:2 (Feb. 2012), 137–144. NCBI.
[8] Goldberg, Joseph. "Antidepressants for Bipolar Disorder." WebMD. WebMD, July 31, 2014.
[9] Harris, Gardiner. "F.D.A. Links Drugs to Being Suicidal." *New York Times*, Sept. 14, 2014.
[10] Kondro, Wayne. "FDA Urges 'Black Box' Warning on Pediatric Antidepressants." *CMAJ: Canadian Medical Association Journal* (Oct. 12, 2004), 837+. Academic OneFile.
[11] U.S. Dept. of Health and Human Services. "Antidepressant Use in Children, Adolescents, and Adults." Food and Drug Administration, April 13, 2016.

BOOK TWO

WHY I STOPPED GOING TO SCHOOL

Nicole was waiting outside for me the first day I went back. The whole car ride over, I'd been imagining walking into those doors alone. I wasn't sure I could do it. She stood next to me, escorted me to class, smiling in a way that seemed both brittle and genuine. Nicole seemed to feel guilty, willing to let me temporarily usurp Ariana, who wasn't around anywhere. I might have felt ashamed or embarrassed by her obvious pity but I needed her too much to care. She met me at break, and, at lunch, got one of her friends in the grade above us with a driver's license to take us off campus. She kept asking me over and over if I was doing OK. Still, it was nice. She was being so nice.

Besides that, the rest of the day was total shit.

Somebody had told everyone why I'd been absent, apparently. All the teachers wanted to talk to me after class. Ms. Novak called me to her desk as the other students were filing out and opened her gradebook. She smiled at me, or it was supposed to be a smile, except her lips were tight and thin. "We'll do this here," she said to me, erasing the F beside my name for the paper I had never turned in on *The Odyssey*. She blew away the eraser dust and wrote a big fat C.

The C was a relief, but also a lie, a fake-ass cover-up because she felt sorry for me.

Ms. Novak said I had until after break to write the *Macbeth* paper that had been turned in by the others while I was absent. She reached her hand across the table and grasped mine, squeezing it, telling me if I needed anything, anyone to talk to, she'd be there for me. Her eyes watered and I thought she might cry, or I might cry, and I felt like if either of those things happened I wouldn't be able to stop, so I mumbled thank you and pulled my hand away and headed out of the classroom and on to lunch, where Nicole was waiting to take me away.

BUT THAT WASN'T EVEN
THE WORST PART

Coach received a note telling him to excuse me from fifth period P.E. I thought, at first, that I was in trouble, that maybe the time I'd missed in the hospital meant I was getting kicked out. But when I checked in with the secretary, she told me to take a seat, and then the guidance counselor came and brought me to her office.

There was another girl sitting in there already. She was wearing a pink polo shirt and glasses. She had shiny black hair and when she smiled at me I could see her neat white teeth. I could tell just by looking at her that she woke up every morning with enough time to shower and blow dry her hair and sit down and eat breakfast. I hadn't even showered since they'd made me in the mental hospital, and my clothes were wrinkled and stained.

The guidance counselor told me she was my Peer Assistant Listener, my PAL, a new friend—someone who would help me figure out my studies and the things I'd been missing. My PAL looked friendly, like she wanted to help.

We walked back over the hill together, to a bench in the quad under a tree where a group of surfers sat during lunch, the surfers with more money and better grades. As we walked, she said mindless things about Christmas break and Christmas trees, to which I smiled and nodded like I knew what she was talking about.

We sat down and she asked me about the problems I'd been having. I thought I should just say I'd been really sick, but then I remembered what they'd told us in the hospital, to be honest, that if we weren't completely and totally honest then no one could help us. I wanted things to be different, I really did—so I told her everything.

She was facing into the sun, and the light reflected off her glasses in a way that made her look like a golden space creature.

The blankness made it easy to talk and talk. When I was finished, I thought she'd know what to do, or at least have something to say.

But it was obvious she had nothing to say to me. Nothing to offer me. She looked at me, looked away, disgusted. She fingered the silver cross that hung on a chain around her neck, me, a vampire, something to ward away. Her mouth opened but she said nothing, white teeth now looking more rodent-like than pretty. I felt my face flush hot with embarrassment. I was so stupid.

I didn't know what to do so I just told her the old standby: I had to pee. I went to the bathroom and peed and washed my hands. The bathroom was empty. The absences, the inability to sleep, the inability to eat, the inability to read, the visions, the suicide attempt, the hospital, the other hospital. I stood at the mirror and reapplied my lip gloss. I didn't look like someone who'd just been let out of the mental hospital. I didn't feel like it either. I didn't feel like much of anything. The new psych meds had turned me cold. A machine.

Someone had scratched the words LIVE FAST DIE YOUNG into the mirror. It was a funny joke.

THAT NIGHT

Neither of my parents would leave me alone. My mom came home early, walked by my door every thirty minutes, like she was checking to make sure I was still alive. My dad came home with pizza and a bunch of videos from Blockbuster. Stupid movies, movies I didn't want to watch—*Air Bud, Liar, Liar, The Nutty Professor*—but I felt so guilty that I pretended I was excited. We watched two movies and then it was time for bed. My dad went upstairs but my mom said she wanted to talk. It turned out she had nothing to say. We sat there at the kitchen in silence for a while, her opening her mouth and then closing it like a fish. "How are you feeling?" was finally what she settled on.

She was looking better, better than before. Her skin was no longer that gray color it had been while I was in the hospital. The bags were almost gone from her eyes. But they were red rimmed, and it made me wonder if she'd been crying. I felt guilty, that I'd made her cry. I told her I was feeling better. It was even sort of true. The hallucinations had stopped and I no longer felt like anyone was watching me. Every night since the hospital, I'd slept like a log. I did feel drugged and sluggish, but it was better than the Other Thing. But underneath the blanket of medicine, I still felt so sad and hollow. Like an alien, this strange interloper that didn't fit in anywhere, didn't have a core or a true self. I didn't want to go back to Carmel Heights, but at the same time, I wished this wasn't true.

At first I didn't say anything about the sadness to my mother. I smiled and said I was feeling good. But then I told her the truth. "I'll be fine as long as I don't have to go back to that school," I said. "I can't go back."

I thought she might be angry, or disappointed. But she slid her hand across the table and put it over mine. It felt good there, warm and solid. "Your father and I will figure it out."

We sat there for while, quiet. Then she said, "You know what I think would be fun? We could have a slumber party. Right here in the living room. We could get out the camping mats and sleeping bags."

I knew what she was doing. I knew she was still afraid of what would happen if she left me alone, if I would try it again. I wouldn't. The whole experience had been so humiliating and exhausting that there was no chance. But I figured I owed her something, more than I could give her, that this "slumber party" on the floor was the least I could do.

We got the mats and sleeping bags from the garage, pushed the coffee table aside and rolled everything out, our pillows so close they were touching. I could feel her watching me as we both lay there. I could feel her eyes on me as I fell asleep, trying to uncover something, trying to figure out if I was really her daughter, or just some maniac who had been left in her place.

Carmel Heights didn't want me to switch to New Hope, the district's continuation school. The vice principal called me into a meeting with my parents and pulled out my scores from the standardized test they made us take every year. He pointed to the numbers, all in the ninetieth percentile, except for listening.

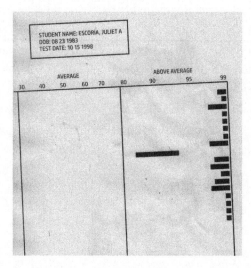

"It's unusual to have a girl score so high in both math and English," he said, transparent. Everybody knew that Carmel Heights was the top-scored high school in the county, although sometimes they lost that title to Reagan High or Sierra Vista, the two high schools just north and south of Carmel Heights, in neighborhoods equally wealthy and white as Santa Bonita. And everyone knew the factors determining this scoring had nothing to do with how much the students learned, or how well they did in college, or how well they did in life, and were instead decided by things that should have been arbitrary yet somehow weren't treated that way, like championship titles, and test scores, and cumulative GPAs, and the percentage of students entering elite colleges upon graduation. I hadn't known the numbers were broken down into gender and subjects.

If he looked at the papers in my file that weren't my test scores, he'd see my shitty grades, and all of my truancies and tardies and detentions. He had even been the one who gave me dirty looks while I had detention, which mostly involved filing things in his office, and he was the one who made the phone calls about the truancies that led to detention and my subsequent endless grounding, and he was the one who had just last month signed a document stating that I had exceeded the acceptable number of truancies and therefore was required to go before a review board, which would probably result in Harry, the narc, following me around from class to class, and would therefore make my attendance a drain of school resources, and not, as he was saying, an asset, a valuable component to the environment that was Carmel Heights High School.

Not to mention the new document that had made its way into my file while I was in the hospital, my IEP, which stated in big bold capital letters that I was the opposite of an asset. I was a liability. Maybe the IEP plus my test scores showed diversity or something. Maybe they got more funding for that kind of thing. Double bonus for smart, emotionally disturbed teenagers.

Julie has **DEMONSTRATED HIGH RISK BEHAVIORS WITH HER FELLOW STUDENTS. SHE HAS NOT RESPONDED TO TYPICAL PRODING OR REQUESTS FOR RESPONSIBILITY, TYPICALLY ASSOCIATED WITH HER AGE.** Her relationships with peers are superficial and poorly sustained. Julie has a tendency to oversimplify difficult situations, which she perceived as being complex and ambiguous. She often overlooked or neglected critical issues that required moral judgement, and **IS PRONE TO OUTBURSTS OF ANGER THAT ARE, ON OCCASION, VIOLENT.** As a result of this, along with her psychiatric treatment, prescribed medication, and problematic school struggle, it appears that Julie would immediately qualify for placement under the category of **EMOTIONALLY DISTURBED.** It appears that these problems impact Julie's ability to learn to such an extent that her schooling cannot be effective without Special Education resources.

Dr. Richard Wood, School Psychologist

Individualized Education Plan for "Julie" [*sic*], December 1998.

I didn't laugh though, mostly because I just wanted to get out of there. Mom and Dad seemed as annoyed as I did, nodding and saying nothing, understanding that this was just a stupid formality. We listened as the vice principal went on, explaining how there were no AP or Honors classes at New Hope, no science past biology, no team sports, that someone with my talents would not be "granted the room to thrive" at a school with limited resources like New Hope. Once he'd finally finished, my dad told him I would indeed be switching schools.

It was three days before the semester was supposed to end. We walked out and my mom told me she didn't care if I finished the week, that I could stay home if I wanted. My dad, who always seemed so interested in following the rules, shivered and said the whole school gave him the creeps. He understood why I didn't want to go; he wouldn't want to either. They both agreed: we were making the right decision.

SO I STARTED AT NEW HOPE

In the mornings I took the bus, which I didn't mind because it re-minded me of being in grade school. A sign that this would be a new start, and things would return to how they were. But the bus stop was at Carmel Heights.

New Hope started at nine, an hour and a half after Carmel Heights, where classes were just beginning. I would have been in Math, at the back of the school, and Nicole in Social Studies. I could see her classroom, but the bus pickup was at the far end of the parking lot, too far for me to see in the windows. The building might as well have been empty. From this distance, my old high school looked cold and lifeless, like some sort of office complex housing a company that specialized in the manufacture of deadened workers and blandly malevolent machines.

The first morning was cloudy and cold. I was the only one waiting because my mom had dropped me off so early. She made me take a piece of toast on a paper towel since I was too nervous to eat before I left. I had nothing in my backpack except for an empty binder, my Discman, and a few pencils. I put on my headphones and sat on the curb. I took a bite of toast, then crumpled the paper towel into a ball and threw it all in the gutter.

SCHOOL RULES

At New Hope, we didn't have classes. Instead, there was a math room with a math teacher, an English room with an English teacher, and so on. You chose which room to go to and when. Right away I could tell that people didn't actually do this, instead holing up in a single classroom for most of the day. I couldn't figure out how you decided which classroom was your home base. I thought it might have to do with your advisor—we were all assigned one, mine was the English teacher, Mrs. Hunter—but nobody spent much time in her room so I figured that wasn't it. Most of the Spanish-speaking students spent the day in the history room because that teacher was fluent in the language. This was the only thing I could piece together.

The Spanish-speaking students were one of the major populations that made up New Hope. There were also the pregnant girls, and people with jobs who needed fewer school hours and a more flexible schedule. Then there were the nerds, kids who'd been made fun of so much they had to be sent somewhere else. Everyone else was some sort of art kid—gay, weird, and/or depressed. I'd never seen so many different colors of hair in my life.

I didn't know who any of the other students were, and none of them knew me.

I was any old kid.

Not crazy. Just weird.

THE SMOKERS

I'd heard rumors that you were allowed to smoke at New Hope. This was admittedly one of the main reasons why I wanted to go there. But I sort of assumed it was mere hearsay, the kind of thing Carmel Heights students told each other while sneaking cigarettes behind the tennis courts, hoping to not get a ticket from one of the cops that patrolled the streets around the school.

The rumors were true. Before and after school, all the smokers gathered at the upper parking lot, in this tiny dirt area next to the main road, cordoned off with a rusty chain-link fence ratted with holes. One of the teachers always went up there too, to make sure we didn't get abducted or leave the property or smoke something that wasn't tobacco. Sometimes a policeman even came by, rolled down his window, talked to the teacher, said hello to us, signaling we were in a safe zone.

But I didn't go up there the first couple days. I wasn't sure of the etiquette, and standing in the small area with a bunch of strangers seemed like too much pressure. When I got to school, I just sat behind a tree in the little courtyard at the center of the school, hoping no one would notice me. It was peaceful under that tree. Its leaves were small and the palest green, and as I sat there the breeze pushed them off the branches, fluttering into my hair.

BUT ON THE FOURTH DAY

This girl I hadn't seen before showed up at the bus stop. She was wearing big platform shoes and pink heart-shaped sunglasses. I didn't recognize her until she came up to me and said hi. It was Holly. Her mother was the secretary at my mom's school, and we used to play together after school when we were little. Now her hair was dyed black. She acted happy and surprised to see me, said she'd been sick the past few days. We sat down on the curb and she offered me a cigarette. Her nails were long and painted bright blue. I hadn't thought to smoke here before, figuring we'd get caught by the narc or something. But I didn't say anything, remembering a conversation I'd had with her when I was in third grade and she was in fourth. She'd asked me if I knew what a condom was. I said yes, thinking she was stupid, because, as I told her, I lived in one. My answer made her laugh and laugh. It took two years before I figured out why.

I took a cigarette from her and figured nothing bad would happen. I smoked it fast, the tip turning narrow and thin like a pencil. I put my butt out on the remainder of my toast from the first day, which was now a nasty beige lump crawling with ants.

At the end of the day, Holly and I got in the back of a truck with three students I'd seen but hadn't talked to. The owner of the truck was this guy Derek, a senior with a blue mohawk. The girl was his little sister Cara. She had a pierced nose and was wearing a belly T with JNCOs. Her hair was neon red. I'd never seen a girl who looked like her until I came to New Hope, and now there was a dozen of them—as good-looking and cool as a popular girl at Carmel Heights, but wearing clothes that made my Calvin Klein T-shirts and Guess? jeans seem prissy and square.

The third person was this guy named Robbie, who was a big ugly with acne scars all over his face, but I gathered everyone liked him anyway because he was funny.

We all went to Derek and Cara's house, which wasn't a house at all, but an apartment they lived in with just their father, furniture old and faded and everything a different color, walls blank except for a photo of the three of them at the zoo in a #1 DAD frame over the doorway to the kitchen. We smoked weed. I didn't say much, worried about how I was coming across, afraid of acting like a stuck-up Santa Bonita girl. But no one seemed to care. It seemed they liked having me around. They passed me the pipe and Robbie told jokes until we couldn't stop laughing, until Holly was snorting and Cara had tears streaming down her face.

FLOCK

Most days after school, Holly and I went to the Palms, this shopping center a few blocks over from Carmel Heights. There was a bookstore, a Walgreens, a grocery store, a brand new Bath & Body Works. The first time Holly brought me there, we'd gone to her house first for hot dogs and Pepsi, pretty much the only thing she ever ate, before walking over. There were a bunch of metal tables in front of the movie theaters, chipped white paint. A small group of boys sat at one of them, playing chess. They were younger than us, maybe junior high, scrawny and covered in acne. I couldn't figure out why Holly wanted to hang out with them. I pulled out a cigarette, said nothing, smoked it, pulled out another, bored. The boys and Holly made dumb jokes that I only half-listened to.

As it grew later, other people started showing up in big trucks and tricked-out cars, shouting from the open windows before parking and walking over to us. The boys wore hoodies and wide JNCOs. The girls wore a lot of makeup, and had long straight hair. I vaguely recognized some of them from Carmel Heights and New Hope.

"Who's this?" one of the boys said to Holly, nodding at me. His black hair was bleached blond and he was old enough to have a goatee. I couldn't tell if he was cute. Holly introduced me. His name was Ramon. He smiled, then told Holly we should go smoke a bowl.

I followed them around the corner, to this corridor behind the theater full of big bags of trash. Ramon pulled out a shitty metal pipe and a tiny baggie of sticky weed, giving me the first hit. I felt funny smoking it right in public like that, hidden only by a tiny stucco wall that separated us from the parking lot, right where someone could see us. But Holly and Ramon acted like it was no big deal.

And later I learned that it wasn't. This was a space I'd smoke in often. Nobody was ever back there besides us. There were other places too—behind the green power box on the far side of the circle, which is what we called the drop-off area for the theater in front of the tables, crouching in the tall grass that grew in the vacant field across the street. During the day, we sat at the tables, the lacy iron pressing curlicues into my thighs, smoking cigarettes until my lungs hurt, drinking cheap beer or liquor hidden in plastic cups and somebody's backpack. The grown-ups and children going to the movies looked at us warily, but nobody ever bothered us. The tables were ours.

As it grew dark, more people showed up and we'd figure out a place to party. Unless somebody's parents were out of town, the parties always revolved around a vacant spot—along the beach or in the canyons, dirt lots off the road where Nicole lived, waiting to be turned into houses and a freeway. We would go there until it got "burned," aka the cops started rolling by as part of their regular patrol.

Our group even had a nickname: PT, Palms Trash. Sometimes the football boys from Carmel Heights drove by the circle and yelled at us from their trucks, throwing soda cans and once a burrito. They meant it as an insult, but I was happy to be called PT, happy to be trashy and not care. Happy to be part of a group.

PILLS, PILLS, PILLS

At New Hope, I joined the literary and art magazine, which some goth girls ran out of my advisor's room. We sorted through the submissions or worked on our own stuff sometimes, but mostly we just sat around and talked. Quietly. Mrs. Hunter freaked out if you made too much noise. A lot of times that meant we passed shared notes. There was Anna, who had tattoos all down her arms and said she was schizophrenic. Tricia, who had big beautiful boobs and a two-year-old daughter. And Lily, who was extra goth, always in a ton of makeup and long lacy dresses, and had the prettiest face I'd ever seen. She lived down the street from me but we never did anything outside school because she claimed she was agoraphobic, had tinfoil taped over her bedroom window, and supposedly shot up speedballs. At school she'd give me pills, Percocet and Vicodin, which I traded for my mother's Somas. After the suicide attempt, my mom kept the medicine in a black lockbox in a cabinet in the dining room, requiring her permission every time I needed an Advil. My mom didn't know I knew where the box was. She also thought the lock on it was secure. It took a while, but it was possible to pop it open with a bobby pin.

At New Hope, there were pills everywhere. Sometimes I skipped lunch and used the money to buy them. Other times I'd trade for what I could find at home. Every now and then people were dumb enough to trade for my psych meds. I hid everything I got in the little silver case my mom made me keep in my purse, just in case I ever decided to spend the night somewhere last minute. I'd nestle them next to a night's supply of Tegretol and Wellbutrin and take the pills right in class. I liked the power that came from getting high in plain sight simply by swallowing a little capsule. Once they'd kick in, I'd sit on one of the beanbag chairs in Mrs. Hunter's room and read, or go into the art room and take out the watercolors. We were allowed to listen to our headphones whenever we wanted as long as we kept the volume down, and every classroom had big windows and warm light, and I'd sit there high and comfortable, a feeling of indulgence, like somebody's favorite cat.

I found out the reason why no one besides the four of us ever stayed long in Mrs. Hunter's room. I was reading one day when all of a sudden she started freaking out. She stood up real quick from her desk, slammed the chair under her desk and stormed over to the tables.

"All right! That's enough!" she yelled. "Everybody out."

I couldn't figure out why she was mad. Some people had been whispering but we were allowed to whisper in class. That was it. That was the only noise.

Everyone got up to go, collecting their things and looking at each other and rolling their eyes. I picked up my books too, but then she started yelling again.

"You! You're fine. You stay." Mrs. Hunter was small and blond, but with her finger quivering at me she seemed like a witch. I did what she said. I didn't argue. I put my book back down, sat in my chair, eyes straight ahead.

"You. You stay also. All you girls. You're fine."

I felt Tricia and Anna and Lily sit back down noiselessly. We opened our books. The classroom emptied. It was silent for the rest of the day. We got a lot of work done.

I got an explanation for Mrs. Hunter's behavior after school let out. Two actually.

She had a coffeemaker in the room, which she drank from constantly, so the room always smelled like burnt coffee. That was the part I already knew. What I didn't know was that she drank two pots a day. Not only that, but once she finished brewing a pot, she used it in place of water and brewed it again—double-brewed, so strong it might as well have been speed.

I also didn't know about an incident that happened a few months before. People used to go into Mrs. Hunter's classroom all the time because she was kind of oblivious, always on the computer doing whatever it was she did, scribbling in notebooks, sometimes just staring off into space. One day, these guys Matt and Robbie—the big ugly—and a few others came up with a plan to smoke weed in class. It was elaborate, involving aquarium tubing from the science room and a student pretending to faint so Mrs. Hunter would have to take her to the office, while Robbie and Matt cut a square in the window screen with an X-ACTO knife. Then they got one of the kids in the gardening club to affix the tube to the wall with the little staples they used to guide vines or whatever. Even the window was chosen strategically—next to the bookshelf, partially obstructed, near the beanbag chairs so it didn't look strange if you were sitting on the floor.

The plan worked. Somebody dropped a book or "accidentally" knocked over a chair or coughed while they flicked the lighter. When they exhaled, the smoke was blown through the aquarium tubing, which pointed away from the open window. It was flawless.

Until, of course, it wasn't. A few of the seniors were former drug addicts, now sober, and they worked as informal narcs for the school. One walked by at the wrong moment, saw the smoke, and ratted them out. Everyone in the room got lectured until Robbie and Matt confessed, figuring as few people as possible should take the fall. They were almost expelled (I didn't even know where the hell you went once you're expelled from New Hope), but in the end got "community service," which involved janitorial chores around the school. Mrs. Hunter got in trouble too, almost fired, so her behavior was close to understandable. Still, she was a freak. Just like the rest of us.

OTHER PEOPLE'S PROBLEMS

We all had group therapy for an hour every Friday. The groups were mostly divided by gender, except for the queer kids who were all together. I tried to figure out why I was placed in my group but I couldn't. Holly wasn't in mine, or Anna, but Lily and Tricia were. I thought maybe ours was the pretty girls because they spent a lot of time talking to us about sex and self-esteem. But there were some hot girls in a different group and some ugly ones in ours so it was hard to say.

Other people had been to the mental hospital, attempted suicide, or cut themselves. I wasn't the only one on psych meds. But most of the other girls' problems stemmed from things you could easily define, things that happened outside of them and made it easy to see them as victims. This girl Jessica, her mom was a drunk and had an endless stream of equally drunk boyfriends. Abby's grandpa molested her. Lily's mom worked long hours and was never home. Cheyenne's family sometimes didn't have enough money for food.

Not once did anyone ever talk about what it was like when your only trauma was yourself. It was all real problems, concrete things that had gone wrong. It made me want to carve out the part of myself that was defective, like a gangrenous limb. My problems didn't seem bad enough to justify all that I'd done to myself. Midway through the semester, I started being sick on Fridays, as often as my mother would let me get away with, so I didn't have to go to group.

MY OLD LIFE

A couple months into the semester, I called Nicole's house after not hearing from her for a while. Her mother said she was gone. She'd been arrested for stealing a car with her new boyfriend, and so her parents sent her away to a reform school in Montana. That wasn't surprising. Nicole's parents had been fed up with her for years.

Sometimes I thought about Nicole, mostly when I was putting on makeup before we went out at night—Holly just wore mascara and lipstick—but really, I only thought about Holly now. It was strange how someone could disappear from your life like that. In a few short months, Nicole had gone from the center of my orbit to a dot so far away it didn't matter anymore.

But Holly was nicer than Nicole. With Holly, I wasn't the weird one. We were the same. We were equal. We were best friends.

I hadn't told Holly about my diagnosis, though. She knew about the suicide attempt, and that this was the reason I'd come to New Hope, but I'd never mentioned the details and she never asked.

One day, Holly and I ditched school. We didn't have a good reason, we just didn't feel like going. Neither of us had skipped out at New Hope before. I wasn't sure if they'd notice or care, or what would happen if they did. The uncertainty was a little bit thrilling, and as we walked the mile or so it took to get from Carmel Heights to Holly's house, I felt excited, like I was doing something illegal. I kept thinking maybe a police officer would drive by, immediately know what type of girls we were and what we were doing, and arrest us.

Of course this didn't happen. We got back to Holly's, turned on her stereo, got sodas from her fridge and went on her patio to smoke cigarettes. We stayed out there for hours.

"The scariest thing was the hallucinations," I found myself saying. "I honestly thought I was completely batshit. I thought I was going to be fucked up forever. But they're gone now, thank God."

I was quiet, feeling both overly exposed for my confession and relieved. I wasn't sure how Holly would take it, the fact that her new best friend was nuts. I wasn't sure what she would say. I looked her in the eye and in my stomach I felt a new dread. But she surprised me.

"I'm bipolar too," she said. She'd never hallucinated, but right before she started at New Hope, there was a time when she couldn't sleep. "I'd be so tired but as soon as I lay down it felt like my heart was going to beat straight out of my chest. Like I'd done crank or something. My mom was so freaked out, she skipped work and took me to the doctor. That was when I switched to New Hope. I'm on lithium now, but I hate it."

I was shocked. I knew Holly wasn't exactly normal. But hearing her say the thing about her heartbeat. My experiences coming out of someone else's mouth.

As it grew later, our pagers started going off, friends from New Hope and the Palms. We didn't answer them. Instead, we continued listening to music, smoking, talking. I felt safe, like we were on an island, a safe island of two where nothing could get us, just Holly and me, bipolar best friends.

HATE-CRIME SATURDAY

It was a Saturday night, right after Valentine's Day. I'd called my parents from Holly's house and told them the usual lie: we were going to the movies and then I was sleeping at her house. For some reason they always believed me.

Instead, we were going to a party. Danny Smackball was meeting us in front of his work at nine. That wasn't his real name. I don't know why anyone called him that. It was a stupid nickname. He worked at the Italian restaurant in the shopping center down the street from Holly's house. I think he washed dishes.

The party was at an abandoned Vietnamese church. Some of the boys found it when they went off-roading. It seemed like it had been vacant a long time.

Danny Smackball's truck was black and shitty. We got in, me in the middle because I was the smallest. It was a stick so he had to bang his hand against my thigh each time he switched gears. I didn't know what to do in response. Leaning into his hand felt wrong. Scooting away felt wrong. Just sitting there and not moving made me feel like a corpse, but that, in the end, was what I settled on.

The drive took a while, over winding dirt roads I didn't know existed. The moon was almost full and we were far enough from the city that the stars shined sharp and bright, the way they did in the desert. There weren't any streetlights, and it seemed like we'd been transported far away, somewhere in the middle of nowhere. By the time we got there, my leg had fallen asleep from sitting so stiff.

The party hadn't really started yet. There were just a handful of cars out front. We walked inside and it was empty and dark, with only a couple people sitting on a pew in the corner. They didn't acknowledge us. A few candles were in front of them, the glass kind with the Mexican saints, their faces distorted by shadows. They were smoking something, it was hard to tell what.

I felt a surge of panic because Danny never had a lot to say and

I hated awkward silences. But then I heard Junk Dog, whose real name was Matt, his voice muffled like it was coming from the ceiling. Holly heard it too. "Junk Dog!" she said. "Where are you?"

"Up the ladder," he yelled.

It took a few minutes of flicking our lighters around in the dark to find the ladder in the back corner. It was wooden and old and I was afraid of heights, so I didn't look down. It led into an attic, one with a bunch of windows, completely empty except for another candle and Junk Dog and Ramon. They were sitting cross-legged, smoking weed.

Holly wanted to go out on the roof because of the stars. We climbed through one of the windows and it led to a flat section, just big enough for all of us. It was cold that night, the air thin, so the shadows were sharper. Junk Dog had a big bubbler but no more weed. Holly and I had most of a gram. Ramon had a handle of shit vodka. We smoked and we drank, until everything became dry and muffled, until my eyes and throat burned.

At some point, the noise of their talk blurred out. I was alone on that roof, no people, just me, everything empty and black. I wanted to jump into it, to become it, forget my name. Not die. A desire to be a void, not a person.

I stared at the trees, the branches long spikes pointing up at the sky, and I thought about falling into them, puncturing my chest and heart. Then Holly's voice broke through. She told me to get away from the edge. I looked down. It was hard to say if I'd die from that height or merely fuck myself up.

From the roof, we couldn't see or hear what was going on inside. When we finally went downstairs, I was surprised to see the church was packed. It was dark, people towering over the few candles on the ground, a bunch of stretching demonic shadows. There was no music but the conversations followed the same beat, throttling like a bass drum, sounds but not words.

My breath quickened like I might have an anxiety attack, so I headed back up the ladder. I tried to tell Holly to follow me but it was too loud. I stopped before I got all the way up, because something ran across the attic floor. It moved like a cat but it was too big to be a cat and then it seemed to disappear.

"Are you gonna go up there or what?" It was Junk Dog, behind me on the ladder. I didn't know he'd followed me.

"One second," I told him. "There's something up there. Some sort of animal."

"Let me see," he said. I went up, alone in the dark with whatever it was, waiting for it to latch onto me.

Except when Junk Dog flicked his lighter, there was nothing there. He told me I was crazy and for a second I was worried he knew about what had happened last semester, but the only person I'd told was Holly and I knew she wouldn't tell anyone.

I'd always liked Junk Dog because he was the kind of person who never said no. If you couldn't sleep and wanted to go down to the beach but didn't want to be alone, you could call him up, 4:00 a.m., and he'd be sleepy and grumpy but he'd pick up the phone and then he'd come get you. He did drugs and drank in the right way, until they were gone, and then he did his best to get more. There was something solid about him, something that made me feel protected and calm. But recently we spent a lot of time alone. It didn't mean anything but I couldn't get him to see it that way. He kept trying to kiss me, and I kept saying no, and each time it made me feel so bad that all I could hope was he wouldn't do it again. So I tried to avoid situations that could be taken as romantic. The attic above an abandoned church seemed easy to interpret as a good place to make out. Part of me wanted to like-like him, because he was fun and nice, but I couldn't do it. I think it was because he was too short.

I was relieved when Ramon came up the ladder a moment later. He was sloppy drunk, clumsy and too loud but at least there were three of us now. His girlfriend had broken up with him. They were always breaking up but this time she'd gone and fucked someone else, this guy Larry who sold us weed sometimes.

"I'm so fucking pissed," he yelled. "I want to punch something."

"So punch something," I said.

I didn't think he would but then he took off his shirt and wrapped it around his fist, and then he punched it through one of the windows. The glass exploded over the noise of the party. The shards glinted off the candlelight and it was beautiful and I wanted more of it, so I went over to one of the other windows and kicked it. I was wearing boots and jeans, except a shard of it tore through my pants. I felt wetness on my leg and then I looked down and saw the blood. I liked it there. I didn't stop to see how deep the cut was. Ramon's wrist was bleeding too.

He punched another window and Junk Dog punched the fourth, his jacket protecting his fist, and then all the windows were broken and we were bleeding and breathing heavy, hot and destructive and alive. The floor was sparkling with glass, crunching under our shoes. There was nothing left to break. We stood there, still for a moment, looking at each other, saying nothing, but something crackled through us anyway. I let it hit my blood, and then I went down the ladder.

I walked around for a bit, the two boys following me, bumping into people but it was too crowded for anyone to notice, a mob. Holly and Danny seemed to have disappeared, which was exactly why I loved parties like this. You could show up with some people and they could disappear, and it didn't matter because they'd soon be exchanged with new ones. It made everyone seem interchangeable, in a comforting way that meant I'd never have to be alone.

The whole room was packed and too hot, but I saw some empty space up front so I headed there. It was a stage, where the preacher must have preached.

The last time I'd been in a church was last summer, when I went to this creepy Bible camp with Nicole. At the end of the week, a Ken-doll preacher showed up and lectured us about Hell, sweat stains blooming on his denim shirt. At the end, everyone went up to the stage, crying, as they let Jesus enter their hearts. Even Nicole went up there and cried. The only person who didn't was me. I'd thought about it; it seemed nice to have somebody else permanently in my body, but in the end, I couldn't do it. I couldn't save myself from Hell. I wondered if this was the kind of church where people went to cry and be saved. It was hard to imagine it inhabited by anything other than darkness and fucked-up teenagers.

And then I saw the perfect thing: a giant stack of old Bibles. I picked one up. They must have gotten wet at some point because the paper was stuck together in ridges. I took my lighter from my pocket and held the flame to the pages. The fire licked up my hand so quick I almost dropped it, startled by the heat and flash of light. The pages floated away, dead and black. I threw it on the floor, lit another. And then Junk Dog and Ramon were doing it too, and we were laughing, ripping pages out and lighting them on fire and there were ashes in the air, flaking apart into a fine white powder like snow. Their eyes looked black in that light, all pupil and no whites, like something had taken hold of them. Something had taken hold of me too; my legs and arms pulsing in the heat and with the movement, and everything around us flickered in stop animation. Other people started doing it with us, for no reason, just to see what would happen, people I didn't recognize and people I did, and there was so much fire that it felt like we were burning in Hell. I thought we might take the whole place down, I could practically hear the roaring of the flames and the screaming. We belonged there. It was home.

A FEW DAYS LATER

An article appeared in the local paper. It talked about the church. It said it had been the victim of a hate crime. It said they didn't know if it was related to race or religion, but windows had been broken and Bibles burned.

A LETTER FROM THE FUTURE #2

For a while, I kept thinking about how the fictionalized version of myself should lose her virginity. Maybe I should write it just the way I lost mine. Maybe I should write it where she was so fucked up, she didn't even know if she'd lost her virginity or not. Maybe I needed to make a statement, about teenage sexuality.

But then I decided, fuck that. My first credit card had way more of an impact on my life than losing my virginity. Just know that this version of Juliet was having sex. Bad, boring, teenage sex. The kind of sex not even worth writing about. Sex in party houses, sex in pools, sex on the beach, sex in cars. The places and details aren't important, and neither are the boys. The important part was the act. Juliet had found a new way to lose herself, a new way to disconnect. A new way to shut off her brain.

DEAD MAN'S PARTY

The next time there was a big party, it was a costume party at the Heaven's Gate house, that suicide cult with the Nikes and purple blankets. The house they'd died in was owned by the father of this shy Russian girl, Elena Orlovsky, who was a grade ahead of me at Carmel Heights. He'd rented to the cult and hadn't been able to find a tenant since. I wasn't friends with Elena but it didn't matter because everyone was invited. It was the two-year anniversary of the deaths.

I figured my mom would let me go to the party if I told her where it was and I was right. She'd been a lot nicer ever since I switched to New Hope, now that I was getting better grades and hanging out with Holly instead of Nicole. She seemed excited, helping us go through the old costume box in her closet. We found old bell bottoms and a sequined vest so Holly could be Cher. I wore my mom's old wedding dress, which fit perfectly once she pulled the seventies-style lacing as tight as it would go. Then she did our makeup—thick eyeliner for Holly, smudged shadow under my eyes and a lipstick trickle of blood at my mouth. I was a dead bride. I tangled up my hair and imagined I'd drowned.

We were supposed to get a ride with Eli, who hung out at the Palms and lived down the street, but at the last minute he said he was sick. We tried to find another ride but it was too late. Out of desperation, I asked my dad. I figured it was the kind of thing he could brag about to his friends: *My daughter went to a party at the Heaven's Gate house.* He even said he'd give us the ten dollars to get in.

We got in the car, both of us in the back seat, embarrassed to be dropped off at a party by a dad. The house was in Laguna Lakes, fifteen minutes away, a neighborhood of windy dark roads and eucalyptus trees and millionaires, home to old money and aging celebrities. Sometimes we'd drive in our friend Sarah's car, smoking weed and listening to music, not going anywhere except up and down those dark hills. Other than that, the only reason we had to be in Laguna was the house parties, like this one, that happened frequently in the mansions. Usually the parents were gone and unaware until they got back, but there were times, like now, when the parents knew about and even encouraged the parties, trying to buy their poor little rich kid some friends.

I asked my dad to let us out down the street. He wanted to see the house, but finally agreed to drop us off at the bottom of the driveway. Which was more like a street anyway—long, lined with trees, and pitch black. He made us take the flashlight he kept in the glove box for emergencies. I was secretly grateful. It was dark as shit.

We turned it on and illuminated the path in a pale tunnel, the beam dusty and gray from the thin wisps of fog that always got trapped in the hills. The entire driveway was filled with people and cars. My dad wouldn't have seen the house anyway. I didn't even know how many people were in that driveway, getting beer out of their trunks, yelling to their friends, fixing their costumes, kissing, laughing, on the stairs waiting in line. Holly and I got to the end of the line, smoking as we stood but not talking.

I didn't know what I was expecting, especially considering I'd already seen so much footage of the house on TV. I knew there weren't any fountains or creepy sculptures or white columns— nothing that made the house look spectacular or spooky. Still, it was surprising to realize this was just an ugly stucco house, the same as a million others in Southern California, only bigger, with a swimming pool and tennis court out back. Only this one had seen thirty-nine people die.

We gave our money to the person at the door, an older man not quite old enough to be Elena's father. I waited for a feeling of doom to wash over me as we walked in, but I felt nothing. It was a little creepy because the walls and floor were covered in filmy plastic, and besides a couple strobe lights in the corners, it was totally dark. That was it. I could have been anywhere.

There wasn't any incentive to be inside. We had nothing on us, no weed, no pills, nothing to drink. "Do you want to go outside?" I asked Holly, figuring we could at least see better out there.

"Sure," she said. "But I want to find the bedrooms first." We tried to find them—the bedrooms all over the news, plain and ugly, empty except for the bunk beds where the Heaven's Gate members had laid down to die. But the strobe lights made me dizzy, and the room was so crowded it was hard to move, and when I finally saw a door that might lead to a bedroom, it was locked. We asked around until this girl from Carmel Heights told us the bedrooms were downstairs but cordoned off. We gave up and went outside.

Everyone in the front yard seemed wasted and too loud, a parody of drunk teens, saying shit about his dick and her ass and his mother's pussy. There were people pissing in the corners, and I almost stepped in some vomit. "I don't want to be around these idiots," I yelled. "Let's just keep walking," Holly yelled back. We walked until we found a path through some bougainvillea bushes to the backyard.

Once we broke through, it was less crowded, almost peaceful, with small groups standing and smoking. The tennis-court lights were on, and the neon bounced off the smooth green ground. Everyone in the backyard was just an outline, dark faces and shapes, the tops of heads and edges of limbs lined in silver. I saw a gazebo, some steps, wicker chairs. A bunch of people from the Palms were supposed to be there, but we had yet to see any of our friends.

Then I saw the Ryans, sitting a few feet from us on lounge chairs under the gazebo. In junior high, they'd been half nemeses, half friends. The less cute Ryan's mom taught with my mom, and the cuter one lived down the street from Nicole, so the four of us all carpooled. Sometimes we traded CDs or notes, hung out together after school, but often they were downright mean to Nicole and me. They called Nicole "Jiggly Tits" and me "Pimple Girl," and the two of us "SB," short for "stupid bitches." Sometimes they asked us if we liked nonexistent bands and if we said we weren't sure but thought we did, they called us posers. Shit like that.

I hadn't seen them since junior high. I hadn't even thought about them. I knew they were going to private school now, but I had no idea they were still friends. For some reason, it surprised me to see them together, as though Nicole's disappearance from my life meant they should have disappeared from each other's too.

Ryan D, the cute one, waved, his palm pale in the refracted neon light. I thought they'd make fun of me, wandering around the party with just Holly and no beer. Then I remembered a year had passed, we were in high school now, no longer total assholes, and they were also alone. We walked over and I introduced Holly. They offered us some of their weed, topped with red rock opium. The shift between sobriety and the drugs was fast, a curtain falling, and the high was both intense and smooth. The noise from the party seemed to die down. The light from the tennis courts was painfully brilliant, a feeling of being too close to the stars. The four of us finished the bowl, lit cigarettes, and sat there, quiet in our contemplation or absence of thoughts. When we spoke again, of course it wasn't to ask how we'd been doing, what we'd been thinking about, or anything real or meaningful. Instead we just talked about the drugs, which were good, and the party, which wasn't as cool as we'd thought it would be, and the house, which was a disappointment. I told them I wanted to go in the bedrooms but they were locked. Ryan M pointed.

"They're right there," he said.

"Right where?"

"Behind you. Those windows. Those are them."

And he was right. We walked up to the windows, which were blank black boxes until we got close enough to put our hands up around our faces to see in. I could make out the room, completely empty except for two sets of bare bunk beds, no blankets, no mattresses. I couldn't believe it. It had been two years since the suicides, enough time that you'd think they'd have destroyed everything. But here were the same bunk beds I had seen in all the news footage, now silent and dark and right in front of me.

The windows were large and low to the ground, the kind that slid open side to side. I had experience with this type of window. So did Holly. They were the kind in her bedroom, the type we'd snuck into and out of dozens of times. I knew exactly how to open them from the outside: push the frame up and then over. And so I did that. And then I crawled on through.

The air in the room was hot and stale, like crawling into someone's attic. I had thought the Orlovskys were living in the home, to make the place seem more hospitable. That was the rumor. But it felt like no one had been in the room for decades.

I wanted to feel something more. I wanted to feel something other than the feeling that comes from stale air and bare beds. I wanted the feel of the dead. But it was nothing more than a sad and empty room. I crawled into one of the beds, the pair in the corner, a corner I could almost remember seeing on TV. I put my feet where I thought I remembered the feet being. I put my head where I thought I remembered the head being. The metal slats pressed into my spine, cold and hard. I put my hands at my sides, the way I'd seen on TV, dead fingers peeking out from a purple shroud. I closed my eyes, there was a blanket over my head, there was a plastic bag, I was dying, I was dead. I was ready to get out of there. I was ready to take a ride on a comet that would deliver me to heaven.

CANYON TRIP

One night me, Eli, Junk Dog, Danny Smackball, and this girl Rachel were sitting on the bluffs in the canyon behind my house. We had split a quad of mushrooms because it was one of those weekends where nothing was going on, hardly anyone was at the Palms, and it seemed like everyone had disappeared. I didn't know where Holly was.

The mushrooms took a while to kick in. They were a lot stronger than we'd first thought. The night seemed strange, spooky, the moon low and dull gold. In the branches of the Torrey pines that loomed over the sandstone bluffs, I saw things hiding, mostly animals—monkeys, pelicans, fanged bats with gnashing mouths, all tangled in tendrils of fog.

Torrey pine (*Pinus torreyana*).

The boys definitely felt it because Junk Dog couldn't figure out how to light a cigarette, and Danny refused to stand up, and Eli was talking nonsense to things only he could see. But I couldn't tell about Rachel. She was my age but no longer in school, had taken her GED to work full time. Her parents were Jehovah's Witnesses, real assholes that made her pay rent and buy her own food. She didn't talk much in general so it wasn't too strange that she wasn't saying a whole lot.

At some point the two of us went to pee. The moon was bright enough that if we stayed on the pale sandstone we could see where we were going. As I sat there crouching, careful not to piss on my shoes, I saw something glint in the bushes.

I cut through the bushes and found myself in a clearing, mysteriously and oddly circular, like the brush had been burned away. I found the shiny thing, thinking it might be something special, a geode or talisman. But it was just an old beer can, so rusted it made no sense that I'd seen it flash at all. I picked it up. The logo was worn away, a pull tab, the kind that hadn't existed for twenty or thirty years. Trash but also a relic. I crouched there, holding it, and then noticed there were more of them. A pile. Like someone had sat right here decades ago, getting fucked up in the canyon, same as us.

I heard Rachel coming through the bushes, quiet as a deer. She sat down next to me, smiling her big snaggle-toothed smile, pupils shiny black in the moonlight. "What are you doing?" she asked.

I showed her the beer can. She picked one up from the pile, shook it. It made noise. She tilted it over and out poured sand and then something else, something fuzzy and black. Spiders. But they sparkled in neon and so I knew they weren't real. I reached out to pet them anyway. The difference between drug spiders and Biology-class skulls.

"We should hide from the boys," she said. "Make them think something happened to us."

I liked that idea. We sat there for a while, talking and making jokes, the kind of things you think are funny or clever only if you're high, careful to whisper so the boys wouldn't hear. But they didn't come looking.

And then in the sky I saw something falling, golden and wild, and I couldn't tell if it was a real shooting star or something hallucinated. I lay back and closed my eyes and a fountain of color rushed through my skull. I felt Rachel lay down next to me, her arm warm against mine. "What do you see?" I asked.

"I see," she said carefully. "A rainbow. It's all rainbow, like a waterfall. But also a horse."

We told each other what we saw, and soon we started seeing the same thing, like telepathy, like mind control. The things became pornographic, moving patterns of people having sex—men with women, women with women, rabbits with bats—and they kept on moving in the same motion, all of creation in one act of creation, of copulation. Of magic. We laughed.

I thought I heard footsteps so I opened my eyes. I figured it was the boys. It wasn't.

A man was in the clearing, standing a couple inches from my feet, torso long and lean in a button-up shirt, face lit in blue. He had long hair and a beard and big aviator glasses. He was smiling at me, but his face looked sad and lost. I had no idea who he was or why he was standing there but I didn't feel scared until I noticed he had no legs. He was dead. He was a ghost.

I didn't mean to scream, but I screamed. Rachel screamed. She'd seen him too. A strange man, all hippied out, a dead guy. We leaped up, and we were running, and when we found the boys my heart was thudding and they were acting like they hadn't noticed we were gone. They didn't even believe us about the ghost.

HAUNTED

I thought he was just a part of the drugs until the dead man followed me home that night. I didn't realize until a couple days later, when I was trying to do homework and felt someone reading over my shoulder. I thought about telling Rachel, but in the end I didn't. He was mine. My vision, my ghost.

Over the next few weeks, sometimes I saw his shape out the corner of my eye, heard him talking to me. I never could understand what he was saying. I don't know what he wanted. One morning I was putting on my makeup before school, and I watched him watching me in the mirror, his eyes filmy and cold under his glasses. I said hi to him.

He put his finger up to my temple, slid it down, like he couldn't believe I was there.

Sometimes at night I saw him in my dreams, standing at the foot of the bed, sometimes hovering over my body. One night he climbed right on top of me, ran his hand up my leg and down my shorts. I felt his finger slide inside of me. It was cold. I liked it. I liked the weight of him, pressing down on my chest, as he fingerbanged me with his ghost hand.

RESEARCH

I walked to the library one day after school, telling Holly I wasn't feeling well. I figured he'd died in the canyon, that the beer cans were his and he'd fallen or overdosed or had a heart attack. On a microfiche machine, I went through all the old issues of the *Santa Bonita Gazette*, from the late sixties and most of the seventies. It took hours. The librarian asked if I needed help, more than once, but I said no. I couldn't think of a way to explain what I was looking for in a way that didn't make me sound insane.

I found nothing that mentioned the death of a young man. But maybe I was merely looking in the wrong place.

EXORCISM

One day I saw him in the bathroom right as I was getting into the shower. I was completely naked, and every hair on my body went up in needle pricks, so I told him to get the fuck out. Said it right out loud, like he was real.

And he left. I didn't see him ever again.

I sort of missed him.

HISTORICAL SIGNIFICANCE

On 4/20, we ditched school to go to a party at this guy Shea's house in the middle of the day. I didn't like Shea. He had sunken-in cheeks from smoking meth, wasn't very bright, and always threw loud, overly dramatic tantrums, the combination of stupidity and drugs. But all our friends were going, so Holly and I went too.

In the morning we walked back to her house after we were dropped off at the bus stop, so we wouldn't be the first ones there. We smoked cigarettes, listening to her stereo and fucking with our makeup. I did Holly's eyes like mine, heavy shadow on the lids and smudged eyeliner. Her hazel eyes popped in the makeup, vivid and outlined and she looked just as crazy as me. We talked about what we'd normally be doing, probably sitting in the art room, drawing pictures and passing notebook pages back and forth. Dumb games of MASH, gossip in code names, recycled jokes, *communism is just a red herring* and *Horace is pretty good looking for a choad.*

We went to Shea's around 10:00 a.m. It seemed funny that the usual party times had been pushed up twelve hours—you *could* get to a party at eight, but you wouldn't want to show up until at least ten. The sun was bright and I felt too tight in my bones, eager to get there and get high. Holly sang as we walked, the Sublime song we both liked. Her voice trilled like a princess in an old Disney movie, and I always wanted to sing with her but never did. I was tone deaf.

A bunch of people were there already, but nobody we cared about. Holly and I went out on the patio, which was tiny, furnished only by two grimy plastic chairs that we brushed off before we sat on them. Holly pulled out the padded bag she always carried, which contained her pipe, a lighter, and the eighth of weed we had purchased the night before. We hadn't let ourselves touch it until now.

I loved the way Holly smoked weed. It was like watching someone who was born to do one thing. Her actions were both effortless and improbable, like a gymnast in the Olympics. With her always perfectly painted long nails she plucked a perfect-sized nug from the baggie, packed the bowl, and held the pipe up to my mouth, an offering, the first bowl of 4/20. She knew just how long to hold the lighter without looking, then took the pipe and lit it for herself. Her inhales were deep, seemingly endless, but never like she was doing it to show off. Her exhales left the patio in a fog, and she never, ever coughed.

We smoked two bowls, more than enough to get us stoned. I felt my body settle, soft and heavy. The chaos in my mind—all the worry about who would be there and if I would act OK—was swept away. When Holly said something about Shea's appearance—he was shirtless, despite the cold, to show off his idiotic tribal tattoo—it was easy to laugh, and I didn't have to think if my laughter seemed canned or too short or too long, the way I found myself doing when I was sober, my special talent of overthinking just about anything.

Shortly after, Ramon showed up, with Junk Dog and this guy named Logan. If I had a crush on anyone it would have been him. Logan was really cute, with blue eyes that seemed perpetually sleepy, long black lashes, and a kittenish jaw. He lived half an hour north of Santa Bonita, had taken his GED, and sometimes toured with a band, so he didn't come around all that much. He didn't say much, so it was impossible to tell what he was thinking, which of course made him mysterious. Holly claimed she didn't like him. When I asked why, her reasons were vague, things like, "He seems skeevy," without any evidence or specifics. I thought she just didn't like that I liked him.

We stood on the patio for a while, squished and smoking cigarettes, sharing a blunt. Junk Dog and Ramon went inside to get beer. Logan said it was too early for drinking and stayed outside with us. "I've got a little bit of coke," he said, once the other boys had closed the door. "You guys want a line?"

"So it's too early for drinking but not too early for coke," I said.

"Yup," he said, smiling at me. "It's coke o'clock."

"We probably shouldn't do it out here," Holly said.

"I don't want to share with everyone," Logan said. "I don't have enough."

We ended up sneaking into Shea's mom's room, which was bare and under-furnished. Just a bed on the floor, no bed frame, and a small dresser in the corner, covered in expensive cosmetics and perfume. From there, we went into the walk-in closet, which was crammed full of clothing, the ground littered with dozens of purses and shoes. Holly flicked on the light and shut the door. We crowded into a corner, clothes parted over us and it felt like we were children playing hide-and-go-seek. Holly seemed to feel it too because she giggled, suddenly OK with Logan now that he had drugs. There was a CD in the back pocket of Logan's insanely baggy pants. Holly chopped and lined out the coke using his Vons Club Card, her movements just as fluid and graceful with the coke as they were with the weed. We each leaned over the CD case with a rolled twenty. The coke wasn't good. It burned, probably mostly meth. It didn't matter too much because the high kicked in quick, a surge of electricity, and I felt good and excited to be at this party with this boy and my best friend.

In the muted light of the closet, Logan looked so pretty, almost like a girl. I wanted to kiss him. His hands were thin and pale with knobby knuckles and splayed tips. Artist fingers. I wanted them on me, inside me.

I didn't know if Holly got the picture or if she was just bored sitting with the two of us, but she got up right after, saying nothing before turning off the lights and shutting the door. Not mad, but like she thought it was funny. We were alone in the dark.

Logan laughed, and I wasn't sure what his laughter meant but it didn't matter because a second later and his hand was on my face, and then his mouth was on mine, and then we were both on the ground, him on top of me and me on top of something that felt like a shoe. I pushed it away. The walls in the apartment were thin, and we could hear all the voices from the rest of the party in the living room: Shea saying, "Yo yo yo," like the poser he was, people changing CDs, never on one album for more than a song.

I closed my eyes so I could concentrate on the taste and feel of Logan's mouth. He kissed just like I had hoped he would kiss, like he meant it. Somebody turned off the stereo and put on MTV instead. Ricky Martin was playing. People started singing along, but turning the chorus into death metal—livin' la VIDA LOCAAAAA—and Logan lowered his hand, unbuckled my belt while still kissing me soft and slow. I moved my hand to his pants, but then the Ricky Martin abruptly cut out. I heard somebody, maybe Ramon, say, "What the fuck?" and then somebody else, maybe Junk Dog, say, "Shut up. Turn it up," and after that, the entire party went dead silent, the only noise Kurt Loder's voice on TV.

As much as I wanted to keep messing around with Logan, the silence of the party seemed more urgent. "What the fuck is going on?" I said.

"Who cares," he whispered into my ear, and then kissed my neck, his teeth sharp against my skin.

"I gotta see," I said, and pulled myself out from under him, buckling my pants and smoothing my hair as I went into the living room.

Nobody noticed me walk in. Everyone's eyes were stuck on the TV. The room pulsed, except everyone in it seemed caught mid-movement under glass, bottles and pipes hovering near mouths. Kurt Loder's voice was grave, playing over footage of teenagers running across the street, hands over heads, flanked by cops. Wearing clothes like the ones we wore, sneakers and T-shirts and denim. In my drug haze, it seemed unreal but too real, hyper-real, some dystopian novel come to life. The coke-meth and weed turned, and I felt the itchiness of paranoia. The TV seemed way too loud and although I usually found Kurt Loder's voice soothing, it was all I could do to not walk across the room and turn it off. I wanted it to go back to a fun party. Logan came up behind me and reached for my hand. I wanted to push him away because suddenly he made me sick. But I didn't move, staring at the TV, like if I looked at it hard enough it would melt away.

The images seemed to float out of the screen: flickering security footage stamped with the time and date, just a few hours before, as boys dressed like characters in video games, gloves and boots and harnesses and guns, skulked around a cafeteria, a bunch of black blobs in the background, barely recognizable as people, maybe dead, hiding behind fallen chairs, food abandoned on tables, police standing around a body on the ground, a shot of a sprawling, institutional-looking school, surrounded by a gigantic parking lot and a perfect lawn, so similar to Carmel Heights, a sign in front of the school reading GOOD LUCK BAND, betraying the normalcy of the morning, boredom and routine and the insular world of high school, suddenly blown up by the gaze of all of us, invading the privacy of that one school, no longer a school but a spectacle. If we hadn't ditched to get high, had parents that raised us in Colorado instead of Santa Bonita, we could be dead. The only difference between us and those kids. The things they'd always told us were dangerous—they were wrong. Instead, the dangerous things kept us safe.

AN EXPERIMENT
IN DUMPSTER DIVING

One night in May, I was spending the night at Holly's. Her mom was really sick, cancer or something. She fell asleep early a lot. We'd snuck out and had a bonfire off Black Creek Road. The cops broke it up. Most everyone else went home. Me, Holly, Ramon, Junk Dog, and Rachel went back to the Palms—we were all that was left. It was late, really late, two or three in the morning. I don't know why we decided to look in the dumpster. We were back in the dark alley behind the Walgreens because we didn't want the cops to find us and make us go home.

The first thing we found was the clothes. They were lying right on top of the garbage in cardboard boxes. A fake fur jacket that fit me perfectly, some miniskirts and tube tops and sparkly dresses, expensive brands like Guess? and bebe, all new, some with the price tags still attached.

We didn't notice the blood at first, not until some of it had smeared onto Rachel's hand. It wasn't much. Maybe it was paint.

Underneath the clothes was a single pair of shoes, Nine West with the heels worn down to stubs, and a purse. In the purse were girl things—a few tampons, some lipstick, a folding mirror. I got to keep the mirror. There was also a wallet, some receipts. A bunch of credit cards, an ID. No cash. The receipts and the ID all had addresses in Arizona.

We stood there for a while, trying to figure out what to do.

"We could call the cops?"

"We'd have to give everything back."

"Maybe the credit cards work."

"Not worth it."

In the end, we divided up the clothes. In addition to the jacket and the mirror, I also got a skirt, some brand I'd never heard of but real cute, with the tag still on it. Rachel got the purse and the nicest clothes because she needed them the most. Holly got all the tops and a bleached denim jacket.

We never talked about the things in the dumpster, just looked at each other with secret smiles when we wore the clothes. Whenever people complimented me on the jacket, I just said thank you, but in my head, I added, *I got it from a dead woman*. I tried to feel bad about it, but it never worked out. I really loved that coat.

THE DRUG TRADE

I was so angry. I couldn't figure out why. I was getting along with my parents, Holly was great, it was nearly summer and my horrible freshman year was almost over. Things were fine. I was fine. It was terrible.

I was in my bedroom, curled in a ball on the floor. I couldn't stop shaking. I wanted to cut myself or break something, but I was sick of cutting myself and I was sick of breaking shit. Everything was pointless. The diseased feeling was erupting again, spilling filthy out of my chest. I was broken.

I got up, went downstairs into the garage. We had a lot of shit in there—old toys, Christmas decorations, tools, stuff from my mom's classroom. Camping equipment. I opened the door. Tents, sleeping bags, pots in a bag that all folded into themselves like nesting dolls. A lantern. A tiny stove. An ax. An ax!

It was really a hatchet. Small, heavy, in a leather sheath. I'd watched my dad take the blunt end to hammer in tent stakes so many times. It was perfect.

I unsheathed it. The blade was rusty and didn't look sharp. I swung it at the wall. The noise it made: *Woosh-chink*. The slice was dark and perfect, a nice even line. I hacked again and again. *Woosh-chink. Woosh-chink*. The anger faded into something contained in that noise.

I realized if I did it too many times, my parents would notice. I was right in front of where my mom parked her car. I wanted to chop more. My closet.

I only chopped a few times, on the wall behind my dresses, before the phone rang. It was Eli. He told me to come over. He had something I'd like. It sounded like drugs.

The only problem, though, was the ax. I didn't want to put it away. It had made me feel OK again, and I wasn't sure it would stick. I put the ax in my purse, but the handle stuck out.

Eli noticed it right away. "What the fuck is that?" he asked.

We were standing in the doorway of his house, me still on the porch, him blocking the entrance. I could see his dad behind him, sitting on the couch with a gigantic book. I'd met him plenty but he was acting as though I wasn't there. He was a philosophy professor at UCSD and was always doing things that didn't make sense.

"We're going to get pizza," Eli told his dad. "Eat it at the beach."

His dad looked up, confused. "OK," he said and returned to his book.

We walked down the road in the direction of the pizza place. "Sorry," Eli said. "I didn't know he'd be home." Then he pulled a little white baggie out of his pocket.

"Coke?" I asked him.

"Nope. K."

I'd never done ketamine. I only knew it was used by veterinarians as a tranquilizer, and too much of it would put you in a "k-hole." I didn't know what that meant, but it sounded kind of nice.

Where to do it. We decided on a power box a couple streets over. It was positioned off the sidewalk in the bushes, on the hill I used to walk down to get to the bus when I was in elementary school.

We had to rail it out, so I took out the little dumpster mirror. It was small but it worked. There wasn't a lot in the baggie, just enough for three little lines each.

The K was weird. It wasn't a high exactly—no warm fuzzy feeling, no giggles, no rush. All it seemed to do was separate my body and the space it inhabited, a strange disconnect I found pleasant. The anger became an object, something placed beside me. The sun splintered in streaks, warm and golden on our faces, as a bumblebee dove drowsily through the air. The cars on the street flew by in a roar. I pulled the hatchet out of my purse and swung the weight of it against my hand, solid and heavy. I don't know how long we sat there. Eli didn't mention the hatchet.

Then his pager went off. "Shit," he said. "I forgot I was supposed to meet these guys. You want to come?"

We walked down to the Circle K to use the pay phone. A few minutes later, two of Eli's friends pulled up in a big Suburban. I knew who they were—Dylan and Luis—two older guys who dealt drugs. I'd bought weed and E from them, but we'd never hung out before. They kind of scared me.

They looked at me warily, like they hadn't known I would be with Eli. "We have to go on a run," Dylan said.

"Can you guys drop me off at the Palms?" I said.

Junk Dog was sitting at the circle, along with Ramon and some of the younger boys. It was still early. Junk Dog was saying he wanted to visit his sister in Vegas, but his car was broken and he didn't have the money to fix it. He was trying to get Ramon to take him, but Ramon wasn't having it. Then they noticed the hatchet in my purse and started making fun of me, calling me crazy. I didn't care. I was used to it. The ketamine made their voices sound far away. "Uh oh," I said.

Nobody had anything to drink or smoke, so we went over to Walgreens, me and Ramon spotting Junk Dog as he tucked a bottle of coconut rum into his sweatshirt. Then we went to Togo's, where our friend worked, and he gave us free lemonades to mix with the rum. We drank our drinks and more people showed up and it seemed like it would be a good night—two parties, both in houses.

The whole time Junk Dog was attempting to harass anyone with a car into driving him to Vegas. It wasn't working. Right before it got dark, he announced he was going hitchhiking. I tried to tell him it was stupid and dangerous, but he said he'd done it plenty before. The only thing was, he didn't have a weapon for protection. I hadn't eaten anything all day and was pretty drunk, no longer angry, so when he asked to borrow the ax I said yes.

Junk Dog came back a few days later, with this big long story about how he'd gotten a ride with someone in a Jeep, and they'd taken it off-roading in the desert. The Jeep had flipped and wrecked, the ax lost in the wreckage. Junk Dog's jaw had been broken and wired shut. He could only eat things from a straw for the next month, couldn't talk clearly, wasn't supposed to smoke, sometimes drooled. I felt bad for him. It was hard not to.

But the minute the wires were taken out, I was on him. "That was my dad's ax," I said.

"It was an antique, belonged to my great-grandfather." It was a lie, but the ax looked so old I hoped it was believable. He needed to pay me back.

He acted annoyed but finally agreed. He asked how much I figured it was worth.

"Probably a hundred dollars. You could get me a quarter ounce and I'd be happy."

Junk Dog said no, which I figured would happen. I was hoping to get an eighth out of him. But he refused to go that high, said the most he'd give me was a gram. I could see he wasn't going to budge, so I said OK. Holly and I had no money that day, or weed, so a gram seemed a hell of a lot better than nothing. We smoked it all before it grew dark.

At the end of the year, I was in more photos for the yearbook than I could have ever hoped to be at Carmel Heights. The group shot with Mrs. Hunter and all her advisees. The group shot with the girls who did the literary magazine. A picture of me and Holly smiling at lunch. Me and Lily laughing over some dumb thing in the courtyard. The version of me in the photos was perfect: high cheekbones and shiny hair.

Except for one. In the photo of our therapy group, they made us put our legs up like we were doing the cancan. In the photo, all the other girls looked excited, hamming it up for the camera. I was on the end, barely smiling, blurry and looking lost because I couldn't figure out which way to look at the camera. Better than before, but still very much a ghost.

It was late June, the first night of summer warm enough to not need a sweater. Something had been in the works for weeks now, and I'd taken the hot weather as a signal of its culmination. Dylan and Luis had picked us up that afternoon, straight from Holly's house. Somehow we'd become friends with them recently. They had cars and money and drugs, and didn't seem to want anything more from us than our company. They just thought we were funny. Liked our taste in music. This had seemed like a sign too, of an elevated status. I'd finally figured out how to act in a way that made people like me. It was a full moon, so bright that when night fell it wasn't even that dark. I felt a pull that evening, as though I was directed by magnets. I thought it was all knitting together into something good.

But later, as I sat in the back of a police car, it seemed like I must have read the symbols all wrong. They were indeed symbols, and it was true they'd meant something; the mistake wasn't finding significance where there had been none. But I'd been looking at them backward, or sideways, when I should have been reading down. I felt so stupid for misreading the code.

The cops were saying something, but I didn't know it was directed at me until I heard them say, "She's too stoned."

They were right. I was too stoned. Not just on pot, either—a little cocaine, a lot of acid. I was having a hard time looking at their faces because they kept turning into the shapes of other things. Demons and trolls and skulls. They wanted to know where I lived. I considered telling them something other than the truth, but then they told me the options were for them to hand me over to my parents or spend the night in jail. I gave them my address.

I spiraled out in the dark of that police car. It started with me doing the thing where I removed myself from myself. I saw a girl sitting in the back of a police car and she was too skinny and her hair was all tangled up, with a gaze so flat and pupils stretched so wide that she might as well have been dead. She looked so lost, like she had no idea who she was or where she was going. And I felt so sorry for her. I hadn't seen any shadows for so long, not since the mental hospital, but now the shadows surrounded her, mutating and pitch black, flocks of birds the color of sulfur, all engulfing her, returning to poke their long dark claws into her chest and around her throat. I saw there was no hope for her, no turning back, no finding her way again. It was pointless.

I had been weaned off Wellbutrin and put on Paxil a week before because I still felt depressed. It was an exceptionally boring strain of depression. This new type didn't make me sad or tragic, so much as listless. I cared about nothing—not myself, not anyone or anything around me. I didn't care what happened to my body, so I smoked until my lungs hurt and I was coughing up dark yellow phlegm. I couldn't remember the names of the last two people I had sex with, because I was so fucked up when it happened and because they were strangers. I only ate when I remembered, and I only remembered when I felt like I might pass out. I was so skinny that whenever I sat on something hard, the sidewalk or the metal chairs at the Palms, it hurt because basically all that was left were my bones.

I still had a bunch of Wellbutrin left though, red and yellow pills the shape of M&M's, plucked from the black lockbox. I had discovered that if I drank while taking it, I got full-blown fucked up off only a couple beers. I figured I might as well bring the leftovers to the party.

Earlier that evening, we'd driven around for a while, just listening to music and smoking. When we'd gotten to Dylan and Luis's, it was only the four of us and the sun was just beginning to set. I'd put the Wellbutrin in a glass bowl on the table and it looked just like a dish of candy, and then Luis handed me a beer. They had a big stand-up bong, four feet tall, and they put weed in it, and Holly and I took turns until we were dizzy and almost too high. By then, there were probably a dozen people in the apartment, and someone started railing out lines on the coffee table, and then Holly and I did that too.

And so it went. More people, more drugs. Sometimes when I got high everything turned into a blur, but that night it had the opposite effect. The more I consumed, the higher I got, the more clearly everything popped in its outline. Charged and trembling in a way that made it almost too real. I felt like I was orchestrating it all, in charge of the direction and aligning everything into its exact right place.

Shortly after midnight, Holly, Ramon, and I decided to eat some acid sugar cubes. Ramon had never tripped before, not on acid, not on anything. Holly and I told him we would guide him, make sure everything went OK.

And it started out well. We were all sitting on this giant velvet beanbag chair, and it felt like we were an extension of it, something fuzzy and sinkable. We were laughing. Ramon was convinced he was stuck to it, that he had actually become part of the chair, and it seemed like one of the funniest things we'd ever heard. This was around 2:00 a.m. There were only a handful of people still left in the apartment.

We pulled Ramon out of the couch, and he was shrieking like a little girl because he thought we were tearing him in two. When we got him standing up, away from the beanbag chair, he hugged us, saying that we had saved him. Luis was sitting on the couch a few feet away, counting a stack of bills. "Look at this," he said, handing me a twenty.

I looked at the face and it wasn't Andrew Jackson but Satan. Then the face flicked back to Andrew Jackson. Then it went back to Satan and pentagrams and flames appeared. It was not a mystery; it was an obvious message that all money is evil. So we burned the bill. It was fun.

And then shortly after, there was a knock at the door. We weren't expecting anyone. And it wasn't a knock really. It was more of a pound. Three hard raps. Luis went to the door. There wasn't a peephole, but there were some little frosted glass windows. I don't know what he saw when he looked through them, the flash of a badge or lights. But he walked away from the door quickly. He told us to be quiet. He told us it was the cops.

He and Dylan flew into motion. Luis got a paper towel and glass cleaner and wiped the coke residue off the table. Dylan grabbed the bong and the money and headed to his bedroom, where he had a safe hidden behind clothes in the closet. Holly and Ramon sat there, not doing anything—we had nothing to hide; we'd smoked or eaten all the drugs. But something in the movement of the room frightened me. I wanted out—out of my body, preferably, but since this wasn't possible, I wanted out of that apartment. The cops were at the front door, so I went out the back.

I made it over the seven-foot wall around their tiny patio without even trying. And then I was on a hill, behind the apartment complex, covered in ice plant. The hill was very dark, and the ice plant grew deep, and it was hard to get decent footing.

Dylan and Luis lived right next to this Mormon temple that was built a few years before. It was white and garish, lit up 24/7, glowing with pointed turrets, like a spaceship or a building in Oz. It loomed there, shooting white out of nothing on the side of the freeway. The lights from the temple and the moon illuminated the road that ran below the ice plant–covered hill. I took it as a sign to head down there.

I didn't have a plan. The closest I'd gotten was that maybe the road went to the shopping center nearby, and maybe I'd walk there and call someone from a pay phone. But I didn't know if I had enough change, and I didn't know who I could call. I was just walking. This was when they got me.

I think they saw me hop over the fence, figured I had something on me, Dylan and Luis's main supply. But all I had was an old aluminum foil pipe I'd made, dark with resin, and a pack of cigarettes. They got me for all they could: paraphernalia, tobacco possession by a minor, curfew. Stupid charges. But it was enough for them to take me home.

I was watching myself in the back of that police car, and I was watching the shadows, and I was watching the demon cops. And the signs focused until they were pointing to one thing, and again it seemed inevitable. Something mandated by the universe. This was the second time I decided I needed to die.

THE FIGHT

It started the moment my parents closed the door. I hadn't been paying attention to what the police were saying to them, because I was pretty fucked up and also because I was more interested in reading the expressions on my parents' faces. Whatever was going through their minds, it wasn't good. Furious, sharp creases in their brows.

Also I was thinking about the black lockbox.

All I had to do was get the box out of the dining room without them seeing, and then figure out a way to be left alone for several hours. If I could get that to happen, then everything else was easy.

I thought I could tell them I was exhausted, that I needed to go to sleep and we could deal with it in the morning. But my dad—he wanted to yell.

I'd never seen him so angry. I was a failure, he said, his voice so loud it kicked off the walls, face red, eyes gleaming. A disappointment, there was something wrong with me, he gave up. It was the giving up part that made me totally lose it. I felt my chest turning in on itself, something hollow, and then the tears just started falling. I found myself backing into a corner in the hallway.

And then my dad hit me, palm across the face, the noise sharp and sudden as the crack of a whip.

He'd never hit me before.

He really didn't hit me that hard. I think it was just the shock of it that made me fall over. As I lay there on the cold tile floor in the corner of the hallway, what I had to do cemented in my mind.

The worst thing was he didn't even seem to care. He crouched over me, his finger in my face and it felt like he was pushing me, and I was falling, falling into a crack in the earth, my heart sucked into my stomach, and then lower still, until my stomach was just a pit of death. "You're disgusting," he said. "Despicable. You're not even worth my attention. You're a nothing, you'll always be a nothing, a throwaway *piece of trash*."

And it hurt because it was true.

My mother pulled him away from me. "I think we all need to go to bed."

He didn't say anything for a moment, and then he agreed with her. "We'll finish this in the morning," he told me. He was still furious. And with that, they went upstairs.

We had a rule in our family: never go to bed angry. No matter how shitty I'd been acting, my parents always told me they loved me before they went to bed. But that night, they just went upstairs.

I made myself quit crying, and I sat in the hallway, listening until I no longer heard movement coming from their bedroom. Then I walked, quietly as I could, into the dining room. I opened the cupboard. I grabbed the box. I went into the bathroom.

I swallowed all my pills. There was a handful of my mother's muscle relaxers left, and I swallowed them too. There weren't any Tylenol or Benadryl in the box, just Advil, which I wasn't sure would do anything, so I left it there. I wished I hadn't left my Wellbutrin at Dylan and Luis's. I hoped I had taken enough. It was still a lot of pills.

I went into my room. It was almost 4:00 a.m. I figured I had at least six hours before my mother would come check on me. It seemed like enough time. I thought it might take a while, because of the coke and acid, but it didn't. That night we went to bed angry. I fell asleep right away.

SAME SAME BUT DIFFERENT: DOCUMENTS

And so I went to the hospital again. Everything was the same as it was seven months ago. Except this time my mother found me in the middle of a seizure, and somehow this time I didn't need to be intubated and so I didn't get pneumonia. This time my parents looked less devastated and more just tired. This time they marked *Catholic* on the patient information sheet for some reason, and so a priest came to see me, and when he asked why I was there I told him the truth, it was a suicide attempt, and the look on his face was pure shock, and when he left the room my parents laughed and I didn't know why until they told me about cardinal sins, and then I laughed too. This time Holly came to see me in the hospital, and she had a bouquet for me and also a gigantic card that everyone had signed, everyone at New Hope and everyone at the Palms, and it was full of inside jokes and compliments. The kindness of it, of all of it.

I was so sad when I heard what happened. I just broke down and cried and cried. You are not alone. Anytime you need to talk, I want to listen. I've been there before and I know how much it hurts.
♥ Lily

Please feel better soon and please know how much we all love you. Nobody is a pirate princess like you!
Love,
Junkdog

If you die, who will be there to find the red herring? Who will be there to shine flashlights on yellow ghosts? I would miss you too much.
Love,
Rachel

Get-well card, June 1999.

SAME SAME BUT DIFFERENT:
INVASIVE SPECIES

And this time when I woke up, I felt even stupider and guiltier. This time when I woke up, I truly felt like I had a broken brain. Except it wasn't even my brain. It was the brain of a homicidal maniac. She was trying to kill me.

But everything else was the same. Hospitals. Always the same. I was in there for the same amount of time, even. Three days, same as last time. The same, the same, the same.

SAME SAME BUT DIFFERENT: PATRIOTISM

Patient Evaluation, June 1999.

And so I went to the mental hospital again, and everything was the same there too. Same sexist doctor, same milk bags of glue, same needle in the arm every morning, and the patients were all the same except different. This time it was less crowded; it was a holiday. This time my roommate was a girl named Carrie, who was very fat, and everyone called her A Lot of Carrie, and she didn't say much to me and so I didn't say much to her. On the Fourth of July, I imagined all my friends at the beach eating hamburgers and drinking beer while I was in my slip-on shoes (same as last time) with Band-Aids all over the crook of my arm. At 9:00 p.m. we both sat on Carrie's bed, stiffly so we wouldn't touch, and looked out the narrow window, where we could see just a sliver of the fireworks at Sea World. And it made me feel like what I was: someone removed from society, who was therefore only able to see a tiny reflection of the outside world. The fireworks were small and far away but they were beautiful, because it turns out society is something that looks best from a distance.

SAME SAME BUT DIFFERENT:
THE OUTSIDE WORLD #2

And this time Holly tried to see me every day, but my parents made her skip a couple days so we could have some alone time. I thought "alone time" would be bad, but they just sat there and held my hand and told me they loved me over and over.

This time. When Holly came, she always brought someone with her, sometimes two someones, Rachel and Junk Dog and Ramon and Lily and people I wasn't even that close to but who wanted to come anyway because they wanted to make me feel better. And this time they didn't stand there awkwardly, looking as though someone had forced them to be there. This time they told me what was going on in their lives, what they'd done that day, gossip from the outside, laughing and lighthearted as though there was nothing too weird about any of it.

SAME SAME BUT DIFFERENT: DEFICIENCY

But it also made me feel like: What the fuck. All these friends. I nearly died. Again. Totally different than last time, but also exactly the same.

SAME SAME BUT DIFFERENT: SAINTED

And this time I wasn't given my medicine because they were worried about "the levels," since I'd OD'd on it twice now. Instead of giving me Zyprexa or something similar they gave me nothing, and so I was more awake in the therapy sessions and CBT made a lot more sense. But at night, I couldn't fall asleep till late, midnight or one or two, one night not until four, which is a very long time to be lying on a thin mattress in the dark only to get awoken a couple hours later and stabbed with a needle. And by day six I was feeling pretty wild, and in group therapy I started talking and couldn't stop. I was saying things that didn't even seem like my thoughts, comparing people in the group to people in the Bible, saying I had come back from the dead twice now, I was a miracle, and there was a war in my brain between good and evil, and Jesus would help me because I was just like Him. Part of me was watching and thinking, *What the fuck are you saying? Shut up, you sound insane, where are you even getting this?* And another part of me was thinking, *Oh good one, Juliet. Clever delusions. Biblical. Way to be a total cliché, you loser.* But the biggest part of me was the part that could not stop talking. And that night was one of the nights where Holly wasn't allowed to come, it was just my parents, and I told them what was happening, and they looked at each other nervous, and our visit was cut short because they went to go talk to the people in charge. And even though we'd switched insurance since the last time and now were covered for ten days instead of seven, my parents arranged for my release the next day because they thought I wasn't "receiving adequate care." So again, I was in there for seven days. Three and seven, both times. Something biblical.

BOOK THREE

DEPARTURE / ARRIVAL

We were going to see my Uncle Paul. He lived on Whidbey Island, in Puget Sound, where we had lived when I was a baby. Except he was staying in Northern California for the summer; his health was bad. A special facility, beautiful, all big sunsets and trees. The change of scenery would be good for me, my parents said. Besides, Uncle Paul was bipolar, creative, too smart for his own good—just like me. A transition between the hospital and real life. This is what they said.

That day I was just so sleepy. I fell asleep on the plane and then I fell asleep on the other plane and then I fell asleep in the rental car. It might have been the heat. It was July and so sunny that it wrapped around me like a blanket, dulling my brain and slowing my limbs.

It was like when you wake up from a nightmare, suddenly and breathing heavy. We were pulling into a parking lot that was gravel and empty. There was a fence, waist-high and wooden, bordering thick pines and next to it, what looked like a small house. There was a child sitting on the fence, small, maybe twelve years old, skinny. My face felt sleep-bloated and sweaty. The child was how I knew something was wrong.

"Where are we?" I asked.

My parents didn't say anything. They just looked at each other.

"Where the fuck are we?" It was like they hadn't even heard me. The silence that followed had a friction, and after a while of it building, they opened their doors and stepped out.

I just sat there. When they noticed, they told me to get out of the car. I refused. They exchanged a look and went into the little house alone.

I turned the volume up on my headphones, which I'd been listening to the whole way. My Discman was new, fancy, claimed it didn't skip and you could get it wet. My parents had bought it for me when I was in the hospital, a "Sorry you tried to kill yourself again!" present. I closed my eyes, tried to sing along to the music. I pretended I was in my bedroom. I pretended I was in the canyon, sitting on one of the cliffs.

But it didn't matter. There was no uncle. He wasn't in the middle-of-nowhere, California. My uncle was in Whidbey Island, where we had lived when I was a baby. My parents had lied to me. I was trapped.

It was hot in that car. After a few minutes, I opened the door for air, but then I closed it. The door seemed like some sort of barrier; if I broke the seal I'd spin out into space. I reached up into the front seat, found the electric lock, and pulled it, *clank*. The heat closed in like a tomb.

My parents came out after a few minutes. By then, the child I'd seen on the fence had disappeared. My mom had a plastic cup of cold water in her hand, little beads of condensation on the walls. She went to open the door, presumably to give it to me, but, of course, it was locked. My dad unlocked it with a beep of the fob.

He opened the door, and I looked up at them. I saw their heads above me and the sun was behind them, blocking out their features until they were just two shadow people, a couple of menacing ghosts. If I ignored them, they would have no choice but to go away. I shut my eyes.

But my dad was shaking me. "Juliet," he said. "Honey." He took off my headphones, but gently, almost like he was stroking my hair.

"It's so hot, honey," my mom said. "Why don't you get out of the car? Have some cold water."

I opened my eyes. I felt like I didn't know who they were at all. I took the cup and I looked in it, brown plastic, bumpy, the kind you drink from at summer camp. I still didn't know what this fucking place was called.

I threw the water in my mother's face without thinking. The action surprised me. Immediately I felt guilty. So then I threw the cup at my father. It bounced off his head comically: *bonk*. The looks on their faces. My mother's wet hair. I started laughing. It was such a nasty-sounding laugh. I put my headphones back on and I pretended I wasn't there. But the looks on their faces kept swinging back to me: shock, disgust, like I had betrayed them, but also like they deserved it. The exact same way I felt.

They went away. A small man came back in their place. I didn't know he was there until I heard a voice saying my name. I hadn't heard his feet on the gravel as he approached. He was wearing sandals and shorts and had thick beard, younger than my parents but not by much. I wanted to hate him but there was something kind in his face and I was annoyed to find that I liked him right away, and so when he motioned for me to take off my headphones, I took them off.

His name was Nathan. I was at a place called Redwood Trails School. It was a therapeutic boarding school, whatever the fuck that meant. My parents had sent me there because they were worried, they didn't want to, they were scared for me, they hadn't wanted to lie and only did so because they had to, blah blah blah. He asked me to get out of the car and I did. I wanted to be stubborn and stay in that car and fight some more but I didn't fight. I gave in.

After I stood up, he put his hand on my shoulder and for some reason, it didn't bother me. I didn't see my parents anywhere. The sun was making me dizzy, the trees and sky blurring until everything was beige. He was only a few inches taller than me. "I want you to meet someone," he said. He smiled. His teeth were white and straight.

HER NAME WAS ALYSON

Nathan told her to take me on a walk to the lake. She didn't smile, or say hi, or shake my hand, or do anything else you'd expect a person to do when they first meet you. She just looked at me. It was that lack of a response, the lack of an action, that made me trust her.

She was short, thin, had shoulder-length blond hair, a pretty face. Wide green eyes framed by thick black eyeliner. In these ways, she looked a lot like me. But her thighs were thinner and her boobs were bigger, straining the stripes of her tank top. A nose that was a tiny bit crooked, forehead just a tad too big. I think the combination made us the same level of attractive.

A LIST OF THINGS ALYSON TOLD ME ON OUR WALK

She was from Vacaville, a shitty city near the bay.

Her parents were divorced.

Her mother was very sick.

She hated her father.

He had paid two men to abduct her from her bedroom at 4:30 a.m., literally kicking and screaming, and they'd put her in handcuffs and then taken her on a plane and dropped her off here in a rented SUV.

This was three weeks ago.

The boarding school sucked.

They had to have group therapy twice a day.

Group therapy sucked.

There were four phases at the school.

Each phase included a higher level of privileges.

Alyson was on Phase One.

I was also on Phase One.

This was because we were new.

Phase One sucked.

Right now, there were twelve students in the school.

Most of them were girls.

The lack of boys sucked.

It meant everyone got their periods at the same time.

Everyone had to do a lot of chores, all the time, regardless of our phases.

The chores sucked.

There were a bunch of animals: some pigs, a few goats, some chickens, cats.

Sometimes the counselors took them fishing on the lake.

A BRIEF DESCRIPTION OF THE LAKE

There was a little path behind the little house. It weaved through tall brush that was mostly brown and dry. I had thought Northern California was green. There were a lot of briars in the brush and even though we walked on the path they got stuck in my socks. The path went by a barn. I could smell their animal smell, but we didn't go in there. The path grew muddy as it went down closer to the lake, my shoes sucking in the muck. The brush turned into cattails and tall plants with green leaves like spears. The lake was small and muddy and had a lot of flies and mosquitoes buzzing around. Dragonflies too—bodies big and bright turquoise, their veined wings winking thin rainbows. The sky was so bright it wasn't even blue anymore, just white. There was a rowboat next to the lake, so people could go fishing. The mosquitoes started biting me right away. Mosquitos have always loved me. I felt their bites swelling quickly into lumps.

A LIST OF THINGS THAT HAPPENED
AFTER THE WALK

They put me in this little office in the little house with this
  woman Rosie.
Rosie had dyed red hair and was wearing pink lipstick and a
  big smile.
She took my blood pressure.
She took my temperature.
She made me pee in a cup.
She went in the bathroom with me while I peed.
It was embarrassing.
I put my hand over the crotch of my underwear so she couldn't
  see if there was discharge.
I got some pee on my hands.
My luggage was in the tiny office.
A suitcase my mother had brought was in the room too.
That suitcase was filled with my clothes.
It made me feel stupid for not realizing what was going on
  sooner.
The suitcase was big, and I had been told we would be gone for
  just three days, and my father always made us pack light.
I had a pack of cigarettes and a couple lighters in my suitcase.
She took those away.
She let me keep everything else.
She printed my name and date of birth on a label using a little
  label-making machine.
She put the label on a black binder.
She handed me the binder and told me to take it over to the big
  house.
I hadn't seen a big house.
She told me to say goodbye to my parents first.

My parents were sitting in the big office space of the little
    house.

They were crying.

I refused to say goodbye, or say anything, or even look at them.

They hugged me anyway.

I kept my arms by my side.

I finally said something.

I told them I hated them.

My parents continued to cry.

I wanted to cry too.

But I didn't.

Nathan said he'd walk me over to the big house.

The big house was right across the parking lot.

I felt stupid for not seeing it before.

He wouldn't let me carry my bags.

Instead he put them all on his arm and smiled at me, as though
    he was trying to make me less nervous.

It didn't work.

The rest of the students were in group.

Group was in the "great room."

The great room was a big room with a lot of couches, all facing
    each other, except at the end of the room where they were
    turned toward a TV.

All the couches matched.

They were all an ugly plaid.

The same plaid was used over the windows as drapes.

I didn't want to look at the students.

I could feel them looking at me.

Nathan told them my name.

They each said their names but the only one that stuck was
    Alyson's.

I felt like I had felt at every new school I'd ever been to, when I
    had no identity but The New Kid.

I sat down on a couch next to Alyson.

They continued with their group.

I didn't hear what they said.

Somebody put my bags in what was now my room, which was
also Alyson's room, without me noticing.

A LETTER FROM THE FUTURE #3

It is December 14, 2015. I am thirty-two years old. I am writing from the basement of the house where I live in Piney View, West Virginia. My desk is right next to the back door, which overlooks three oak trees and a small patch of forest, and all their leaves have fallen. These sections, I have written them twice before, over the course of five years. Both times, I tried to tell them straight. So this time, I am trying to tell them a different way. I don't know if I will get it right. The problem that always happens is information overload. So many things that make the boarding school different from the rest of the world.

My husband, he always laughs whenever I say I went to boarding school. "Boarding school is for rich kids," he says. "You were institutionalized." And he is right.

I'd searched for Alyson before, at least once or twice a year since social media has existed. I'd never been able to find her before. I thought maybe something bad had happened to her. I thought maybe she'd died.

But today I found her. She is a mother now, two kids, a husband in the military. She looks both exactly like she does in my memory and also totally different. She is a grown-up now, short hair and neat lipstick. And without warning, or me expecting to, I am crying.

I remember the time I talked to my boyfriend from boarding school, the one you will soon read about. That was three years ago. My first love. Like Alyson, I hadn't been able to find him for years, and then I did. He called me one night shortly after I'd found him, late. Neither of us was doing well at the time. His voice, it sounded the same. I didn't know I remembered his voice but I did. I was talking to that seventeen-year-old boy in my memory even though the sixteen-year-old girl who'd fallen in love with him was long gone now. Or my sixteen-year-old self had reawakened, just for a moment, and it was she who was doing the talking. I felt the part of me that was our shared past, such a small strand of our existence, reaching out across what was now half our lives, emerging from the dark and reweaving itself into the same braid. Even from what was once the future, that link glowed, the memories of that intertwining vivid in a way that memories rarely are, the vividness that only occurs when a person is going through intense pain and intense change (which are the same thing). I remembered the look in his seventeen-year-old pupils, empty and black and doomed. It was the same look I had had in mine. The pupil is a hole in the iris that lets the light in. The pupil of a doomed person is just a hole.

Now, on December 14, 2015, my pupils no longer broadcast doomedness or blackness or even emptiness. There is something sad in them instead, even though I am mostly happy now. The sadness is something you can't get rid of. In one photo, Alyson is with her two children and her husband, who is dressed in army fatigues. Her smile is so big and she looks so pretty. She looks so happy, genuinely, the smile obviously not just a pose. But even in this photo—the pupils show something else.

WAKE-UP CALL

I woke up the next day, early. There were no blinds on the window and the sun beat hot on my face. I waited for my eyes to adjust, and the gray lumps slid into objects. Our window overlooked the porch that wrapped around the house, and past it, trees and then the lake. It might have been pretty if everything wasn't so brown.

Alyson was still asleep, snoring softly out of her mouth, hair messy on her pillow. I felt so far away from everyone and everything I knew and loved—a sucking kind of loneliness that made me want to crawl inside myself until I disappeared.

I started to cry.

I was horrified to realize I missed my parents.

Ever since I was a baby, any time I cried my mother would scoop me on her lap and tell me to just get it all out, even after I was way too old for that kind of thing. She'd rub my back while I cried, and whisper *Shhhhh, shhhhh*. But they weren't the kind of *shhhhh*'s meant to convey that I was supposed to stop crying. It was the kind of noise meant to wordlessly tell me that everything was going to be OK. I wished she were here; I wished she cared enough to do that now.

ORIENTATION

I didn't have to think all day. We had breakfast and then chores and then group therapy and then school and then group therapy and then more chores and then dinner. Everything was "orientation," which meant they either gave me instructions or I was just supposed to watch. I pulled out weeds. I ate a turkey sandwich. I paged through a textbook. Nathan led the group therapy, a new language, phrases like "emotional regulation" and "conflict resolution." During the meals, the other students asked me questions. What was my name. How old was I. Where was I from. What was my diagnosis. Too personal and accusatory. The day didn't feel like a day but a series of flash cards, crash studied, too much too quick so nothing could stick.

By the end of the day, I said as little as possible because I didn't want them to think I was stupid. Everyone else knew exactly what to do, knew their role and what would happen next, but I was in a foreign new world, with no map.

We had free time after dinner. Alyson and some of the other kids went down to the barn, but I didn't because I felt like I'd been following her. I figured I'd just go read. It was a nice day so I decided to sit on the porch.

The rails had just enough space between them that you could put your feet through and let them dangle. It was still hot and bright out and the low sun skimmed off the lake in a shimmer. It was very quiet—just the thrum of insects and an occasional shout from the barn.

I only had two books in my bag—a stupid teen horror novel, and *Fear and Loathing in Las Vegas*, which I hadn't started yet. Strangely, it had been a gift from my father. He had said it was one of my uncle's favorites. Guilt. My thoughts were pinging around in my head, all the stuff I'd been told that day, in a way that made it hard to concentrate. I didn't want to think. I picked the horror novel.

I read for five minutes before I heard someone behind me. I turned around. It was this guy I'd met earlier, although I didn't remember his name. He had curly hair, brown eyes, sharp cheekbones, and even though I didn't like guys with curly hair, he was easily the cutest person in the school. I think his girlfriend was this rockabilly girl because I'd seen them holding hands at lunch. The rockabilly girl was chubby but her face was pretty.

"Hey," he said to me. He smiled. His teeth looked sharp.

"Hey," I said.

"Can I sit next to you?"

"Sure."

He didn't say anything for a minute and I felt confused about what he was doing there. Then he asked me what I was reading and I regretted not having picked *Fear and Loathing*. I showed him the cover.

"It's stupid," I said. "I haven't really been able to concentrate lately."

He nodded like he understood. He asked me if I read a lot and I said yes. He did too. His favorite book was called *Youth in Revolt*. Mine was *Geek Love*. I'd never heard of *Youth in Revolt* but the title made me feel less stupid about the horror book.

We started talking about our diagnoses. He told me he was bipolar, an alcoholic, a cutter, and also bulimic. I didn't expect for his list to be that long. He looked boringly normal.

"Your eyes," he said at one point, his voice low and corny. He kept on edging closer to me, which seemed like it must have been uncomfortable because the slats in the railing were digging into his thigh. "They're incredible. What are they, two different colors?"

People were always commenting on my eyes. One of them was blue and the other was mostly brown. It was the kind of thing that was either annoying or embarrassing, depending on who was saying it. He was looking at them so intently I felt my cheeks burn.

"Kind of," I said. I looked at his feet. He was wearing the stupidest shoes. Tevas. His toes were long and skinny. My shoes were covered in dust from the chores we'd done earlier, but his feet looked perfectly clean. I looked up at him, at his brown eyes, so warm they were nearly yellow. Doomed eyes. I still didn't know his name.

I heard the big sliding glass door behind us open. "Luke," someone said. His name was Luke. It was the rockabilly girl. She looked upset. She stood there for a second, then went back inside, slamming the door.

"Fuck," Luke said. He shrugged like *What can you do?* and then followed her inside.

RUMOR MILL

Alyson explained that when something happened at Redwood Trails School, the news spread so fast that everybody, including the staff, knew exactly what was going on within an hour. The rockabilly girl—her name was Julia (which I didn't like—people were always mistaking my name for Julia and it made me furious because it was such a stupid-sounding name, like some nineteenth-century girl with braids—or a chubby girl with a pretty face). "Julia's supposed to graduate in a couple weeks," Alyson said. "She and Luke have been fighting a lot, about what they'll do once she leaves." Then she informed me that Luke was from Seattle; Julia was from Olympia. Luke wasn't supposed to leave until December. The times and locations seemed close enough to make it work—but Luke had been saying he would die without her, that he couldn't stomach it at RTS alone. She didn't understand why he couldn't wait. She thought he was making the options pretty clear by talking to me on the porch—either stay, or he'd get together with me. Which was annoying because no one stopped to wonder if I wanted to get together with him. He wore Tevas. He was a bipolar bulimic alcoholic cutter, which was way too many adjective-nouns. But nobody cared what I thought. I was new.

After Luke went inside, Julia refused to talk to him. She went straight into her room, closed the door, and wouldn't open it for anyone other than Rosie, including her roommate, Angel. She was crying real loud, the kind where the person is doing it mostly for attention. The rest of us were in the great room by then, watching the news because the only two channels we got were that and cartoons. We could hear her from across the house. She finally fell asleep.

BEDTIME STORIES

Since everybody else was so busy with the Julia drama, Alyson and I sat together on a couch in the great room, late. The lights were off and I didn't think anybody knew we were in there.

We talked and talked, about all the times we'd gotten fucked up and all the crazy things we did before we arrived. Alyson told me how she used to wear big baggy guy jeans, take a shoelace and tie it around the cuff, walk into stores and shoplift by putting bottles down the waistband. One time she got greedy, tried to put four forties in her pants, two in each leg, and a shoelace came untied. The forties fell out and broke all over the floor. She took off running, the beer and glass sticking to the bottoms of her shoes. Her friend was waiting in the car, and they peeled out before Alyson could even shut the door, laughing hysterically over what had happened. It's the nights you get the beer that blend together, she said. I knew exactly what she meant.

Alyson told me that she and her mother were best friends, and her father couldn't stand it. She would go over there and they'd play checkers till 4:00 a.m. in the garage, drinking beer and smoking cigarettes. She showed me a scar on her forehead, a perfectly white crescent moon curving up to her hairline, the lasting result of a drunken argument they'd had where her mother hit her with a beer stein. She seemed to think this was funny. By then her father was so sick of her mother not taking care of herself, and of Alyson coming home from her visits tired and hungover. The custody arrangement was modified. Alyson was forbidden from going over there. He didn't care that her mother was dying; if they wanted to see each other, they were only allowed supervised visits at a special center that felt like jail.

The great room was so dark I couldn't see her face, only her outline and the glow from the hallway light glinting off her blond hair. But her voice cracked in a way that made me think she might be crying. I couldn't blame her.

And so, like the time with Holly, I told her my story.

About the hallucinations and the suicide attempts and how I had found myself here, incapable of functioning like a normal person in normal society. She said nothing the whole time I was talking. When I was finished, she touched my hand, just for a second, saying without saying that she got it.

By the time anyone noticed us absent from our rooms it was an hour past lights out. But even then I couldn't sleep, so we continued to talk, gossiping about the other students. Eventually her breaths slowed and steadied. When I went to sleep that night, I closed my eyes, my own breath settling into the rhythm of Alyson's, and for the first time since I'd arrived at the school, I didn't feel alone.

JUST TRAGIC

In the morning, everything seemed fine and normal. Julia and Luke sat together at breakfast, alone at the far table. They held hands again but I didn't see them talking much. But then Julia didn't show up for group. So one of the counselors—Vinnie, this guy with a glass eye and a redneck accent—went to go look for her. He wasn't gone very long. He came back, breathless, sweaty, holding Julia by the wrist. He had a belt in his other hand—one of those fat leather ones rockabilly girls wear, with rivets. Her neck was a bit red. He'd found her in the barn, standing on a fence with the belt around her neck. She said she planned to hang herself.

Everyone acted like it was so sad and they felt sorry for Julia. I watched Luke sit next to her, their knees pressed together, and he stroked her hair as she cried. They were whispering so quiet I couldn't hear a word they said.

It seemed like I was the only one who saw the truth, which was if she really wanted to hang herself, she wouldn't have gotten caught like that. She wouldn't be standing on a fence with just a tiny red mark on her neck. She'd be dead.

Julia had been on Phase Four, since she was about to graduate. You'd expect a suicide attempt, no matter how lame, to bump that back a bit. But nope—no privileges lost, nothing changed. And a few days after that, she was gone. Rehabilitated, but only theoretically.

PATIENT LOG

PATIENT NAME: Juliet Escoria
AGE: 15 yrs 10 mo
SEX: F
DOB: 8/23/83

DATE: 07/20/99

HISTORY: Patient was diagnosed as Type I Bipolar Disorder, Rapid Cycling 11/98. Possible Borderline—reports unstable & intense friendships. Patient is sexually active, admits to past drug use: marijuana, alcohol, benzodiazepines, prescription opiates, prescription stimulants, prescription muscle relaxers, ecstasy, ketamine, psychedelics, cocaine. Reports marijuana is consistent drug of choice; other drug use is "sporadic." Substance abuse began 06/98 approx. Drug test positive for cannabis. Experienced hallucinations (auditory/visual) in past but claims hallucinations have ceased. History of self-harm. Chronic reported insomnia.

Patient admitted to school after recent suicide attempt requiring hospitalization. Attempt was made using patient's own medication, Paxil & Tegretol, in addition to Soma (obtained from mother). 2nd attempt—1st made 6 months previous, approx. Circumstances similar; addit. Benadryl & Tylenol. Tegretol & Paxil were discontinued temporarily in hospital, resumed 7/10. Reported side effects of dizziness, lethargy, upset stomach.

PREVIOUS MEDICATIONS:
Zyprexa—discontinued 01/99 once stabilized
Wellbutrin—discontinued 03/99 (ineffective)
Tegretol—discontinued 07/99 (risk of overdose/replace w Depakote)
Paxil—discontinued 07/99 (replace w Remeron)

TREATMENT:

Depakote, begin at 500 mg/nightly, increase to 1000 over course of 1 week

Remeron (for depression/insomnia), begin at 15 mg/nightly, increase to 30 over course of 1 week

Group therapy, indiv. therapy

PHONE PRIVILEGES

On Phase One, we were allowed only one phone call each week, and only from our parents. The first weekend, I had the idea that I would refuse their call—but then at the last second I felt a pull toward them, a homesickness, a longing—and I was surprised enough by this that I couldn't stop myself from going to the phone.

"Hello," I said, making my voice cold and annoyed so they would know right away I was still angry. I was still so angry.

"Juliet," I heard my dad say. "I'm sorry. Please know we didn't want to lie to you. Please know it broke both of our hearts. It's just . . . " He trailed off.

"We didn't want you to die," my mom said, listening in on the other extension. "We didn't want you to die and we didn't know what else to do."

"The school is supposed to be very good," my dad said. He'd looked and called all over, gone on several early-morning plane trips around the West while I was in the hospitals, trying to find a place that could help me. Somehow this made me feel even stupider, that I hadn't noticed he'd been gone. But then I remembered. I'd been unconscious.

TEENAGE DREAM

Luke, me, Alyson, and Alyson's boyfriend, whose name was Kiran, decided to go to the barn so we could dip without anyone seeing. I'd thought chewing tobacco was gross at first, but soon I understood. It didn't smell and they had cans of Skoal in baskets at the general store that were easy to steal, which couldn't be said about cigarettes. You could do it during school or in the van, as long as you sat where no staff could see and brought something to spit in.

They'd just gotten three goats, a mother and two babies. The babies were like kittens, clumsy and mewing and adorable. Rosie had named the mother Bessie. The baby goats' names were decided in a vote between the students—the gray one was Smoke, the brown Mary Jane. We were petting them and joking around.

Luke and I were sitting on the fence by the goat pen, while the others were trying to get Bessie to do tricks by feeding her baby carrots. It wasn't working. If you told her to sit and held out a carrot, she just bleated until you fed her. I could feel Luke looking at me, and when I turned to him he put his hand over mine, which was wrapped around the fence post. The sun was hitting us straight in the face, bright and neon and beautiful. His hand was very big, completely eclipsing mine. His touch made my palms tingly.

The first time he kissed me, we were down by the lake. It was hot. We were sitting on the big rocks, me on one, him on the other, in the clearing where the boat was, where they could see us from the back porch and make sure we weren't doing anything we weren't supposed to.

Even though the bugs weren't bad that day, I still ended up with a gnat in my mouth. I yelled, spat. Luke knew what had happened without asking because gnats in the mouth was something that happened to everybody.

He walked over to me, crouched down, leaned over, kissed me

softly but firmly on the lips. A quick kiss, so we wouldn't get caught.

"Even with a bug in your mouth, you're irresistible."

Then he laughed.

With that laugh I saw it, the same stabbing madness in him that was in me. The tilting demarcation between "fine" and "crazy." That moment—the pine trees, the laughter, the bugs, the kiss—felt both familiar and strange, like something remembered from a dream.

That was what cemented it. That brisk recognition, that quick kiss, drove home the fact I'd already known since the moment we first spoke. It was impossible to resist it.

I couldn't help it.

I fell in love.

PROMISE FULFILLED

My favorite part was the evenings, right after dinner. Free time. We could do whatever we wanted. Most nights, Luke and I, or me and Alyson, or Luke and me and Alyson and Kiran, would get as far away as we could—the barn, a walk around the lake, whatever it took to get out of sight of the grown-ups, whatever it took to feel like normal teenagers, on a camping trip or something like that. Sometimes, it wasn't even hard, the warm nights when the cicadas rang through the trees and the geese flew in V's over the lake as the setting sun turned it scarlet. My parents had been right—it was beautiful up here, all big sunsets and trees.

Even with Alyson and Luke and the therapy and the big sunsets and trees, sometimes this terrible feeling would creep through me and I couldn't seem to get it out. One morning I woke with an especially heavy feeling of doom. Before breakfast, we were doing chores in the barn—cleaning out poop and the animals' feeders, while Kiran and Bill (the ranch manager, who I totally hated) did repairs—when I saw movement behind a pile of hay in the corner. I thought it was one of the barn cats. We hadn't seen the gray one in a while.

I was right. It was the gray barn cat. Only she wasn't doing the moving, because she was dead. The flicker of movement I had seen was hundreds of maggots. She had been dead so long that her eyes and ears had been eaten away. Most of the maggots were squirming around on her underbelly, with bones poking out. I might not have even known it was a cat if I hadn't recognized her fur pattern. I stood there watching for a few moments. It smelled and looked horrible, but for some reason it didn't sicken me. It seemed a good reminder: this is everyone's future. Rot. A dead cat.

Then Bill saw me standing there doing nothing and started to jump my ass about it. So I showed him the cat. He told us to go back to the house, that he would bury her body. And by "bury," I'm sure he meant "transport to the dumpster."

Later in school, we were on World War II, and guess what? Death, death, death.

We had fried rice for lunch, and it felt like the circle of life. I'm eating this thing that looks like maggots, and someday the fried rice maggots will eat me.

And then in group, no one had anything much to talk about, so Nathan started asking Alyson about how she was doing with her mom's illness, which I had learned by then was MS; severe, terminal. And then we were talking about dying in general. Angel's mom and sister had died in a car accident. It turns out Kiran had a sister who had died before he was born, only three months old. I sat there thinking about how I'd tried to kill myself and how I'd really meant it, but now I was really glad I'd fucked that up. I didn't want to be dead and rotting yet.

When I got in the shower that night, I wasn't thinking about my life, and I wasn't thinking about my death, or anyone else's.

I was thinking about the hole in my chest. The finger prick of it bloomed until I was only the hole, a sucking void of darkness and sick. In it, I was floating alone. No matter who I was friends with or who loved me, there was no way to kick through the cavern that held me in.

I did my old razor trick, biting the head until it split and I could remove the thin blades one by one. I was careful to make only little cuts, surface level, the kind that hurt but barely bled. I'd meant to make only a couple, but once I started I didn't want to stop, so I didn't until the top of my whole right thigh was a crosshatch of lines, until you wouldn't have even known a thigh was the thing under there. But it didn't work. I still felt just as rattled and doomed, like something dead and rotting. I sat under the shower nozzle and cried until the water changed from hot to warm to cold.

Rosie was waiting in our room for me, sitting on my bed. Just the tip of what I had begun to think of as my pain quilt showed below my towel, but somehow she saw it right away. She made me pull up the towel even though I was naked underneath, and when she saw it her face looked like it had broken. She sat me down next to her on the bed, and then she held me, still wearing nothing but a towel and with dripping wet hair, but she didn't care, and I cried, and she rubbed my back and whispered *Shhhhhhh*. Like my mother.

I thought the pain quilt would be my and Rosie's secret, but I had all of my razors taken away. I wasn't allowed to use them at all anymore, the staff said. I asked what the fuck I was supposed to do with my hairy-ass legs and my hairy-ass armpits. I told them they were being cruel, that they wanted to take away any self-esteem that I was able to maintain in this demeaning shit-hole, that they wanted me to feel ugly and gross like Sasquatch. They gave me a twenty-minute time-out for the swearing and told me to ask my parents for an electric razor. So I did. The cuts turned into little scabs and my hair grew in dark and straight and a couple weeks later the cuts were mostly gone, a pale pink stippling, and an electric razor arrived for me in the mail.

Later, on the porch, the cuts healed to scars, peeking out the cuff of my shorts. Luke and me, sitting on the rail, waiting for everyone to get ready so we could go into town. His fingers on my thigh, touching the pink bumps. "Beautiful," he said. Quiet, like he didn't even know he was saying it.

PATIENT LOG

PATIENT NAME: Juliet Escoria
AGE: 15 yrs 11 mo
SEX: F
DOB: 8/23/83

DATE: 08/10/99

HISTORY: Patient's acclimation to school—fair. Involved romantically with other patient LUCAS WEBER. No reported hallucinations. Experiencing anxiety, suicidal ideation. Self-harm incident in past week.
Reported side effects of lethargy, muscle pain, upset stomach, hair loss (mild), weight gain.

PREVIOUS MEDICATIONS:
Zyprexa—discontinued 01/99 once stabilized
Wellbutrin—discontinued 03/99 (ineffective)
Tegretol—discontinued 07/99 (risk of overdose/replace w Depakote)
Paxil—discontinued 07/99 (replace w Remeron)
Remeron—discontinued 8/99 (weight gain/replace w Zoloft)

TREATMENT:
Increase Depakote to 1500mg/nightly over course of 1 week
Begin Trazodone 25mg/nightly (for insomnia)
Begin Zoloft 50mg/nightly (for anxiety/depression)
Cont. group therapy, indiv. therapy

We were sitting on the logs, me and Luke and Kiran and a couple of the others. The new kid, Dennis, was with us. It was his second day. Yesterday was orientation, and like everyone else during orientation, he didn't talk much, unsure, trying to get his bearings. We took him to the logs to find out who he was.

He was a big kid, tall, overweight, with a grown-out buzz cut and acne. We asked him why he was here.

"No idea," he said. "My parents are dickheads. Just wanted to get rid of me."

This was a fairly standard answer so we didn't press him. The conversation shifted, as it often did, to drugs. Dennis hadn't done coke, hadn't done E, hadn't done acid. He didn't like pot. He didn't like drinking.

"I only like one thing," he said. "Huffing."

I'd never huffed anything before I came here, and the first and only time had been a few weeks before Dennis arrived. We were making crafts, popsicle houses decorated with paint and glitter. There was a big craft box, full of all types of art supplies. We were supposed to only use the stuff required for whatever shitty craft they came up with for us, but still I liked to go through it. Sometimes it was hard to imagine that it hadn't ever been just us, that there were dozens of kids who had come to the school before we had, and there would be dozens after, and, just like us, they all had their own unique problems and pains and joys and desires, yet we would never know each other. We had one big thing in common. This school. These craft supplies. And you could see the traces of them in that box. Who knew where they were now, if they were better or the same or dead. The only thing I knew was that at one point, they'd sat at this same table, making the same bullshit crafts, writing their name on a collage: *Kelly*, or carving their initials on the foot of a misshapen clay elephant: *J.S.*, or at the bottom of a really good, really detailed drawing of a tree: *Taylor*. I'd been going through the box, looking at the scraps. That's when I saw it. Airplane glue. The thing that stood out was the label on the back, the big yellow skull and crossbones. I slipped it into my pocket for later.

I didn't know how to huff, but Alyson did. She got us a brown lunch bag from the kitchen, and we squeezed the glue into it, and then breathed in and out through the paper bag until we got high. I don't know why, but I was surprised when it worked. It made me warm and tingly and we giggled, over nothing.

Kiran was trying to be nice and started asking Dennis questions. Why did he like huffing, how often did he do it, what did he prefer to inhale—paint or gasoline? Dennis answered all the questions sullenly, looking at his feet instead of us, until Kiran got to the last question. That last question got him excited.

"Nah, man, that shit's for pussies," Dennis said. "If you're really down with it, you huff fucking Raid."

I thought maybe he was mistaken. Maybe he was saying Raid but meant Rave, the hairspray. Kiran thought the same thing.

"Raid? Are you sure?" he said.

Dennis insisted yes. "Roach spray is the best, gets you super fucked up. Way better than lame pussy shit like glue."

"Are you fucking serious?" Kiran said. He pointed out that Raid was used to kill bugs that supposedly would be the only things to survive a nuclear war, that huffing Raid was beyond idiotic. "I don't believe you," he concluded. "You're just trying to front."

I watched Dennis's face slowly turn from pale to red to pale again. I watched his pupils get tiny and sharp.

Kiran was angry now. "That's bullshit."

"I huff Raid," Dennis said again. "Raid is the best."

"You do not huff Raid," Kiran said.

Dennis lunged forward, grabbed one of the big rocks that made up the fire pit in the center of the logs. I assumed he was going to throw it at Kiran, and moved to get out of the way.

But instead he hit it against his own head, and then he did it again. And again. His eyes zoned out, and there was something scary and dark in them—two holes. The noise it made. Bowling pins. A noise a head wasn't supposed to make.

I felt something like fear rising in my stomach, along with nausea, sick and afraid I'd see a cracked skull and brains falling out. "Stop him!" I yelled at Luke. "Get him to stop!"

Luke didn't move. I didn't either. Blood began to appear and then pour out of Dennis's forehead, and then a small trickle ran out from his ear.

The noise had drawn attention, and soon Nathan and Vinnie were out there, and with Luke and Kiran's help, they tackled and restrained Dennis on the ground like he was an animal. He was moaning like one, drool coming out of his mouth like he was rabid. Once they finally got him calmed down, Nathan told us to leave. We all went back to the house in complete silence.

Dennis didn't come in for lunch. He didn't come in for group either. In the middle of it, I watched an unfamiliar van pull up. I watched Nathan lead Dennis into it, his hands bound together in what looked like zip ties. The van was black, unlabeled, had mesh on its windows, the kind they sometimes have in the back of police cars. I watched the van drive away with Dennis in it. He had his head down the whole time, and I couldn't see if it had been bandaged or if he was sad to be leaving.

We never saw him again. When we asked, all anyone would say was he went somewhere better equipped to deal with his diagnosis. They wouldn't even explain what that meant. A lot of us had diagnoses the other reform schools wouldn't touch—me and Luke with bipolar, Stephen with schizophrenia, Angel and her bulimia. Until then, I'd thought that Redwood Trails School was the worst place you could go, the place to hold you when there was nothing else left. I was wrong. I could slip further.

FARMER TAN

I learned that late summer is hay time. The fields of long grass surrounding us weren't just fields. They had a purpose, had been growing for a reason, and now that the sun had bleached them blond it was time for the harvest. We would be the ones to turn them into hay.

There were two tractors behind the barn that I hadn't noticed before. We learned that making hay is a three-step process. First you cut it, then you rake it, then you bale it. The tractors had separate attachments for each step. The cutting and the baling were dangerous, so I wasn't allowed to do it. Only Bill and his favorites, Kiran and Gavin, were. I said this was sexist bullshit. I was told I could help with the other steps if I wanted to spend six hours of my free time training with Bill, the way Kiran and Gavin had done. I said no thank you.

But it turns out it didn't matter. It turns out that one of the spokes of happiness is raking hay in a field at the end of summer as the sun glints off the grass and the tractor's windshield, and you're listening to country music because that's the only channel the radio picks up (previously, I'd had no idea tractors had radios), chewing tobacco because there's no one around to tell you to stop, spitting out the open doors of the tractor, feeling just like a farmer, feeling just like a man.

Hell yeah.

THE BANISHING

Two of the other girls had been caught with cigarettes, so that meant the rest of the school got searched. Alyson and I were out of chewing tobacco. We had nothing to hide.

Bill stood in the doorway and watched as Rosie looked under our beds and under our mattresses and through all of our makeup and clothes, arms crossed over his stupid pearl-buttoned cowboy shirt. When she didn't find anything, he got mad.

He went over to our bookshelf, where I had my books and Alyson had a bunch of photos in frames, and he looked through them until he found something he didn't like.

It was *Fear and Loathing in Las Vegas*. The book I'd entered the school with. The book my father had bought for me.

Bill took one look at the cover, with Johnny Depp's distorted face, and one look at the back cover, which cataloged all the drugs Raoul and Dr. Gonzo brought on their trip, and declared it contraband. I tried to explain that my dad gave it to me, that I'd had it since I'd arrived, that I wasn't hiding it from anyone, just ask Nathan, but Bill didn't care.

I was sent out to the logs.

It was after dinner but before it got dark. I sat on the logs and because there was nothing else to do I watched as the sun lowered in the sky through the trees. I watched as the shadows they made changed from silvery gray to black, as they stretched out long and thin inching toward me. I listened as the bird sounds grew softer and the cricket sounds swelled, until it was the only thing I could hear.

It took me a while to notice. I felt a tickle on my leg, and then when I went to itch it I saw blood. Mosquitoes. And there was one on my other leg, and my elbow, and my forearm, and my face, and my neck. By the time I was allowed back in, I was covered in bites, all red and swollen and itchy.

I itched so much I couldn't sleep that night. Rosie put calamine on all the bites but it didn't matter. The bite on my ankle would start itching, and then the one on my leg, and then the one on my forehead, and then they'd all be itching, so bad I wished I could slip out of my skin. I tried not to scratch because I knew it would just make it worse, but I couldn't help it. In the morning my sheets were streaked copper with blood.

FIRST TIME AT THE RODEO

It was Vinnie's idea. Sometimes on Saturdays the counselors took us to Yreka, the closest city, for bowling or a trip to the movies. But that weekend, he hadn't taken us anywhere. It was now Sunday afternoon, and we were bored.

Vinnie said that when he was a kid, he'd visit his uncle who lived on a farm, and when he was there he was never bored, so there was no reason for us to complain. He insisted there were more things to do on a farm than in a city. When we pressed him, all we got was tipping cows, fresh milk, fishing. So we pointed out that the farm was only fun because he was probably high, which made his tan skin flush red, his glass eye staring hard at nothing.

It was just him and his wife, Shauna, on staff that night, so there was no one more sensible to talk him out of it. The two of them were our favorite counselors. Neither cared too much about our behavior as long as we weren't blatantly breaking the rules. They were recently married, childhood sweethearts, had met and grown up in Redding—two hours away, which seemed close because we weren't really close to anything. They both got sober a couple years ago, he from heroin and she from alcohol. That was the only thing that made them qualified to work with us. Vinnie was stocky, prone to wearing things like basketball jerseys, and Shauna was beautiful in a casual way, with brown eyes and shiny hair always up in a ponytail. With just the two of them on, it felt like being left at home with a babysitter.

So we all went down to the barn. I'd never seen anyone but Bill move the pigs from the dark pens, where they spent most of their time, to the big pen where they got exercise. I thought we'd have to do something to guide them, but they knew the way, seemingly anxious to get out, noses snuffing the air and eyes blinking in the sunlight.

I had a strange fascination-repulsion to the pigs. I'd heard pig meat is the closest thing to human meat, and it was easy to see the truth in that. They looked like old men, pale pink flab covered in sparse and wiry hair poking out in tufts from their veiny ears, eyes heavy lidded with pale lashes, noses thickly pored and obscene. Their feet were especially disgusting, with toes cleaved in a way that seemed vaginal, if vaginas concluded in nails. I loved looking at them, I couldn't stand looking at them. It probably didn't help they were named Helga and Betty.

Once we crowded into the pen, it was time for the rodeo. We decided the smallest of us should be the ones to do the riding because we were worried about hurting the pigs. That left us with Tommy, the skinny kid I'd seen the first day, and me and Alyson, who were the same size. We decided between the two of us with a coin toss. I won. I didn't want to win, but I was more afraid of looking like a wuss.

Before I could think of a way out of it, Vinnie had set his watch and the rest of them started counting down . . . 3 . . . 2 . . . 1.

I hadn't really thought about what I'd do to stay on once I got there. I ended up wrapping my arms around Betty's neck, which caused her to scream. I could feel the vibrations against my wrists, shrieking so loud it hurt my ears. She bucked and started to run, and I tried to hang on but I slid off and landed smack in the mud. I was filthy. Betty was now all the way across the pen from me, glaring like she was offended. I expected everyone to be laughing, but Luke was the only one paying attention. The rest were all standing silently in a circle around Tommy. He'd fallen off right away and Helga had trampled his leg. Luke helped me up and we walked over there, wiping the dirt off my face and pants. Tommy was crying silently, and Vinnie was crouched over him inspecting where he'd gotten hurt. He was fine; his leg was red and would later swell into a bruise, but no blood. Still, Vinnie had a panicked look in his one good eye. I think this was the first time it occurred to him that the pig rodeo was a bad fucking idea.

None of us wanted to see Vinnie and Shauna in trouble, so when he said the rodeo was over, we listened. Shauna and Tommy headed up to the house so she could put ice on his leg. The rest of us went to put the pigs back.

Except the pigs didn't want to go back. It had been fine getting them into the big pen because they wanted the space and the sunshine, but they absolutely did not want to go back into the barn. When we opened the pen, they bolted. We split into two groups, each chasing one pig. They were fast. Vinnie was with my group, going after Betty, and totally freaked out. He kept on saying, "Oh shit oh shit oh shit oh shit" over and over, not caring about cussing in front of us.

A pig is not like a dog. It doesn't wear a collar and it has no bred-in desire to please. It turns out pigs can be incredibly deceptive. Betty ran us like a losing football team, faking us out by going left and then heading right, and a couple of the boys went to tackle her but missed. Finally we cornered her, all the way past the parking lot, in the circle of log benches. Once we trapped her, we had to figure out how to get her back to the barn. We ended up surrounding her like pallbearers, Vinnie in the front in case she decided to charge, Stephen at the rear, hitting her on the butt with a stick and saying "Yah yah" in his monotone voice, like she was a wayward horse. It took a while to make it back down the hill, but finally we got her in the pen.

Helga didn't get as far and was already inside, with the other kids waiting for us to come back with Betty. By then, a good forty-five minutes had passed. Most of us were filthy, covered in dirt and sweat and briars. Before we went to shower, Vinnie made us promise to say nothing about the pigs. The dirt on our clothes and the bruise on Tommy's leg were from an especially competitive soccer game. The grass had been muddy and we all got really into it, but it was a good release for our aggression. The score was tied forever, two to two, until finally Kiran made the scoring goal.

He made us repeat this. He made us promise. We repeated. We promised.

The pigs had won.

REVENGE IS A DISH

The next day, Luke and I were assigned to feed the pigs. I snuck two raw eggs and some leftover bacon up my sleeves.

The barn was mostly quiet and the sunlight sliced through the cracks in the wood. The pigs were making little grunting noises, their hairy backs the only things visible. The noises were making me sick so I made Luke put the feed in their trough by himself. He didn't know I'd brought the bacon and eggs.

I threw the eggs. I missed with one but hit Helga, the spotted one, square on the neck. Betty, who had been snorting in wait for her grain, suddenly lurched at the egg-covered neck, licking it off hungrily, shells and all, making slurping noises that sounded oddly sexual, and I hated the noises so much that I threw the bacon at them. They ate it down so quick it was like they'd been eating bacon their whole lives.

Like all they'd ever wanted was to taste themselves.

ALYSON'S MOM

A few days later, I had a session with Nathan that ran over and so I was late to school. I went into my room to grab a sweater before I headed to class. The heat of the summer was dying off and lately I was always freezing in the classroom, which was downstairs in what probably used to be a cellar.

I expected the room to be empty. But Alyson was in there, curled up in a ball on her bed, so all I could see was her folded-up limbs and her hair. Rosie was sitting next to her, not saying anything, just stroking her hair in silence.

I knew what had happened immediately, but I stood there in the doorway for a second. A good friend would rush to her, hold her, tell her everything would be OK. So I crossed the room, stood in front of her, snaked my arm behind her back.

She screamed into her lap when I touched her. It wasn't a scream, though, not really. It was just a noise, something jagged and loud that tore into my bones. I pulled my hand away. I stood there in front of her but she didn't look up, didn't even move. I waited for Rosie to tell me what to do but she just looked at me and I couldn't tell what the look meant. I patted her again, on the head this time, like a puppy, and it felt so stupid I left.

After school, I stood in the hallway listening to Alyson talk to her father in the office. I couldn't make out a whole lot, just her talking and crying softly, until I heard her yell "FUCK YOU!!!!!!" She slammed the phone down so hard I was surprised later when it wasn't broken, and then she ran past me into our room. I thought I should go and try to comfort her but I didn't know how to begin. I imagined a spider's nest—something that looked manageable until you touched it too much and found yourself in a mess of swarming baby spiders.

I ignored it. I pretended that nothing had happened. I went outside to go finish my chores.

We didn't talk until bedtime, because she punched the bathroom mirror shortly after. It shattered and busted her knuckles; blood spattered all over the sink and floor.

No one got mad at her. They took her to the clinic to get stitches. I felt guilty, so I volunteered to clean up the bathroom. I got a splinter of glass stuck in my finger.

I didn't bother to pull it out. I hoped I got gangrene.

But later, in the darkness of our bedroom, the two of us in our separate beds, I asked her what had happened. I pretended I didn't already know. She didn't cry while telling me. Instead, her voice was flat and dead.

Her father wouldn't even let her go to the funeral. He said she was still too new to the school, that he didn't want to risk it. He refused to explain what, exactly, he thought she would be risking. "I'm never talking to him again," Alyson said, in a tone so cold I believed her.

THE SHIT BABY

The boys had a new nighttime counselor. His name was Hank. He was cute in a TV-dad kind of way, but I thought he was mean because he didn't say much and always looked at me slanty eyed in the hall. But all the boys seemed to love him. They said he told dirty jokes and let them go to bed late and didn't care if they dipped as long as they didn't walk upstairs with one in. Meanwhile, most nights we had Rosie, who was great and everything but she was such a stickler for the rules.

But then Hank started taking us to AA meetings in Yreka once a week. All the kids with "substance abuse issues" got to leave, while the nerds like Tommy and schizophrenics like Stephen had to stay. In the van, Hank let us listen to whatever music we wanted—he didn't care if it had curse words, or was rap or punk—all the music the other counselors hated and forbid. He drove fast with the music loud, taking the turns of the mountain so fast it felt like we'd fall in, and we all told war stories from our drug days and laughed.

Hank was sober, had been for eleven years. Before that, he'd liked coke, and also weed—but it was the liquor that got him in trouble. He had stories about getting kicked out of bars, thrown in jail, various dates and jobs ruined by puking.

The best story involved too much weed and a bottle of Tums. One night, he'd had a bad case of the munchies, could have killed someone for a candy bar, but there was nothing in the house except stale bread and condiments, and going to the store seemed impossible. In the bathroom he came across a bottle of Tums. He figured they tasted like fruit—same as candy. In his stoned stupor, they tasted good. He ate the whole bottle.

In the morning, he tried to take a shit first thing, just like usual. Nothing. No shit the next day either, or the one after that. He was so constipated, it felt like he was pregnant with a shit baby.

The fourth day, though. That day his shit was gigantic, and it was also solid white. He guessed it was the calcium in the Tums. "Looked like a fucking iceberg," he said. "All white and hard and so big it stuck out of the water. So big and white I should have named it." We couldn't stop laughing. Every time the van finally grew quiet, somebody would start giggling and that would set the rest of us off, and by the time we got to the meeting my stomach hurt. Hank and his massive iceberg shit baby.

SHORTLY AFTER THAT

Nathan left. He didn't say goodbye. We didn't know he was leaving until he was gone. He wasn't the owner, just the person in charge. The owner was some woman named Donna, who lived in Sacramento, who I'd never met. Maybe they got into a disagreement. Either way, one Monday we woke up and he wasn't there, and they said he wasn't coming back. It felt like a bit of a betrayal, this man who'd listened to me in counseling and then disappeared with my secrets.

In the meantime, Bill the ranch manager would be in charge. Bill, who wasn't even a counselor but a fucking cowboy, and, even worse, a Christian.

THE BRIGHT SIDE

But then they hired this woman Carly. Not as a headmaster, like Nathan. Her title was Wilderness Counselor. She came in a couple times a week, met with us for counseling, not the hour-long sessions we'd had with Nathan, just a quick check-in for ten or twenty minutes. If something bad happened, she might talk to us for longer, but mostly that was it. We were told that once we got to know her and vice versa, she'd take us backpacking and rock climbing, Death Valley and Mexico and Alaska. I liked her right away. We all did. She was cool, knew about good bands and had funny jokes.

Carly was no help when Bill did things like go into the classroom and decide we weren't allowed to listen to music anymore, and since I ignored this new rule, I had to stay in my room during free time for three days.

And sometimes he'd do stuff that was really fucked up. One morning he was yelling at Tommy during breakfast because he'd made his bed all messy.

"How about you stop being a dick," I told Bill.

He flipped out. "Until you learn some respect, you're not going anywhere. Not down to the barn, not to watch movies, not on a walk, not to town. The only places you'll be going are your room and the schoolroom and to do chores."

"Um, hello," I said. "I have an appointment with my psychiatrist tomorrow."

"I don't care. You're not going anywhere. You can go next week, after you've learned your lesson."

Naturally, I ran out of medication.

Rosie was dispensing, and she seemed so confused until I explained why there was nothing in my bottle.

She muttered, "Good Lord," and then dug through other people's medicine until she came up with my doses. "Here," she said. "Our secret. We'll solve this problem in the morning."

I don't know what happened, if Rosie yelled at him or something, but the next night my medicine had been refilled, and not only that, Bill apologized. To me. His voice was soft and you could tell he was embarrassed and I tried to not revel in it but it was hard. "It's OK, Bill," I said.

Later, once I was in bed, I played that moment over again in my head. Bill's embarrassment. Bill's apology. Rosie could get anybody to do anything. What an amazing woman.

VETERAN ADVICE

At the AA meetings, we were the only people under forty. Hank had formerly been the baby of the group. Mostly it was crusty old men, old-timers who could quote whole passages from the Big Book and loved repeating all the stupid AA catchphrases. *It works if you work it. Keep coming back. Meeting makers make it.* But they also had great stories, about robberies and prostitutes and prison. They loved us, gave us extra cookies and cigarettes, which Hank didn't mind us smoking as long as we didn't smell like it when we got back. Between that and the coffee, the handholding and the corny phrases and the God and prayer bullshit hardly mattered.

The first few times we went, Hank had instructed us to just watch and listen and take it all in. He told us we didn't have to like or relate to everything we heard—the point was to pay attention to the parts that sounded like us. "It's like a cafeteria. Take what you need and leave the rest behind," he said. Another stupid fucking catchphrase. But we did what he said.

And he was right. When I listened to the old men, I found traces of myself. One night, this guy—he was wearing a hat like the ones my grandpa wore, with the name of his navy ship from WWII stitched on the front, white hairs sticking out of his nose—was saying the only time he felt whole was when he was fucked up. The generations between us were nothing; there was something in him that also existed in me. I heard what he said like he was talking straight to me. Like I was the only person in the room.

I DECIDED TO TRY SOMETHING NEW

It was late and I couldn't sleep. I kept watch on the clock until it read 12:03, because Rosie was on night shift, and she said I had to try to sleep for at least two hours before I could get up to read.

But this time I didn't start reading right away. This time I asked her if we could talk.

She smiled like she'd been waiting for me to ask that question a long time. "Of course," she said, and I sat down next to her at the table. I told her about my loneliness. I said it felt like there was something wrong with me. I felt like I was missing something.

"Loneliness, huh." She leaned back in her chair, and looked at me for a moment like she was assessing me. Then she said, "That's something I know a lot about, sweetheart."

I knew Rosie was married to a truck driver named Denny, but I hadn't really considered what that meant. Turns out it meant she was alone a lot of the time. Her kids were alone a lot, too—the oldest, her son, had to be the parent sometimes. He put the others to bed when she worked the night shift, prepared breakfast in the morning, made sure everyone got to school on time. She said she felt the loneliness in herself, but it was worse when she saw it in him because she knew it was her fault.

"But I have to look at the positives," she said. "Denny's gone a lot of the time, sure. But we have good health insurance, a nice home. Plus with him being away so much, we don't have time to argue or get bored with each other the way most people do. I swear, his job is what's kept us going for these fifteen years."

She put her fingers on her hair-sprayed curls, twisting them in a way that was almost girlish. "You know, there's good in everything," she said. "It's just sometimes you have to dig a little harder to get it out."

She was quiet for a bit, and I was too. "Now you," she said. She reached across the table to hold my hand. Hers were warm and plump. Mom hands. "You're sensitive. And that means extra pain, extra loneliness, extra sadness. But it also means extra joy." She said, "Your job is to dig for the gold. God's given you a shovel, you just have to figure out how to use it."

We sat there for a while after, me reading my book, her reading some women's magazine that told you how to be a good woman. I kept looking at her over the pages, how her face was both hard and soft, tired and youthful, at the same time. I wondered what she thought about the magazine, if she was reading things she cared about or just killing time. I wondered what she thought about me. But I didn't ask. Soon I grew tired. I said goodnight to Rosie, and she said goodnight to me. I fell asleep within minutes, like magic.

SITUATIONS THAT USED
TO BAFFLE US

After we'd been going to AA for a month, Hank told us it was time for us to share. So after we finished reading from the Big Book, Hank nodded at us, which meant we should raise our hands.

Alyson went first. She talked about her mom, and getting arrested for stealing, and how much she hated her father. And then Luke went, sharing about his blackouts and how he always felt like he couldn't stop betraying the people he loved. And then Kiran—the fights he'd gotten into, his DUI, how his mother told him she didn't love him anymore. These were things that only came out in group, and I felt so proud of them for not being afraid to say them aloud here in that room, outside the school, to people we barely knew.

And then it was my turn.

I wanted to be honest. It was weird, standing up in that room. I didn't know where to look or what to say, and I felt the hot spread of embarrassment crawl up my neck and face. I told myself it didn't matter, but I couldn't talk while looking at anyone so I just stared at the ground, at the worn industrial carpet covered in weird stains and cigarette burns. And then I was talking, saying that drugs were the only thing that seemed to fix me, the only time I could shut up my stupid brain. I told them I wasn't suicidal anymore, but sometimes all I wanted was to die. I told them I couldn't stop hating myself. When I finished, everyone was looking at me—the old men, Hank, my friends, everybody. But it didn't make me feel uncomfortable. They weren't looking at me like I was a freak. They were looking at me like they understood.

At the end of the meeting, they gave out tokens—for the people who had been sober a month, six months, years. Unfathomable amounts of time. They offered all of us, "The most important token of all. The one for a new way of life."

We went up one by one, and everybody clapped, and they gave us a token and a hug. At other meetings when other people had gone up for that token, it had felt cheap and corny to me, celebrating something just for showing up. But when I got that hug—the old man, I think his name was Stu—he smelled like cheap cologne and tobacco and something else, maybe beef jerky. That smell and that hug actually meant something to me—starting as tingles at the back of my neck, shooting into my arms.

As I walked back to my seat, fingering that white piece of plastic, I realized I was in danger of crying. I didn't even know why. I didn't feel sad.

I felt something new.

I felt . . .

happy.

LET'S TWIST AGAIN

We were having a dance. The first ever at RTS, in all of its three years. We'd spent almost two weeks deciding on a theme, making decorations. The challenge of finding songs we liked that didn't have curse words or talk about sex or drugs or violence. We decided on the theme Lost in Space, so we cut planets and stars out of cardboard, painted them and covered them with glitter. Rosie went into town, bought us shiny star-shaped Mylar balloons—even one that looked like an astronaut—a big pack of tissue paper, a purple strand of Christmas lights.

Of course none of us had prom dresses, prom shoes, or prom hair, but we did the best we could to get ready. Alyson put a mix CD on her Discman and turned the volume all the way up, fuzzy through her headphones but loud enough that we could hear, and I pretended it was like the olden days, when I'd go over to Nicole's after school on Fridays and we'd spend hours listening to music while picking our outfits. I put on the long black nightgown I bought at a vintage store, and over it my fuzzy pink angora sweater, my rhinestone choker and my silver bracelet. Alyson French-braided my hair so it was like a headband, and then we put little flower clips to pin it in place. We did our makeup with the brightest shadows we had, to fit the theme, sparkly purple on my eyes and electric green on Alyson's. We put glitter on everything, our cheekbones and brow bones and collarbones. I didn't have any prom shoes, so I just went barefoot, painting my toenails silver. When we were finished, we didn't look prom-ready, but it was close.

The kitchen almost looked like a normal dance too. The "decoration committee" had put purple butcher paper on the tables, sprinkled glitter on top. The tables and chairs had all been pulled back and pushed together. There was a big bowl of punch, soda cans, a tray of cookies. The tissue paper was bunched up in things you could almost imagine were extraterrestrial landscapes, lit up from behind with the purple Christmas lights, glinting off the glitter on the planets and stars.

And then Luke and the rest of the boys came up the stairs. Somebody turned on the music, oldies because we couldn't find anything else that fit the criteria, and as "Angel Baby" swelled through the speakers Luke walked up to me, his eyes glowing in the cloudy light. He had a corsage for me, pine needles and a couple bright yellow oak leaves bundled together with white yarn, because there was no florist and any flowers outside were now dead. He tied it around my wrist and I almost felt normal, almost like I was going to prom. He placed his hands on my waist and I put mine on his shoulders, because we weren't allowed to get any closer, and he smiled at me like I was the best thing he'd ever seen, and I felt like I was, like I truly was good, beautiful and alive and special and loved.

The dance didn't last all that long but it didn't need to. There was a meteor shower that night anyway. It was cold and clear, so first we went into our rooms, and I put long johns under my nightgown and my fake fur coat over. The staff gave us a bunch of old blankets and towels so we could lie out on the front lawn but the grass was wet and crunchy with frost, so we went down to the basketball courts. Maybe that's why they let us go out alone—we'd be on the lawn so they could watch us—but no one came out to stop us from moving. We lit up a cigarette, one that Alyson had stolen from Rosie's purse, menthol and skinny, passed it between us and waited.

Nothing happened at first, so we pointed out all the stars we knew, or thought we knew. Venus, the North Star, Orion. I'd never seen stars the way they looked in Redwood Trails. There were so many you might really think the sky was just a sheet of black paper with pinpricks, dully masking the glowing afterworld.

I tried to recall the stories I'd heard during that Christian camp, but all I could remember was the one about Ursa Major. Once a giant bear roamed the earth but he and a hunter got into a fight, and the hunter grabbed him by the tail and flung him into the sky. That was why the tail was so long—it had gotten stretched out in the flinging. I thought the bear might fall down. It bothered me that a little mistake like fucking with the wrong hunter could lead to an eternity of embarrassment and consequence—alone in the sky with a stretched-out tail.

Then Alyson spit on her hand and started to give Kiran a hand job under the blanket, mostly joking, and we told stories about all the funny places we'd had sex. Except by then I'd heard all the stories before—Alyson getting fingerbanged on the teacups at Disneyland, Kiran in his little brother's bed, me in the bathroom at a Burger King, Luke in church.

That was when the shower started. First I saw something so slight it might have been a trick of the eye. Then one more. I made a wish. And then more of them, dozens of them, dozens of wishes falling down from the sky.

PIZZA PARTY

Hank got permission for us to leave for AA an hour early, so we could have pizza. It was a bit of a celebration, really. Alyson and I had finally been promoted to Phase Two, and so had Beto.

It was kind of humiliating, getting to Phase Two the same time as him. Beto had only been at the school a month. Plus he barely spoke English. He was from Guadalajara, said he'd been sent here for smoking crack—which made no sense because why didn't he just go to a rehab? Still, I liked Beto. He had pretty brown eyes and a mean sense of humor and said a lot of shit that was unintentionally funny. Like how he was going to "broom" the floor, or the time he couldn't remember the English word for "confused" so he said his brain was like scrambled eggs.

The annoying thing was the staff clearly wanted to make an example out of him. Beto claimed it was his choice to be here, because he wanted to quit smoking crack and wanted to get better. So he followed all the rules and never talked back and here he was, not even at RTS for a full month but already on Phase Two, could already drink caffeinated soda and go into town to help with the grocery shopping and make phone calls twice a week. Things that had been kept from Alyson and me for four long months.

I thought we'd go to a Pizza Hut or something, but instead we got some delivered to Hank's house. He had gifts for us, he said, and then pulled out a paper bag. We each got two containers of dip in the flavors we liked. Cherry for me and Alyson. Copenhagen for Luke. Spearmint for Kiran and Beto.

His house was kind of a dump, with shitty wood paneling and dark brown carpets. His kitchen table was too small, so most of us ate while sitting on the floor. There were dishes in the sink. Cheap furniture. You would've thought he lived alone if it wasn't for the pictures on the wall, which showed him and his wife, a chubby blond. And then there was the existence of his stepdaughter, which surprised me because Hank had never mentioned a stepdaughter before. She came out of her room and had pizza with us. She was our age, looked like someone I'd be friends with, with her dyed pink hair and nose ring. When we were done eating, she showed me and Alyson her room. It was just like mine before I'd left home— clothes in piles, an unmade bed, pictures from magazines taped to the walls. Our room at school was neat because it had to be, and we weren't allowed anything on the walls. I didn't stay in there long.

She was just like us, except she wasn't at all.

When I came back into the living room, all the boys and Hank went silent, looking at me like I'd caught them doing something wrong.

"What?" I said. "What are you guys doing?"

But they just giggled and looked at each other.

"That was some good pizza," Hank said.

"Sure was," said Luke.

And that was that. And then we left for the meeting.

TROJANS

I found out why the boys had been acting weird a few days later. After group, Luke gave me back the sweatshirt I let him borrow a few weeks before, saying he had finally gotten around to washing it. Except I hadn't let him borrow a sweatshirt. The sweatshirt he'd handed me was his to begin with, but I was smart enough to not say that. Instead, I took it into my room and closed the door. Tucked inside the pocket was a whole strip of condoms, eight of them, in shiny silver wrappers like candy.

I didn't even know what we were supposed to do with eight condoms.

They'd increased the security recently because a few weeks earlier, two kids got caught having sex in the barn. The funny part was who the two kids were. The girl was Angel—who was cool enough but was so chubby and shy. The boy was Gavin, who was short and had braces and a shaved head, and was always trying to act tough and fit in with Beto and Kiran and Luke but actually just had bad ADD and a shoplifting problem. I never thought they would have tried to fuck anyone, and I especially never would have thought they'd try to fuck each other.

After they got caught, all excess freedom was revoked. Boys and girls weren't allowed in the same room together unless they were in direct sight of a staff member. This was complete bullshit, especially considering there were rarely more than two staff on at a time anymore, so we were often stuck in some room until a staff person came to get us. The staff seemed annoyed with the new rule too, because instead of doing paperwork or anything that mattered they had to sit around staring at us like we were specimens—but that was better than somebody getting pregnant. It also meant a lot of sneaking around, and a lot of getting caught.

The new rule was one of the things that had kept me and Alyson on Phase One for so long.

I put the condoms back in the sweatshirt pocket, and then folded it and put it in a drawer, pushing it underneath my sweaters. I sat on my bed for a couple minutes, so I didn't seem suspicious. Then I went back into the great room, with Luke and a few of the others. Rosie was in there, sitting on the couch with a magazine, making sure nobody was doing any touching.

I took some paper and markers from the shelf, like I was going to draw something. Then I sat down next to Luke. I wrote in very tiny letters:

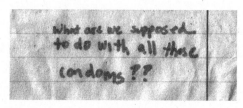

But Luke didn't say anything. He just smiled at me.

Later, during school, Luke and I were supposedly quizzing each other on science, but actually we were talking about condoms.

"So Hank gave them to us, a strip to each of the boys, when we were at his house," Luke whispered.

"Damn. That's cool of him."

"He even said he would help us use them. We can get in the back of the van when we drive to AA."

The teacher walked by. "Which is the heaviest noble gas?" I said, pretending to be very absorbed in our flash cards.

"Easy," Luke said. "Radon."

I lowered my voice again. "That's kind of creepy."

"I think he just knows how sexually frustrated we are. He said it would help relieve stress and anger and all that shit. But he doesn't want anyone pregnant, which is why he's so big on the condoms."

It made enough sense to me. Then Luke said we were up first, that he'd beat Kiran in a game of rock-paper-scissors. We were scheduled to fuck the very next day.

SEX TAPE

I thought about it all during breakfast and chores and school and group and lunch and chores and group and dinner. Finally it was time to leave for the meeting. I was nervous. I hadn't had sex in so long. The lyrics from Madonna's "Like a Virgin" kept playing in my head. I had shaved my legs and shaved my pussy the night before, or at least done the best job I could with my shitty electric razor. I was wearing my cutest underwear and cutest bra, a black satin set I'd stolen a lifetime ago from Victoria's Secret with Nicole.

We got in the van like normal, with me and Luke in the back row. I was wearing the sweatshirt. I tried to smile but my hands were shaky and I kind of felt like I might cry. Then Luke put his hand over mine, and I looked up at him and his blue eyes met mine and I could feel something crackle between us, a force that was equal parts blessed and damned.

Hank stopped the van right before we got on the main road, turning the volume up on the music. We crawled over the seat into the very back, where we always put the groceries. There was a pillow and a blanket back there. I guess Hank had snuck them in before we left.

We pulled the blanket over us and lay with both our heads on the pillow, just looking at each other for a second. And then he kissed me, his hand in my hair, his hand on my back, his hand in my pants. We both slid down our jeans and there was that awkward moment when he put on the condom and then he was inside me and the pleasure surged in a slow wave up my back, crashing into my head. I closed my eyes to concentrate and I no longer had a body, was no longer a human but an object and I let the feeling swirl around me. I rolled on top of him and it wasn't like the sex I'd had before, which always felt frenzied and awkward.

This felt like being in love.

At one point I splintered out of it, turned back into what I was, a teenager having sex in the back of a moving van full of other teenagers.

I caught Hank's eye in the rearview mirror.

He was watching us.

He held eye contact for a fraction of a second, then looked back at the road, and then back at me.

For a second I wanted to stop.

But—the creepy feeling was quickly overridden by something else.

I shook my hair, threw my head back, bit my lip. I was beautiful. I was glorious.

It didn't last long. I curled into Luke's chest and kissed his mouth and then it was over. We pulled up our pants and climbed back into our seat.

I kept waiting for somebody to say something but nobody did. I kept waiting for somebody to make a joke. But everyone acted like nothing had happened. So Luke and I did the same.

Except we held hands all through the meeting and for once it didn't feel pathetic or desperate or virginal. His palms were hot and moist and I couldn't stop thinking *He's been inside me.*

LATER

For some reason I didn't tell anyone about Hank watching us. Not even Luke.

But it was something I often thought about.

THE KIDS THAT LEFT #2

This new kid was different from all the other new kids. His name was Tasafi, he was from Iran, and he looked middle aged even though he couldn't have been more than seventeen. He didn't speak much English but somehow had a lot of cigarettes and was fine with sharing, so nobody made fun of him for his accent or dorky clothes. New kids at the school were always interesting, watching their stories unspool: a kid who seemed meek might have been sent for stealing cars and fighting, someone who seemed like a typical popular kid might end up slashing their arms. I was curious to find out Tasafi's story because it had to be weird. Since he couldn't even speak English, I figured it would take a while.

The boys went to the gym in Yreka one Tuesday. We did this often enough on weeknights, the boys one night, the girls the next. This time, the boys came back two hours late, the kids excited, Vinnie and Hank panicked. At first I assumed it had to be an elaborate ruse, some prank that was the result of another lapse in the counselors' judgment. When they said Tasafi had run away, it seemed impossible. The school was literally miles from anything—the closest structure was the barn of the neighboring horse ranch, and Redwood Trails was so small that everyone in town knew what to do with an unfamiliar teen. But Tasafi was smart. He realized that if he was going to run away, he would have to do it in Yreka, a place where a stranger wouldn't be noticed.

It happened in the locker room. One minute he was there, one minute he was gone. Cops were called but they found nothing. He'd vanished. Later, someone heard he'd hopped a train, was free for several weeks until he was finally apprehended in Southern California. Maybe that was just a rumor. Maybe he's still train hopping around the coast, smoking his weird cigarettes.

THANKSGIVING BREAK

Bill said
I shouldn't
Be allowed
To go home
For the holiday
There was some debate
Between him and me
And Carly and
My parents
In the end
I was allowed to go
But only because of my
Wisdom teeth
Which were breaking through
Impacted
The doctor gave me
Vicodin
And I spent the four days
In my parents' bed
High
Watching all the R-rated movies
I'd missed
My mother brought me milkshakes
And, on Thanksgiving, mashed potatoes
I wasn't allowed to see my friends
Except once Holly came over
Crying because she missed me
With photos of all the things I
Had ceased to be
A part of

And I felt a twinge of loneliness and
Something not unlike
Nostalgia
But mostly all I felt
Was warm and safe
And high

Because she still wasn't speaking to her father, Alyson had stayed at the school over Thanksgiving. Everybody else went home. There was a question of what to do with her. Finally, Vinnie and Shauna said she could stay with them.

I found out what had happened as soon as I got back because Alyson was waiting for me in our room. I put my bags down and she closed the door. Her face was all swollen, a scrape on her cheek and a big black eye, so bad that the white was blood-red.

"I've got something to tell you," she said. I figured it was a fight, with another student or some kid in town. I was wrong.

Apparently things with Vinnie and Shauna had gone fine at first. They'd played board games and watched movies at night; Alyson helped out with their two kids during the day. They had Thanksgiving dinner at their house, just the five of them, a family, everything homemade by Shauna. But on Saturday, Vinnie and the kids went to Redding to see his parents. Shauna and Alyson stayed home. They ended up getting drunk—really drunk—on cheap vodka purchased at the general store. Both of them blacked out. Alyson didn't know how she got the black eye, she just woke up that way, sore and bruised.

They had sworn to each other they wouldn't tell anyone. Shauna said she didn't see the harm in one night, wouldn't even consider it a relapse because it was just temporary. But Vinnie got home early the next day. So early that Shauna was still drunk. She thought she could pull it off anyway. But then she started puking.

Alyson had been sleeping in the kids' room when he got home, and the two children were put in there with her while Vinnie and Shauna fought. "Really brought me back," Alyson said, "listening to Mom and Dad scream from the other end of the house, closed up in a room with my little brother." Vinnie was yelling like he thought it was the old days, back when he and Shauna used to get in the epic fights they'd told us about, before they both got sober and had kids. He was yelling like he hoped Shauna might throw something. She didn't. He even threatened to leave her. But all she did was cry.

In the end, they decided to work things out. Shauna would go to AA every night, she promised. Vinnie made her confess, which seemed stupid of him. That was this morning. Now, Shauna no longer worked at the school. She'd been fired.

By the time Alyson finished telling the story, I was so jealous of her black eye my stomach hurt. We were sitting on the floor, our backs against her bed. I moved my finger near her cheekbone, where the bruise was darkest, the skin swollen taut in violent smudges of purple. I wanted to touch it. I didn't touch her. It looked too painful. I hovered there for a moment, and she was perfectly still, staring straight ahead like she was waiting for me to hurt her, before touching my own cheekbone instead. The skin under my finger was smooth and soft.

PATIENT LOG

PATIENT NAME: Juliet Escoria
AGE: 16 yrs 3 mo
SEX: F
DOB: 8/23/83

DATE: 11/29/99

HISTORY: Patient's behavior log continues to indicate impulsivity issues. Cont. involvement romantically with other patient LUCAS WEBER. No reported hallucinations. Experiencing increased anxiety; mild depression.

Drug test positiv e for opiates due to recent surgery (oral). Otherwise clean.

Reported side effects of lethargy, muscle pain, upset stomach, hair loss (mild) (cont.).

PREVIOUS MEDICATIONS:
Zyprexa—discontinued 01/99 once stabilized
Wellbutrin—discontinued 03/99 (ineffective)
Tegretol—discontinued 07/99 (risk of overdose/replace w Depakote)
Paxil—discontinued 7/99 (tremors)
Remeron—discontinued 8/99 (weight gain/replace w Zoloft)

TREATMENT:
Cont. Depakote at 1500mg/nightly
Cont. Trazodone 25mg/nightly (for insomnia)
Cont. Zoloft 50mg/nightly (for anxiety/depression)
Begin Buspar 15mg/nightly (for anxiety)
Cont. group therapy, indiv. therapy, 12-step group

GAY SEX

A new girl arrived at the school. Christina. She was shy, not as pretty as me and Alyson, not quite as funny, but she was cool, did drugs and had sex, told interesting stories, and liked cute clothes and makeup. She slid into her place at school, halfway hanging out with Angel, her roommate, when she wanted to be good, halfway hanging out with us.

One night we were all in the kitchen before bed, the four of us girls, along with Beto, Kiran, and Luke. We were talking about being gay. It seemed weird that none of the kids here were. We didn't even suspect anyone. "Maybe there's a rule against it here," Kiran speculated, but we decided against it, figuring it discriminatory. It also didn't make sense, because RTS accepted students that other schools wouldn't.

Then we started talking about gay sex, and whether anyone had had any. All the other girls had—even chubby nerdy Angel had once felt up a girl. The most I'd ever done was kiss Nicole at a party, but that was just because we were drunk and somebody told us to, and it was just for a second anyway. Luke had even made out with a couple of boys, had thought for a while he was bi. All these secret-world stories, right beneath the surface, a range of possibilities I'd been too boring to think of on my own.

A couple nights later, no one was paying much attention to any of us. Stephen, who everyone liked because he was so nice, even though he was schizophrenic and only ever really talked to Kiran, had spent the entire evening in a fit, crying and cursing through dinner so loud they ended up making him eat alone in the bedroom, where he punched a hole in the wall. He did stuff like that sometimes. So the staff did what they always did—put out the cot in the office, where somebody could keep an eye on him all night. That was what Carly, the girls' counselor that night, was doing.

Hank was downstairs with the boys, so we were left to ourselves.

I got an idea. I told it to Alyson. She liked it.

Christina and Angel's room was next to ours. Both rooms faced the lake, had wide sliding glass doors that locked with a security bolt, allowing them to open just a few inches, enough to put an arm through, but not a whole body. Once it was officially bedtime, I sat in front of the door, waited until I heard someone walk out of Christina and Angel's room. I peeked through the crack at the bottom: I could see fuzzy purple slippers walking away, Angel's feet.

"Now," I said to Alyson, who was sitting on the floor next to the sliding glass window, which was closed to keep out the cold. She opened it, slid her arm out, holding the wire coat hanger we'd prepared, untwisted and stretched out, with a note taped to the hook. I heard it scraping against the glass next door. I heard the sliding glass door open. A moment passed, the door shut. Then a knock at our bedroom door.

Christina's short brown hair was still pinned back in the sparkly barrettes she'd worn that day. She'd taken off her makeup, and I could see her freckles, traces of blue shadow still smudged in the corner of her eyes. I noticed her lips were chapped. She looked cute, standing in the doorway, but not sexy. I told her to come in. She was holding the note, which Alyson had written in red pencil:

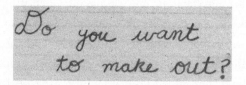

"Yes," Christina said. We stood there in the doorway for a second, the three of us, before Alyson took both our hands, led us to her bed, and flicked off the light. We sat awkwardly for a moment, Alyson's knees pressed against mine, Christina farther apart, sitting formally, her back straight and feet flat on the floor. None of us looked at each other.

I grabbed Christina's chin and kissed her, her lips rough under mine. I could feel Alyson move away from me, and when I opened my eyes I saw her kissing Christina's neck. I was jealous, which surprised me, so I stopped kissing Christina, scooted across the bed so I could put my mouth to Alyson's. She tasted different than Christina, almost salty, her mouth hotter and dryer. I felt Christina's hand lightly on my shoulder, her fingers trailing down to my elbow, back up, almost but not quite tickling, across to my chest. She gave my left boob a squeeze, laughed, and I laughed too, opening my eyes but not moving my mouth from Alyson's. Then Alyson started laughing too, pulled away from me, and the three of us sat for a moment, just giggling. The only light in the room came from underneath the door, in the hallway, and I looked out our window into the dark night. You could see our outlines in the glass, the forms of three girls, three heads and three sets of shoulders, sitting together.

I thought for a moment that that would be it, a pathetic foray, barely hitting second base, but then Christina leaned in to kiss me again, harder and more serious this time, reached to unbutton my jeans. I stood awkwardly to take them off, feeling a little dizzy. I got back on the bed. She went down on me while I made out with Alyson and it was good, better than any boy.

I put my fingers down Alyson's pajama pants. I had no idea what I was doing. I pushed my finger between her lips, found her clit, bigger than mine, not sure if I was doing it right, but she started to moan softly so I figured I was. Christina went to work getting Alyson's pants off, and we both fingered her, me on her clit, with two of Christina's fingers sliding in and out, Alyson's breath getting faster, finally dissolving into whimpers.

"Holy shit," Alyson said, breaking away from our hands. "I just fucking came. I've never come from anyone before besides myself."

She leaned back on the bed, and Christina curled up next to her so I did too. There wasn't enough room for the three of us unless we squeezed in close together, Christina's arms around the both of us to keep me from falling off. I turned my head, pressed my cheek against Alyson's, and everything in that room felt so still and soft.

We lay there for a few more minutes, listening to each other's breaths, as something buzzed around us, something I could only describe as warmth.

SPY GAME

One night Rosie called in sick last minute, so the only person on the night shift was Hank. After dinner, Hank said we would play a game called Spy. We gathered on the back deck and split into pairs, me and Alyson together. Each team got a flashlight, and we were supposed to hide in the woods. If another team shined their light on you, you were dead. The winner was the last team standing.

As soon as Hank yelled *GO!* Alyson and I ran down the path that went around the entire grounds of the school, out to where the trees were the thickest. We whooped, and then we were laughing, our feet thudding fast on the dirt at the same rate as the beat of my heart. We got into the brush and I felt wild as a wolf, darting through the snow and sticks by instinct. Once the light from the house was just a tiny dot we stopped and got quiet. My face was hot and I could feel the blood pulsing through the veins in my throat.

It felt so good to run, and to yell. Ever since I got on the Buspar, I felt sluggish and thick, like there was a swaddling of cotton around my body. But that night, the cold air cut clean into my lungs and my eyes blinked tears. The moon glinted off the snow in bright swords, and the branches of the trees webbed black and still, and the only thing I could hear besides my breaths and Alyson's breaths were the far-off shrieks of my friends. For once I felt alive and I felt sharp and I hadn't felt either of those things in so long.

We made a plan. If we walked on the path, someone could spot us in the moonlight. If we walked in the forest, the snow crunched under our boots. It was prey that spent their lives running and hiding. If we wanted to win, we would have to think like wolves. So we decided to lie in wait.

It was pitch black next to the trees, so we found an especially dark patch close to the path, figuring someone would walk by sometime. We crouched back-to-back so no one could sneak up on us.

For a moment everything emptied and stilled, and the only things that existed were the blackness of the forest and the movement of Alyson's shoulders rising almost imperceptibly with her breaths, at the same slow, steady rate as my own.

I was just starting to get bored when we heard it. Movement. The crunching of snow, the snapping of branches.

We both stood up, slowly slowly slowly, careful to not make a sound.

It was Beto and Luke. They were headed our way, padding down the path.

"What should we do?" Alyson whispered.

"Stay here. We can see them, and they can't see us."

"You better kill him," Alyson said. "I don't care if you love him, you better shoot him."

"Shut up."

It was hard not to laugh at them as they crept down the path, whispering to each other to be "stealth" and "chill." They looked so stupid and blind. I had to squeeze Alyson's hand to keep from giggling. We waited in silence until they were about ten feet away, and then I flicked on the flashlight.

"Bang bang, motherfuckers," I said. And then Luke and Beto were dead.

It turned out that their team and ours were the only ones left. Which meant we'd won. Not Kiran or Gavin, who knew so much about the grounds from working with Bill. Not Luke, who was so fucking smart. Not Beto, the former soccer star. But us. We won because we thought like wolves.

All the others were waiting on the porch. Hank had two big ice cream sandwiches for Alyson and me that he'd stolen from the deep freezer in the supply room. Everyone else got freezer-burned Otter Pops. I split mine in half to share with Luke, and we ate our ice cream out there in the snow, flat on our backs, staring at the rippling black sky—all fifteen of us, Hank included. It was twenty degrees but it was the best ice cream I'd ever eaten. It tasted like victory.

After that, we went inside. Hank got out hot chocolate, three liters of Pepsi, and two party-sized bags of chips he'd bought for us on the way over. We took the boom box out of the office and turned off the lights and it almost felt like being at a regular party. We started to play Never Have I Ever, but since we had no alcohol we took shots of Pepsi instead. We could say things like "Never have I ever killed a cat with a pellet gun," and "Never have I ever been beat by my dad," and somebody would have to take a shot.

We were about ready to start playing Fuck Marry Kill when I noticed that Christina was no longer in the room. Then I noticed Hank wasn't either. I said I was going to the bathroom but I decided to find them instead.

I went to her room, but it was empty. I went to the bathroom. I went to the kitchen. I went to the office. I went downstairs, into the boys' room and the boys' bathroom. I tried to get into the schoolroom but it was locked. The only place left was outside.

I went through the boys' back door so no one upstairs could see me. I couldn't hear anything so I walked around to the front. Nothing. Totally quiet, totally dark. I'd almost given up when I saw a tiny flash of movement.

The windows in Hank's truck were fogged with condensation and there were no lights on, but the movement I'd seen was a hand. It had made finger-shaped trails along the glass. I couldn't really tell what I was seeing, but I thought I saw Hank's face, and Christina's face too, pressed up against each other like maybe they were kissing.

I didn't know what I saw.

I snuck into the house through the back door and went straight to my room without saying anything to anybody. I tried to read, but I couldn't concentrate. I was about to paint my nails, just to have something to do, when I heard a knock at the door. It was Hank. He told me it was bedtime, that I needed to take my medicine.

I looked him in the face and it didn't seem like he was hiding anything. He was acting the same as he always did. I followed him into the office and he handed me my pills. "Did you have fun tonight?" he asked.

I told him the truth. It was the funnest night I'd had in I couldn't even remember, the funnest night I'd ever had without drugs. He smiled at me, like he was genuinely happy he'd been able to make me happy, and I couldn't say exactly how I felt about him overall, but in that moment he was simply my friend, someone who wanted me to know there were still things in this world worth enjoying that had nothing to do with getting high.

Still, I wanted to check on Christina. I decided to say goodnight to her and Angel, which was a little weird because I never did that, but it had been a different sort of night, so it wouldn't seem strange. I knocked on their door, heard laughter, and then Angel's voice telling me to come in.

Angel was already in her bed, tucked underneath the covers. I don't know what I expected from Christina—crying seemed too dramatic—but she was just sitting on the ground next to Angel's bed, like the two of them had been talking. I tried to figure out if it was a serious conversation, but it didn't seem to be. I looked closely at Christina. She didn't look like someone with a secret. She smiled at me, her expression soft, like absolutely nothing could be wrong.

I had mixed feelings about Christmas break. I wanted to go home—to see my friends, my parents, my room, to have a choice about what I did that day and the freedom to decide what I'd eat. To see the water and the canyons I'd missed so much. To not have to put on socks, boots, long underwear, a sweater, a coat, gloves, a hat, a scarf, just to go outside.

The only thing was: Luke would be gone. He was leaving the school five days after me, for good. We didn't talk about what was happening until a few days right before I left. We were in the great room, the weak winter light staining everything in pastels. Rosie's country music was coming in tinny from the kitchen, and we'd discovered that if I lay on the couch upside down, my head where my legs should be, I could make my voice sound not dissimilar to Patsy Cline's. My hair was dangling on the floor, next to where Luke sat on the ground beside me. He was stroking the ends, removing tangles, when he suddenly grabbed it hard. It hurt, but I didn't say anything.

"What are we going to do?" he said.

I forced my voice bright. Like I had no idea what he was asking. Like it was October, November. Not December. "About what?"

"Me leaving."

I wanted to make him say it. "What do you want to do?"

He didn't say anything for a while. I sat up, watching the top of his golden head, not his face.

He wrapped his hand around my heel, and I felt it, the magnets locking us in place, simple as science. "I want to stay together." His voice was quiet but firm.

I worked very hard to keep my face neutral. But inside I felt ecstatic. I'd won. He loved me more than Julia. He was willing to wait for me.

"I don't know when I'm leaving, though," I said. "My parents just said sometime in the spring, maybe early summer."

"I applied to UCSD," he said. "I've got the grades, the SAT scores." In January, Luke would go back to his regular high school and graduate at the end of the year. That was all I knew. He hadn't told me anything about his college plans because I hadn't asked. Sometimes at night before falling asleep, this dumb picture of Luke wormed its way into my brain, him holding hands and kissing some blond college girl at an ivy-covered school, a pink cashmere sweater straining over big tits. But now the picture floated away. Instead, I saw myself visiting him in his dorm room, us doing grown-up things like having coffee, staying up late with old books, reading the best parts aloud to each other. We'd take our medicine but not drugs. I could bring up my GPA, go to UCSD too. I saw myself piecing back together the picture I'd held at the beginning of my freshman year. I wouldn't be in New York and I wouldn't be in San Francisco but the image looked bright, this future with Luke. It would work. The two of us. Happy and sane together.

FLIGHT

I had to leave for the airport early, 5:00 a.m., two hours before wake-up call. I brushed my teeth, washed my face, pulled on my clothes, and wheeled my suitcase into the hall. Luke was waiting for me, sitting on the ground, his face tired and glistening with tears.

"I'm going to miss you so much," he said.

I ran to him, and he wrapped his arms around me and I breathed him in. I didn't want to forget that smell. I thought about our future selves, Luke and me under the eucalyptus trees that grew all over the campus, kissing and smiling. The two of us stable enough to do things like go to class, have jobs, turn whatever we had in boarding school into a real relationship. Not end up in institutions. It didn't seem impossible.

We stood there for a long time, statues, motionless and wrapped in an eternal embrace, until we heard Carly clearing her throat, signaling it was time to go.

I would be home for ten days, an unfathomable length of time to be out in the world. In order to keep myself from crying, I spent the flight planning the days out in my head, the meals at the Mexican restaurant down the street from my house, the parties, my friends, the walks in the canyon, sitting in the sun, listening to the ocean waves. It had been five long months since I'd really seen any of them. Before, I'd never cared about the beach—the only time I liked going was at night, when it was dark and empty. But I'd missed the sound of the waves crashing while I slept at night. I liked knowing it was there, that to one side of me there was always water—roaring, wild, the end of the map.

Then I got home. It wasn't like that. My parents had rules in place, boundaries, obstacles. I tried to convince them there was nothing to worry about. I hadn't gotten high in months, didn't even want to. I showed them my new sixty-day coin. Still, they were concerned about "temptation," "peer pressure," so I had to be with them most of the time. I was allowed only two hours with friends every day, and the latest I was allowed out was ten. It was worse than not being home at all. Close to normal, but not normal at all.

And when I was allowed to see Holly, she brought this girl named Kate with her, who had started hanging out with her since I'd been away. Her version of Alyson. The person she'd been spending all her time with that wasn't me. I wondered if they'd ever been at Holly's house, sitting together for hours, like they were on an island.

Kate was bigger, boyish, used to live in Germany and loved techno. Had a car. She and Holly would come inside, smile, do their best to look wholesome for my parents, and then we'd go eat, or see a movie, or drive around while they smoked weed and I smoked cigarettes. Kate was very nice, and I appreciated the rides, but still. As we all stood around in the kitchen that first day, the thin December sun streaming through the sliding glass windows, I looked at this strange girl, with her baggy jeans and stringy hair, and all I wanted to say was *Who the fuck are you?*

But there was a certain beauty to inhabiting the world with this barrier around me, a space bubble. In it, I was a child. My mother was on break too, and so if I wanted to go outside she had the time to go with me, supervise. We walked in the canyons, her my shadow. I showed her the rope swing hidden by the hills, and we took turns, laughing and skidding our feet, until our legs were brown with dust and there were blisters on our fingers. I showed her the bluffs, bright sandstone pale and looming like clouds, a startling brightness out of the dull greens and browns. I showed her the elephant slides that ran along them: these narrow grooves in the rock—I don't know if they were natural, run-off from rain, or manmade—that curved down, and you could put your foot in them, the grooves just wide enough to fit, and slide down the sandstone like in *The Jungle Book*. Mom followed me through all of it like we were the same age, like she wasn't a mother acting as warden to her crazy daughter—just a friend.

My parents felt guilty. I got so many Christmas presents—a new winter jacket, new boots, new jeans, all the makeup and CDs and books on my wish list. I spent a lot of time reading the books, headphones over my ears as I listened to my new CDs. My parents didn't bother me. Nobody bothered me. Everything I needed took up only the tiny space between my eyes, my ears, the page of my book, and it made me feel powerful, like a tiny god, ruling over a predictable world.

And on Christmas they let me call Luke, even though they didn't approve of me having a boyfriend because they said I was supposed to be focused on getting better. But that night they said we could talk as long as we wanted. I took the cordless out to the patio. It was cold, colder than I remembered Santa Bonita being in December. I was wearing my new jacket and my breath made dusky puffs.

His mother answered. I'd met her once, when she'd visited the school before taking Luke to Ashland, the hippie town a couple hours from RTS, for the weekend. She had a severe haircut and didn't wear makeup, the kind of woman who favored long flowy skirts and leather sandals. She didn't seem to like me, her face pinched and priggish as I shook her hand.

But over the phone her voice got all chirpy. "Oh hiiiiii," she said. She asked me how I was doing and I told her I was fine and asked the same question. Then she went to get Luke.

I heard shuffling, Luke's mom talking to what sounded like Luke. I couldn't hear what they said, but the conversation took longer than, "Oh hey, honey, your girlfriend is on the phone." After a while, I no longer heard voices. A minute after that, Luke finally picked up the phone.

"Hello," he said, his voice completely monotone.

I'd expected him to sound happier, but maybe he was feeling

depressed or something. I asked him how his Christmas was. He said it was fine. I asked him how it was being back home. He said it was fine. I waited for him to ask the same of me, or to say anything, but he didn't. He just sat there, the silence between us growing and gathering edges. Finally he broke it. "I left some presents for you, for Christmas. They're on your bed."

I wondered what they were. I hadn't gotten him anything. I hadn't thought to.

"That's so sweet," I said. "I really miss you."

There was more silence, until eventually he said, "I miss you too." His voice was cracking, like maybe he was crying.

"Are you OK?" I asked.

"Fine," he said, clearing his throat. "Everything is fine."

"OK," I said.

"I have to go," he said. "We're going to some party. Family shit."

"OK," I said.

"I love you," he said. "I really do love you."

"I love you too," I said.

I heard a click. He'd hung up.

I didn't know what to think about that.

I pushed the feeling away, stared out from the patio. During the day, you could see the lagoon and the 101 and beyond that, the shining ocean. The 101 wound up the hill, past the giant reserve full of Torrey pines. On the other side was UCSD—the spaceship library and eucalyptus trees. I conjured up the picture: hand in hand, walking under the trees, reading in the library. In the dark, all of it was just a blob. But still, I knew it was out there. That future.

Towards the end, Holly and Kate picked me up and took me to the Palms to see everyone. It was after dark but still early, and there weren't a lot of people around. We had lied to my parents, saying we were going to a movie at the theater downtown. They thought the Palms was the source of my problems, a den of "bad influence," as though they hadn't once thought the same thing about Nicole.

Danny Smackball was there, and so was Junk Dog, but a lot of the others were nowhere to be found. Everybody seemed happy to see me, but a lot of the people were strangers. I hadn't even been gone that long. And finally I realized how transitory everything was: people in, people out, a revolving door for teen problems. My absence hadn't created a hole. Things kept on turning without me—parties, smoking, drinking, fighting, making out. And again I felt like something in a space bubble, a film of plastic that separated me from the world. An astronaut. A stranger, just visiting.

The last night I couldn't stand it anymore—this ghostlike, passive version of me—so I pretended to go to bed early. It seemed believable because my flight was at 7:00 a.m. I left through my sliding glass doors, just like the old days, figuring if I got caught it didn't matter. What else could my parents do to me anyway.

Holly and Kate picked me up. They had three stamps of acid, the only thing that wouldn't show up on my piss test. There went my sobriety. I imagined it, an object, something tiny and small like the stamp of acid, dropping it off a cliff just to watch it flutter. I waited to feel regret but instead I felt good, like settling back into my true self.

We ate the acid in the parking lot of the park at the very back of Carmel Heights, the side that always got crowded after football games, our windows rolled down as we smoked and waited for the drugs to kick in, and Kate and Holly showed me their favorite techno songs. I imagined the me who hadn't attempted suicide or gone off to Redwood Trails School. I fell into the version of that girl, the one who didn't know Luke or Alyson. The one who knew drugs were fun.

I could tell the acid was starting to work when I had a sudden urge to get out of the car, to inspect the eucalyptus trees. Kate and Holly followed me. We peeled off the papery strips of bark, found sticks on the ground that seemed like magic wands.

Then Holly got a page, so we went to the Palms to listen to the message, bringing our new wands with us. The page was from Ramon, who we didn't have to call because he was sitting in front of the pay phone. He picked me up when he saw me, swung me around like I was a bride and he'd been away at war, and the lights from the light posts shifted and glowed like suns. There was a party, he told us. We followed him over the hill in Kate's car to an unfamiliar house.

It was almost all dudes, and everyone was doing coke, sweating and stinking. There was the creepiest vibe, and Holly and Kate felt it too. I wanted to get out of there but I had an idea. I still had twenty dollars in my wallet, from the money my parents had given me for food and movies. Coke started at forty dollars a gram, but I figured I could get someone to sell me a few lines. I couldn't do it until after I got back to RTS, but I figured I could hide the drugs in my bra, the little pocket for the removable padding.

So I sat next to and smiled a lot at this disgusting troll Larry. He smelled like rotting meat and had the blackness of pure evil pouring out of his eyes. He finally agreed to sell me some, wrapping the coke up in a little piece of paper folded like an envelope. As soon as I had it in my hands I got out of there like I was escaping death, the contagion of a plague.

We got back in the car without saying goodbye to anyone, even Ramon, which I felt bad about, but I was too creeped out. There wasn't anywhere to go, so we drove around for a while, Kate laughing because the lines in the road were twisting like snakes, before we decided on the beach.

We took off our shoes and rolled up our jeans and it was cold and windy, but it didn't bother me. We ran around in the sand, splashing in the shallow parts of the waves, the crescent moon glinting off the water like money. Shooting each other with our wands, because now they were magical guns. Laughing. It felt good and it felt pure, three girls on the beach playing like puppies, and for the first time since I'd been back in Santa Bonita I felt at home, really in the world, occupying it, not just ghosting, and it seemed absurd that if my parents knew I was there on that beach they'd be furious.

Kate and Holly had meant to go home early because the next night was New Year's Eve. They had party plans, a big one with an open bar at what was supposedly Master P's old house, right near my elementary school. I kept pushing the thought out of my head that I wouldn't be with them. Every time they talked about calling it a night, I'd remember "one more place I wanted to see": the hills of Laguna, the elephant slides, the parking lot at New Hope. It wasn't too hard to convince them.

Towards 4:00 a.m., right before they finally dropped me off, I had them take me to the Walgreens. Getting on a plane coming off acid seemed horrible, terrible, especially since my final destination was the school and sobriety. But then I remembered something Gavin had said back at the school: if you take Coricidin, this cold medicine for people with high blood pressure who apparently can't take the regular stuff, the high was way better and more intense than Robofrying. I knew the school didn't include that kind of thing on their drug test, so I bought a box. Then they finally dropped me off, hugging me, Holly tearful, and by then the acid almost gone, just a feeling of giddiness now. The only thing left from the hallucinations were pale trails, which I saw a lot of the time anyway.

I crept back in the window, lay in bed for a bit and was nearly asleep when my dad came to tell me it was time to get ready to go. Right before we left, I swallowed half the box of Coricidin with a glass of orange juice. My mom cried some when they dropped me off, and I wanted to feel sad and I wanted to miss them, but leaving didn't bother me too much.

When I boarded the plane I felt dizzy but that was it. Maybe the half-box wasn't enough. I swallowed the rest in the tiny bathroom with water from the sink even though there was a big sign telling me not to drink from it.

Once we arrived in San Francisco, I stood to leave the plane but it was like there were astronaut boots on my feet. I walked through the tunnel from the plane into the airport in what I hoped was a straight line, and all I wanted was to be away from those people and the stale air pressing against my mouth like plastic film. I wanted a cigarette and fresh air.

I rushed past the security checkpoint, and I hit someone with my backpack. The guy glared at me. He said something, or maybe he yelled it, but whatever it was that came out of his mouth sounded like only noise. I got outside and lit my last cigarette. The winter air felt violent, punishing and cold. I focused everything I had onto that red tip and for the five minutes it lasted I felt OK.

I made it back through security and to my gate without too much trouble, but the plane was delayed. I sat listening to my head-phones, telling myself everything was fine, I would get on the plane soon, but suddenly my head went thick and heavy, my chest tight, and I couldn't breathe. I thought I was ODing but I didn't know how to fix it, so I just sat there until my fingers went numb, and then I made myself get up and go to the bathroom. I splashed water on my face, not bothering to dry it off even though it smudged my mascara. I locked myself in the handicapped stall, sitting on the toilet, head between my knees, trying to catch my breath. When everything stopped, I noticed the ends of my hair were wet from something, wet from something on the floor of the bathroom. Probably piss.

I got up, my pulse still jumpy. The plane had boarded by then. I made it on just before they closed the doors. When Vinnie picked me up in the white van he didn't seem to notice anything, but for the rest of the day I felt dizzy and doomed. Coricidin is a terrible high. Don't try it.

BOOK FOUR

NEW YEAR, NEW YOU

The school was almost empty when I got back—just Christina, and this new kid, Alex. It was his very first day. Christina had only gone home for Christmas Eve and Christmas Day, and Alex's first day was December 31 because his parents followed the same logic as mine: New Year's Eve would be too much of a temptation.

Vinnie left right after he'd dropped me off, so it was just the three of us and Rosie. The Coricidin left things blurry, but still I could tell Alex was kind of hot for a hick. A big nose, construction boots, and a Carhartt jacket—but full lips and long lashes. His hometown was some Podunk place in Montana, and he already chewed tobacco.

Rosie had the whole evening planned out. Her ideas were so depressing that I would have preferred we go to bed at 10:00 p.m., same as always, but I could tell she'd tried and I didn't want to hurt her feelings. We ate frozen pizza. When it got dark, she showed us how to blow out eggs and then we set them on the oven to dry. Right before midnight, she handed us shitty paper hats and shitty plastic noisemakers, sparkling cider in plastic flutes, and tubes of glitter, which we poured into the eggs. The four of us went on the porch, bundled in our coats, paper hats on our heads. We opened the windows to the great room, despite the cold, to hear the TV. When the bell hit midnight, we crushed the eggs, smashing them on each other's heads, throwing them in the air so they crunched on the sidewalk. The glitter glinted and swirled under the porch light like fireflies, and the TV blared "Auld Lang Syne." It started snowing, fat puffy flakes light as the glitter, which seemed a good omen for the year to come. But by then I knew better than to believe in signs.

The phone rang, so Rosie went to answer it. She was gone for a while. Her husband.

I put two hats on my boobs like Madonna, and then Christina

did the same. We rubbed our paper boobs together, looking at Alex to make sure he was watching. I stepped over and kissed Alex on the cheek, and Christina did the same on the other side. We could still hear Rosie's voice from the office. I leaned over Alex to kiss Christina. She opened her mouth and I stuck my tongue in. I pushed her paper cone bra to the side, grabbed her boob. Without opening my eyes I slid my hand down Alex's thin chest until it was on his crotch, and Christina's hand met mine and we rubbed him and kissed, until we heard Rosie hang up. When she came back outside, Alex's face was bright red and he kept pulling his jacket down to make sure his boner was covered, but Christina and I just looked at each other. Her sad eyes were flickering and she smiled at me, and I could tell she felt it too, this odd palpitation of power. I liked the idea that we had been Alex's strange introduction into this strange new world. I liked that we had made it a decent New Year's after all. We had done our best to party like it was a whole new millennium, because it was.

I didn't notice the presents Luke had left me until bedtime because he had hidden them under my pillow—a copy of *Youth in Revolt*, a set of colored pencils, the nice kind you could turn into watercolors, and a Marilyn Manson CD I didn't have yet. There was also a folded-up piece of notebook paper, covered in his neat block-letter handwriting, listing all the reasons he loved me . . . my mismatched snake eyes, my pouty lips, the way I sounded when I laughed, the brilliance of my poems. I didn't want to but I started crying, the emptiness that was him no longer near me rising up in a wave. I smelled the paper, wanting it to smell like him, but of course it smelled like paper. I cried and missed him until I fell asleep, and in the morning my eyes were puffy and red.

Y2K

On Monday, we found that the whole school had changed again. We finally had a new headmaster, a real one. Bill was relegated to where he belonged: the ranch. The new headmaster was a woman. Her name was Stacy, and I liked her right away. I liked the way she dressed—black Western wear with flowy skirts and lots of jewelry, like Stevie Nicks if she'd found herself on a ranch. That day, she met with each of us in her office, to see where we were and where we had been, and I could tell she liked me right away too, smiling big and telling me I seemed so smart and that she liked my ring, a silver snake curled around a nugget of amber. Her office decorations were still in boxes, pictures stacked in frames against the wall. A diploma faced out, a Ph.D. from the University of Iowa. I wondered how she'd found herself here.

The other big change was that Hank was gone.

He had quit. Completely left us, without even a warning or goodbye.

PAINS

Over the next few days, I kept waiting for Luke to call me, to write. I couldn't figure out why he didn't. I wondered if he missed me too much, or if it was too painful. I wondered if he had, but maybe the letters and phone calls had been intercepted.

I sent him letters at first, one every day, just to let him know what I was thinking and what I'd been up to, the changes that had happened at the school. But when I heard nothing back, I suddenly felt desperate. I decided no more letters until I heard from him. There was no way I wouldn't hear from him soon.

But I didn't.

His silence remained a mystery.

PATIENT LOG

PATIENT NAME: Juliet Escoria
AGE: 16 yrs 4 mo
SEX: F
DOB: 8/23/83

DATE: 01/11/00

HISTORY: Patient's behavior log good. Cont. involvement romantically with former patient LUCAS WEBER. No reported hallucinations. Cont. anxiety (panic attacks), sleeplessness.
Drug test negative.
Reported side effects of somnolence, lethargy, muscle pain, upset stomach, hair loss (mild) (cont.).

PREVIOUS MEDICATIONS:
Zyprexa—discontinued 01/99 once stabilized
Wellbutrin—discontinued 03/99 (ineffective)
Tegretol—discontinued 07/99 (risk of overdose/replace w Depakote)
Paxil—discontinued 07/99 (replace w Remeron)
Remeron—discontinued 8/99 (weight gain/replace w Zoloft)
Buspar—discontinued 01/00 (somnolence)

TREATMENT:
Cont. Depakote at 1500mg/nightly
Cont. Trazodone 25mg/nightly (for insomnia)
Increase Zoloft from 50mg/nightly to 100mg/nightly over 1 wk (for anxiety/depression)
Cont. group therapy, indiv. therapy

CLEANLINESS AND GODLINESS

I did the cocaine the next weekend, after my piss test came back clean. My plan had been to do it with Alyson during deep clean, which was how Stacy made us spend our Saturdays now. That day, my chore was dusting and then polishing all the furniture in the great room.

Except that Saturday Alyson wasn't around, and I couldn't even remember where she was. We hadn't been spending that much time together lately, all because of this new guy named Adrian, who'd arrived right after Alex.

Adrian seemed to think he was a cholo. He buttoned his shirts to the top, sagged his Dickies, even had stick-and-poked three dots on his hand to signify his crazy life. It was bullshit. I wanted to tell him that nobody whose parents could afford this school was a thug, and Adrian Calabrese was obviously an Italian name and not a Mexican one, so he could cut it out with the bad accent and saying shit like how so-and-so could *chupa* his *verga*. I wanted to tell him that I knew the city where he was from, Laguna Beach, and that it was full of rich white people and not Mexican gangs. But I didn't say any of this. Instead I kept my mouth shut. And Alyson fell for it. He arrived on a Sunday and by Tuesday she'd broken up with Kiran. Now all they did was hang onto each other, arms draped around their shoulders like they were broken, whispering together all day long like they were conspiring against the world. It was disgusting. And Kiran, who was awesome and handsome and not a phony fuck, was left to mope around alone.

I thought about doing the coke by myself except it seemed important to have someone do it with me, just in case we got caught—two people meant bad influences, while one person meant you were just bad. I ended up asking Christina. We'd been hanging out a lot lately, ever since Adrian had arrived.

I chopped the coke in my room while Christina stood in the hall, pretending to be doing her chore, which was dusting and then removing grime off all the baseboards. I snorted my lines and then headed to the great room so Christina could do the same.

I didn't even notice the high until I was back in the great room, and then suddenly I felt the whoosh straight into my heart. I turned on the stereo, the oldies channel, and it was the Shangri-Las with "Leader of the Pack." It made me remember how when I was little, I listened to oldies at night, and the songs telling stories about teenagers seemed so far away, so impossibly tragic and glamorous—broken hearts, early deaths, the era of James Dean and Marilyn Monroe—the songs in the speakers fuzzy and crackling. Christina walked in, on her knees scrubbing at the baseboards, and we sang to the songs, dusting and cleaning until the pale oak gleamed golden. We kept looking at each other, smiling, our secret, and Christina's cheeks were flushed pink and she looked so happy and pretty.

And I know people act like you can't have any real feelings on drugs, that everything that happens to you on them is a lie, but cleaning and singing with Christina while our hearts beat fast in our chests felt like something real, realer than real, electric and on fire.

PRESCRIPTIVE

They were always saying "Take your medicine." The therapists and the doctors, my parents, the counselors—anyone with an opinion about my illness. They all told me about people who started feeling good again, or decided they weren't actually bipolar, or missed the energy, and stopped taking their medicine and ended right back in the hospital. Back at the visions, back at depression, back at death.

What they didn't say was how much psych meds sucked. They went over the long list of side effects, but nobody seemed to care when I said yes, the medicine made my stomach hurt and hair fall out and gave me diarrhea and turned everything stupid and flat and boring. The sluggishness, the flat gray of the sky and the old snow, the days all the same, same routine, same people, same dramas. I didn't want to go back to hearing things and I didn't want to go back to trying to kill myself, but I also wanted to feel something real and true, life in neon, rather than this dull blanket.

A compromise. At RTS, they didn't check your mouth after they gave you your pills. They were supposed to, but generally the staff was in a hurry and didn't have time. Every third night, sometimes every second, I would swallow my Zoloft, same as always, and then I'd put the big pink ovals of Depakote in my mouth. I'd go straight to my room and spit them in a sock.

The first time, part of the coating wore away by the time I got there. The bitterness of the pill took over my whole mouth. I brushed my teeth, carefully around each tooth and the entirety of my tongue. When I spat in the sink, the bubbles were foamy and the color of Pepto-Bismol. Nothing happened at first.

I think we all felt sorry for Stephen, the schizophrenic. We might've been fucked up, but we could interact with other people like we were normal at least some of the time. Stephen couldn't. Every once in a while he'd say a complete sentence to someone who wasn't Kiran, but mostly he responded in one- or two-word phrases, head nods, and hand gestures.

This changed after Angel's home visit. She came back with gifts for everyone, cheap little toys. She gave me a My Little Pony. Other people got weird sunglasses. Stephen got a plastic microphone.

When the Beastie Boys album *The Sounds of Science* came out, we listened to it in the van all the time. It was one of the few albums everyone agreed on. One day we were singing along to "Intergalactic." I didn't know who first noticed Stephen singing with us, but somebody did. We tried to not make a big deal out of it because we didn't want to embarrass him. But it felt like a big deal, as though we'd finally gotten through to him. As though we'd helped him.

Ever since, we'd ask him to sing the song, and he always would, always happy to oblige. It got so he could do the entire song, hitting each beat perfect. Angel's microphone was for him to sing in. He smiled so big when he unwrapped it, not just with his mouth but his whole face. He tapped the microphone, miming to check if it was "on," and then he said his lines: *intergalactic planetary, intergalactic.*

When an unfamiliar van pulled up a few weeks later, similar to the one that had taken away Dennis, we were surprised. Nobody had gotten in trouble recently, no drama, no outbursts. We were even more surprised when we found out the student they'd come to take away was Stephen. The staff didn't want to tell us why but we wouldn't stop asking.

Finally Carly told us to sit down in the great room. We were pre-

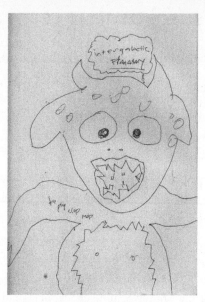

Notebook drawing, January 2000.

pared to hear about some great injustice, the unfair reason he'd been taken away. "We found things," she began. "Troubling things."

Which seemed an unfair description. I was imagining, I don't know, naked-girl drawings or something. I wasn't prepared for what she told us: nearly a hundred dollars in cash, a milk jug filled with water, three loaves of bread, a jar of peanut butter, the big butcher knife the staff concluded had accidentally been thrown away when it didn't turn up in a search. The kind of things that take a long time and a lot of planning to steal. The van keys were the thing that got him caught. He'd lifted the spare set kept in the office and thought no one would notice.

The most troublesome thing, though, was a hand-drawn map of the school, and a checklist that involved students smothered with pillows, a night staff with slit throats. Carly wouldn't let us see the list or the map. She said it was too disturbing.

THE BITCH

I'd been out shoveling snow and I was cold and wet. When I went to my room to change, Christina was in there, sitting on my bed and crying. She looked so sad and broken that I ran over to her, sat next to her, put my hand on her shoulder.

"What happened?" I said.

Her crying broke into sobs, thick in her chest, snot running from her nose. I plucked a tissue from the box near my bed, and she wiped away the tears and snot. "Oh God," she moaned.

"What's wrong?" I asked, thinking she'd had a fight with Angel and that's why she'd come to me.

"I have to tell you something," she said, her voice momentarily clear before breaking again. "I feel so terrible."

A cold feeling shot through me, as though before I knew, I knew.

"I slept with Luke," she finally said, a pause between each word. *I. Slept. With. Luke.* Her voice quiet but wobbling.

Each syllable drove itself home, a series of pinpricks. She was looking at me as she spoke, but she wasn't looking at me. It was as though she wasn't looking at anything at all, as though she was dead, her eyes blank, and suddenly I wished that she was. I didn't feel anything. I wanted her out of my room. I wanted to get out of my wet clothes. I told her as much and she left, slowly like she was going to her death, the door closing behind her.

I didn't know what to do once she left. I changed and then just sat there on my bed for a while, trying to figure out what, exactly, I felt. I could not name the feeling.

When it came time for dinner, I told Rosie I wasn't hungry. I said I was feeling sick. I was still sitting there on my bed. I decided to write in my journal. I figured I'd write a letter to Luke, but I didn't get very far.

Christina, told me what you did. My first love was not actually love. So it isn't good anymore. You broke it. It means nothing now.

Luke letter (draft), January 2000.

Alyson came in after dinner to check on me. I was still sitting there, my journal next to me, the letter unfinished.

"What's wrong with you?" she said, laughing. I must have looked so silly, just staring into space.

I told her, the words sounding different out loud than they had in my head.

Her mouth dropped open. "What?" she said. "That little fucking bitch."

That was when the feelings finally hit me. Brokenness, but also rage, hot and boiling. My chest tight, shaky hands. A tilt to the room, something thick and viscous like milk.

I didn't want to cry but I started to cry. "I'm so fucking pissed," I said.

"You should fuck her up," Alyson said.

"I should totally fuck her up." I imagined pounding her face with my fists, ripping out her hair.

"Let's do it," she said. "I'll back you up."

We went down the hall to Christina's room. I opened the door without knocking. Christina was curled on her bed in a pathetic little ball, which made me even angrier. I walked over to her. She didn't look at me. I wanted her to look at me. I punched her in the face, my knuckles sliding off her cheekbone.

I didn't know how to fuck up anyone. I didn't even know how to properly wrap my hand into a fist. She looked surprised, her hand covering where I'd hit her, but also like she deserved it.

"I'm so sorry," she said. I didn't care.

So I fucked her up the only way I knew how. I stood in front of her, hands on my hips.

"You little slut," I said. "This is just like you. Desperate to be liked, desperate to be loved. You're a nothing. You're a shadow of a person, weak-willed, personality-less, spineless." I went on. Because we'd been in group together for months, I knew just what to say, all her weak points. I hit every one:

Your parents don't love you. You're stupid, passive, have nothing to offer the world. Fat. Dykey haircut. Ugly clothes. White trash. Luke just did it because he feels sorry for you. For Luke, you could have been anyone. You mean nothing. Alyson and me and Luke and everybody else are here for good reasons, because our parents were afraid for us. But your parents just put you here because they wanted to get rid of you. This is what everyone who's ever encountered you wanted to do, to ignore you, to forget you, because you're forgettable. Your pussy smells bad anyway, it smells bad because you're a slut, because that's the only reason people like you, except they don't like you, because you're a nothing. You probably even liked it when your brother's friend raped you, wanted it, it wasn't rape at all, because you deserve to be used. You probably even liked it as a kid, with your uncle, because nobody loves you and that's the only way you know how to be loved. You deserve to be raped, should be raped again. Fuck you.

Christina didn't look at me once, looked down at the ground, curled in her ball, silently crying the whole fucking time, whispering over and over, "I know. I'm sorry." Pathetic.

Once I'd finished, I looked over at Alyson, who was standing in the doorway, her face wide. "Come on," I said, and we left the room, laughing.

"Oh shit," she said once we were back in our room. "Shit, girl. That was some fucked up shit. You fucked her up. You fucked her up!"

I smiled. I had fucked her up.

That night before bed, I wrote a better letter to Luke. This time I knew exactly what to say. I didn't sign it. He'd know who it was from.

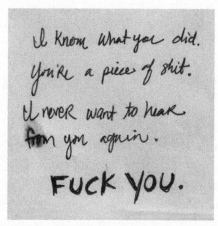

Luke Letter (final: copy, made for personal records), January 2000.

AFTERMATH

I kept waiting for Christina to rat me out, for somebody on staff to notice that Alyson and I no longer spoke to her, refused to sit with her, in the van or class or at meals. I kept waiting for it to come up in group. But it never did. Except for the broken look I'd sometimes catch on Christina's face, it was like nothing had happened at all.

A week later, I got a letter back. *Something something, I love you.* All lies. I crumpled the note up into a ball, threw it in the trash.

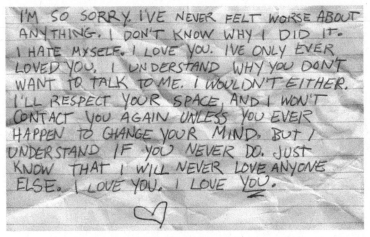

I'M SO SORRY. I'VE NEVER FELT WORSE ABOUT ANYTHING. I DON'T KNOW WHY I DID IT. I HATE MYSELF. I LOVE YOU. I'VE ONLY EVER LOVED YOU. I UNDERSTAND WHY YOU DON'T WANT TO TALK TO ME. I WOULDN'T EITHER. I'LL RESPECT YOUR SPACE, AND I WON'T CONTACT YOU AGAIN UNLESS YOU EVER HAPPEN TO CHANGE YOUR MIND. BUT I UNDERSTAND IF YOU NEVER DO. JUST KNOW THAT I WILL NEVER LOVE ANYONE ELSE. I LOVE YOU. I LOVE YOU.

Luke response (retrieved from trash), February 2000.

A LETTER FROM THE FUTURE #4

These remain the cruelest words I've ever said to anyone. These remain the words I feel the worst about. It is hard to believe I said them. It is especially hard to believe I said them to someone like Christina. But I did.

Our Father who art in Heaven, hallowed be thy name; thy kingdom come, thy will be done, on earth as it is in heaven. Give us this day, our daily bread; and forgive us our trespasses as we forgive those who trespass against us; and lead us not into temptation, but deliver us from evil. Hail Mary, full of grace. Our Lord is with thee. Blessed art thou among women, and blessed is the fruit of thy womb, Jesus. Holy Mary, Mother of God, pray for us sinners, now and at the hour of our death. Amen. Glory to the Father, and to the Son, and to the Holy Spirit. To thee do we cry, poor banished children of Eve; to thee do we send up our sighs, mourning and weeping in this valley of tears. Turn then, most gracious advocate, thine eyes of mercy toward us and after this our exile show unto us the blessed fruit of thy womb, Jesus. O clement, O loving, O sweet Virgin Mary!

SEEDLINGS

My pill sock got crusty and full. I finished my morning chores early, said I felt groggy and was taking a quick walk. I went down by the lake. It had snowed and then gotten warm again. The path was sludgy and sticky, sucking on my boots. I found a place in the cattails thick enough that no one could see me, the dry brown blades rustling like feathers. I found a stick and dug away the muck until I had a little hole. I put the sock in it, a baby grave. I patted the mud down. You couldn't tell anything was there.

MARTIN THE MYSTERY MAN

We didn't realize the quiet guy in the glasses and button-down wasn't somebody's visiting parent until after dinner. He hadn't been introduced. Nobody explained his role. We only knew something was different because he hadn't gone away.

In the weeks that followed, the only thing we found out was his name—Martin—and what he wasn't. He wasn't a counselor, because he didn't do anything with us, didn't tell us to knock it off when we swore, didn't come up with activities when we grew bored. He wasn't a therapist, because he never led group—although sometimes he sat in—and never really talked to us, except for light chitchat during meals. The only thing we ever saw him do was scribble in a notebook, which he was too careful to leave laying around. The few times we'd been able to slip a glimpse, we discovered his handwriting was too messy to read anyhow. For a while we speculated that he was from some accreditation board, but he stayed too long and once said something to the boys during lunch about good food being just as sensual as good sex, so that no longer made sense. Eventually we gave up, called him Martin the Communist in secret, pretending he was a spy from the KGB.

It took a whole month for us to find his purpose, before we realized he was indeed at the school in order to spy on us. Not for the Russians. But to make us feel like shit.

WHAT IS CONFRONTATION?

Therapeutic confrontation has been defined as the process by which a therapist provides direct, reality-oriented feedback to a client regarding the client's own thoughts, feelings, or behavior (Forest, 1982)... In the mid-twentieth century, addiction counselors developed and advocated a particular style of direct verbal confrontation of those with alcohol and other drug problems. These communications varied from frank feedback to profanity-laden indictments, screamed denunciations of character, challenges and ultimatums, intense argumentation, ridicule, and purposeful humiliation. Confrontation marked a dramatic break from earlier therapeutic traditions premised on the importance of neutral exploration, empathy, compassionate support, and positive regard for clients... Four decades of research have failed to yield a single clinical trial showing efficacy of confrontational counseling, whereas a number have documented harmful effects, particularly for more vulnerable populations.

White, William L., and William R. Miller. "The Use of Confrontation in Addiction Treatment: History, Science and Time for Change." Counselor 8.4 (2007): 12-30.

Confrontational therapy (research), January 2016.

VERBAL ABUSE

The first time, he did it to Adrian. Martin called us all to the great room, slid the coffee table behind one of the sofas, told Adrian to stand in the blank space. So he did, reluctantly but with a smile, as though he was expecting a game.

Adrian's smile turned plastic as Martin spoke, his voice thorny and cold at the beginning, gradually growing louder, so subtle it was difficult to register the change until it had risen to a yell. The things he said were things I'd wanted to say: Adrian was a phony, a fake, a liar. His gangster masquerade was disgusting, completely failing to hide the fact that he was pathetically insecure. His haircut was stupid, only "illuminating the odd mushy shape" of his head. I might have liked what was happening, but all at once just seemed cruel.

And then there was the fact that the rest of us had to listen. We'd all been called in to sit there and watch, the counselors and Bill and Stacy and even Linda, the cook. I watched everyone's faces. They all looked blank, refusing to look at the center of the room. All eyes on neutral things—the ceiling, the window, their shoes. But I wasn't afraid to see. I watched Adrian's face, as he stood in the center of the room, the mush pot, his arms crossed and his mouth streaked in a sneer. I watched Martin's face, sparked eyes and the occasional spittle flecking out of his mouth, as though he was enjoying this, as though he was genuinely angry and not acting. I didn't feel creeped out until I looked across the room, saw Stacy standing near the doorway, hands at her sides, head down so I couldn't see her eyes. But I could see her mouth. It was shaped like something. It was shaped like a smile.

The next week, he targeted Tommy. Tommy, who had never done anything to anyone. He was always so good it was confusing why he was at the school in the first place. I'd never seen him angry or unruly, even when he was the target of our jokes, which was often.

There was the time the boys took Angel's Nair and put it on a patch of his hair while he slept, waking up to a bald spot and a chemical burn, pink and raw. There was the time the boys tricked him into masturbating with Tiger Balm. When he first arrived at the school, long before I got there, everyone convinced him to take a fat lip of chew, then told him you were supposed to swallow the juice it made. Tommy puked. It happened outside during chores, right onto the dirt, and Vinnie saw it and saw the tobacco in it, and they all got in trouble even though Tommy refused to rat anyone out, because Vinnie was smart enough to know Tommy wouldn't have chewed dip on his own.

Then there was the one that was my fault. A few Saturdays ago, it was cold and wet all day, so we had been cooped up and bored in the great room. We started measuring ourselves—foot to foot, hand to hand, back to back to compare heights, just to have something to do. In everything, Tommy was the smallest, coming up only to my shoulder, fingers reaching only halfway up my tips. Somebody said he was so tiny he could fit in the dryer, and we managed to talk him into it—just as an experiment, just to find out.

I hadn't thought about turning it on until he made me promise I wouldn't. That was the thing about him—it never really felt like bullying so much as something we were obligated to do in response to his behavior. The only option was for me to hit the button.

I opened the door a fraction of a second later. He was curled up like a fetus, nearly upside down, his eyes all big and round and afraid like a big dumb baby. I couldn't help laughing, we all couldn't help but laugh. Tommy was mad, you could see it in his face, but it didn't take too long for him to be laughing too.

I couldn't get the way he looked when I opened the door out of my head. Helpless and hurt.

So it seemed wildly unfair for this adult to pick on him. It was bad enough that we did it, but at least we knew him. And of course

Tommy wasn't like Adrian. Tommy started crying immediately, as soon as he got to the mush pot. You could tell he was trying to hold it together at first, his mouth quivering, but Martin was only a few lines in before Tommy's face was blotchy and streaked with tears, his mouth pinched up and whining.

Martin used it as ammunition, telling him this was exactly what he expected, for Tommy to act like a pathetic, blubbering baby, because that's all he was, a spineless puddle of Jell-O.

I wanted to say something. I wanted to stop him from berating someone who was helpless and so easily hurt. But I didn't know how. I sat there, squirmy, a feeling not unlike needing to take a shit. I considered it for a second, just standing up and loudly announcing I had to use the bathroom, in an attempt to get Martin off track. I looked across the room, where Vinnie was standing in the corner for some reason. I thought I could catch his eye. Vinnie wouldn't allow this type of cruelty. But Vinnie didn't look at me, or anyone.

I twisted my bracelet around my wrist. Martin was trying to get Tommy to name one positive quality about himself but he just kept crying. The bracelet was the same as the one on Alyson's wrist, plastic beads we'd strung in matching colors. I picked at the biggest bead, a sparkly butterfly, snapping it against my wrist. I was trying to figure out what to say, but instead I accidentally muttered under my breath.

"God, shut up."

I knew I'd said it too loud because Martin stopped immediately.

"Who said that?" he said. He wasn't yelling anymore. His voice was low and hard.

"Um," I said. "I did."

"What did you say? I couldn't quite hear."

"Um." I stared at my bracelet, pulled the bead again. Snap. "I just thought you could stop yelling at Tommy. I think he got your point."

He stood up from where he was sitting, in the big recliner, a dictator on his throne. He walked slowly across the room, until he was standing in front of me, hands on his hips, khaki crotch right in front of my face. He must have realized because he quickly leaned down, so close I could see tiny blackheads on his nose. "You want to help him? Is that it?"

"Um," I said again, like an idiot. I didn't know what to do or say, which pissed me off because the last thing I wanted was to be intimidated by this dumb sadist.

Martin smiled. "Maybe you're right," he said. And then he told Tommy to get out of the center, and for me to take his place.

I did so, walking fast like I didn't care but I kept my eyes on the ground. My face began to burn. My knees went quivery, and I felt thin and naked like a skeleton. I was trying not to care but it wasn't working. I snapped my bracelet again, hard this time, just to keep myself from crying.

"Typical," he said. "Typical, typical, typical. Can't stand to not be the focus, to be off to the side. Ego so big it almost masks your insecurity, but we all know very well how much you hate yourself. And all that makeup, all that eyeliner, you might think it makes you look glamorous but really you just look like a cheap whore."

It seemed so insane for him to call me a whore that I just didn't care anymore. I felt the old throb in my temples, the blur of black anger at the edges of my vision.

"What the hell is your job anyway?" I said. "Are you paid to point out the obvious? Because it's really not that hard to figure out that yes, I hate myself, considering I'm here for suicide attempts and can't even have razors because I'll cut myself. Or that Tommy doesn't stick up for himself, or that Adrian thinks he's a thug. I don't understand the point of this, and I don't understand the point of you. You're pointless. You're worse than pointless, you're a bully, a fatboy bully disguised as a grown-up. In fact, you can go fuck yourself."

I wasn't thinking, not really, as I was talking, but I meant every word. Once I shut up, I knew I had to get out of there, so I walked out of the circle, and then I ran out of the room. I ran through the hallway, the kitchen, the front door. I ran across the lawn, the parking lot, past the logs, the little house, until I was in the forest, my feet crunching the dead leaves. The forest a blur of thin trees. And even though I was running as fast as I could, I could see the beginnings of springtime, the sprouting of pale yellows and greens in the branches, the first true spring I'd ever seen. The brightness startled me, but I didn't let that slow me down either. I felt like Athena, I felt like a deer.

I didn't stop until I reached the path, at the far end of the property. My heart was pounding and I was breathing hard and jagged. But I felt clean.

The path ran by the fence that was the property line, wood posts and rusted barbed wire. On the other side there was a field, owned by the neighbor, a horse rancher, and in the field stood a single horse, head in the tall brown grass. He heard me, looked up. I didn't know anything about horses but I could tell this one was young, with thin legs and knobby knees, its thick mane a golden yellow, a color I wasn't aware horses came in.

I heard something coming through the forest toward me, fast, and I thought I was caught and in trouble. But it was only Little Dan, Carly's collie dog. I hadn't known she was at the school that day. She must have just gotten there. I went to go pet him, but he ran away from me, not afraid, but like we were playing, except then he ran under the fence, heading straight for the horse, who got spooked, rearing up on its hind legs and snorting. Little Dan didn't seem to notice.

I knew I had to save him. Not thinking too much about what I was doing, I hopped over the fence. It caught on my jeans and cut me. I didn't care, didn't even feel it. I ran to the horse, grabbed Little Dan, wriggling and heavy in my arms.

Then I heard somebody yelling. It was Carly. She was coming down the path, a tiny outline, but even from that far I could tell she was freaked out. That was when I realized how close the horse still was, frightened, legs kicking and eyes wide and wild. I felt a whoosh of air and I ducked and ran like an army man, waiting to be knocked out, waiting to be dead. I made it to the fence, pushed Little Dan under and Carly grabbed him by the collar. This time, I gingerly pinched a hole in the fence, dipped through, careful not to cut myself.

I didn't get in trouble. Carly took me back to the little house, cleaned off my cuts, bandaged them. She said I was stupid for going over the fence, unbelievably stupid. Little Dan could think for and take care of himself. But she said nothing about me running away, or me yelling and swearing, and, once I was back at the big house, nobody else did either. Martin had left. He wasn't there the next day. He didn't come back. Nobody asked about him. Nobody missed him. It was like he'd never existed, nothing more than a collective bad dream.

PROMOTION

Even with me flipping out on Martin, they promoted me to Phase Three. I called my parents as soon as I saw my name moved up on the whiteboard, next to the other people on Phase Three.

They were happy, proud of me. Lately they'd been discussing me leaving and this seemed to cement it. Late spring they said, April or May. They didn't care if I officially "graduated." They just wanted me well enough to return home.

STARSEED

We were driving back from Wal-Mart. It was raining and Vinnie was taking the turns too fast. I was sitting in the back next to the window, Alyson on the other side. My body slammed, no seat belt, as the van grinded the curves, her hips and the hard plastic. The electric thing was back in my bones, and I'd missed it, missed feeling wild and special. I could feel my pupils dilate, my brain chemicals sizzling in my skull and getting me high. The rain on the windows pelted by in streaks, and the headlights from the van sliced the trees into spears, black shadows pooled like blood. Everything felt black-white, strobe light, the cockpit of a spaceship or a shooting star. We were listening to Metallica loud, all of us singing, and I felt something lifting me like wires hooked in my sternum, pulling me from the van to the sky, and I was no longer human, I was dazzling.

ATIVAN DAZE

We got a new psychiatrist. His name was Dr. Hult. What an ugly name. He was an ugly guy too, balding underneath a frizzy blond comb-over. A big nose, red and acne scarred. The square and yellowed teeth of a horse. Disgusting.

He asked me for my diagnosis, which seemed strange because my file was sitting right in front of him. Maybe he was trying to see if I'd lie. He asked if I'd been having any issues, and I told him as always I was having problems sleeping. He said he'd add a new medication. Ativan.

It felt like winning the pharmaceutical lottery.

I was getting a prescription for something that got you high.

I left the office feeling giddy.

PATIENT NAME: Juliet Escoria
AGE: 16 yrs 6 mo
SEX: F
DOB: 8/23/83

DATE: 02/22/00

HISTORY: Patient exhibits aggression, impulsivity, grandiosity, distractibility.
Reported side effects of lethargy, muscle pain, upset stomach, hair loss (mild) (cont.), dizziness, dry mouth, tremor (mild).

PREVIOUS MEDICATIONS:
Zyprexa—discontinued 01/99 once stabilized
Wellbutrin—discontinued 03/99 (ineffective)
Tegretol—discontinued 07/99 (risk of overdose/replace w Depakote)
Paxil—discontinued 7/99 (tremors)
Remeron—discontinued 8/99 (weight gain/replace w Zoloft)
Buspar—discontinued 01/00 (somnolence)
Trazodone—discontinued 2/00 (replace w Ativan)

TREATMENT:
Incr. Depakote from 1500mg/nightly to 2000mg/nightly over 1 wk
Decrease Zoloft from 100mg/nightly to 50mg/nightly over 1 week (for anxiety/depression)
Begin Ativan 4mg/nightly; up to 6mg additional as needed
Cont. group therapy, indiv. therapy

The only problem: almost everybody got a prescription for Ativan, either for anxiety or insomnia or both. Word must have gotten to someone who actually knew what they were doing, Carly or Stacy. Either way, the Ativan prescriptions went unfilled. I kept asking about mine, trying not to sound eager, just concerned. All the horrible medication and now finally one that was actually fun. Not a "relapse," a prescription. But all anyone would say was they were working on it.

In the meantime, the staff must have been given a big bottle of Ativan to use on us as needed. If someone threw a fit, or if they still couldn't sleep and it was really late, we got a pill.

I started throwing fits a lot. There's a way to have an anxiety attack that is sort of real and also sort of fake. If you're feeling anxious, all you have to do is breathe shallow and think about all the things you hate about life and yourself. Like this:

I'm a piece of shit.

I'm a fuck-up.

Batshit crazy.

A fucking mess.

A failure.

A piece of shit.

A piece of shit.

I should die.

And soon enough, you'd be hyperventilating. Soon enough, they'd be handing out Ativan. If you did it well enough, you'd get two. Like magic.

I'd woken up feeling like I was going to die soon, like a shroud had descended over my head. I kept seeing my parents' deaths, sometimes bloody and violent, sometimes decrepit and blanched. We were supposed to go grocery shopping, something I normally enjoyed. But I couldn't get rid of this feeling, that if I left the house I would die or my parents would die or at least my brain would spin out of control. I tried to push it away, explaining to myself that I was being illogical. I put on my boots and I put on my hat, but my chest felt so heavy I thought my ribs would crack if I moved.

Rosie crouched beside me, put her hand on my knee. "Are you OK, sweetie?"

I couldn't say anything. I remembered what I was supposed to do. I tried to take deep slow breaths from my stomach but the air came in shallow and jagged. "I'm having an anxiety attack," I finally managed to say.

One of the other kids was sick anyway, so Rosie stayed with the two of us at the house. She gave me Ativan, and I lay out in front of the TV with my blanket and a pillow. The only thing on was the Snorks, so I watched the Snorks. I fell asleep, and dreamt I was a Snork. I guess I was missing Luke, because Luke was also a Snork and we were floating underwater, alternating between fucking and holding hands, blowing bubbles out of the Snork tubes in our heads, and the lights and the seaweed glittered. Then I woke up and Alyson was beside me, sitting on the sofa, her body warm. Her green eyes were bright and she was smiling, and in that moment I loved her so much. My best friend, here with me and not with stupid Adrian. They'd stopped at the candy store on the way home and she'd brought me two pieces of marzipan shaped like flowers. I felt so soft and floaty, from the pills and the dream and her presence, that I wished I had anxiety attacks every day.

But then something with the Ativan started to misfire. A couple nights later and Vinnie told me I couldn't watch the movie with the others. I had to go to my room. I asked him why and he looked at me like I already knew. I didn't. Finally he said it was because of the incident the other night.

I hadn't done anything bad lately, not since Martin had left. "What are you talking about?" I asked.

Vinnie sighed deep like I was being annoying on purpose. "Fine," he said. "Let's go look at your behavior log."

I followed him into the office, and he pulled out my binder from the big filing cabinet. We sat at one of the kitchen tables, while everyone else went into the great room for the movie. He pointed to one of the entries, the night of the Snorks. Tilting blue cursive reported I'd broken into the office and stolen my Discman, which had been taken away for a month because a while ago I'd called Bill a fucking asshole.

But I never broke into the office. I didn't even know how to go about it. I was good at picking locks, but I had no idea if that particular lock required a card slipped through the door or a bobby pin in the knob. I looked at the door, trying to figure out if it was even pickable. A tiny hole next to the lock. Bobby pin. The easiest kind.

"Who wrote this?" I asked Vinnie. It seemed a little extreme, even for Bill, to write some random thing to fuck me over.

"Let me see," he said, checking the signature. "CR. That's Carly."

Carly wouldn't make shit up about me. I really had done it. The Ativan made me completely black out. I thought about the other times I had taken it, the fuzzy mornings and afternoons, hours soft around the edges. Finishing a novel in school but not remembering what happened at the end, a blank space when I thought about what I'd had for dinner. But nothing like this. Hours gone, a prank pulled by myself on myself. I opened my mouth but didn't say anything. I'd sound like a liar, and even if he believed me, it'd guarantee that I wouldn't get the Ativan again.

"I'm sorry," I said instead. "I must have forgotten."

An elevator dropped in my chest, a betrayal. I looked down at my hands, and they seemed both darker and paler at the same time. A graying. As though I was shifting into a ghost.

I wasn't the only person who'd had weird shit happen to them because of Ativan. One day they took us to the public park, which had a playground and big fields and was down by the river. It was the first warm day in weeks. It was supposed to be a good day, a reward. Me and a couple of the other girls were hanging out down near the water, throwing stones and talking. The boys were playing baseball. Then Tommy started crying, which didn't seem odd at first. He cried a lot. But then he was clawing the air like he was swatting at bugs, and saying stuff about food and animals and fights. Soon after, he was totally melting down, sobbing and flailing his limbs around. It was so extreme, they packed us back in the van, Tommy wrapped up next to Carly in a blanket, shivering like someone who'd been saved from drowning. We figured he'd had some sort of psychotic break.

No one made fun of Tommy after. He calmed down, and for a couple days no one spoke of it. But then Tommy's parents showed up at the school, and they were *pissed*. He'd been feeling nervous so one of the staff gave him an Ativan, which reacted adversely with the medication he was on. Nobody had figured on that. So Tommy's parents took him from the school, which seemed reasonable, but also made me sad, like it was something we had caused by being mean, rather than a fuck up by the staff. I don't know where he went next, if he simply stayed home or went to a better school.

Shortly after Tommy left, so did Dr. Hult, taking the Ativan with him. Bye-bye, ugly doctor. Bye-bye, lovely pills.

PHYSICAL EDUCATION

They started taking us snowboarding each week. They called it PE. Every Tuesday instead of class, we got in the van and drove two hours to Mount Shasta, always asking to stop and pee at the gas station in Weed whether we had to or not. They always let us.

We had an instructor the first couple weeks to learn the basics. He was kind of cute, reminded me of the surfer boys in Santa Bonita, sun-bleached hair and a sunburned nose. We tried flirting with him but he was clearly not interested, just looked up at the sky like *Help me Jesus*, and then he'd get real quiet. I didn't know if he knew we weren't from a normal boarding school. I didn't know if he could tell we weren't normal teenage girls.

I wasn't very good at snowboarding, had never done it before or even skied, but soon enough I was better than all the other girls and half the boys. I could go down the trails faster than any of them. I was uncoordinated and clumsy, but it didn't matter. All that mattered was fearlessness, going down completely vertical, until everything was a streak of whites and blues and greens, until the whoosh of the air drowned out any other sounds, the mountain air cold and clean, the sun reflecting off the snow like lava.

Every time, I wouldn't stop snowboarding until I had to. After a couple hours, I didn't go warm up with the others as they drank hot powdered cocoa in the lodge. I didn't loiter at the top of the summit like they did, taking advantage of the relative privacy. I didn't even wait to ride the ski lift with Alyson or anyone else I knew, unless somebody from school happened to be at the bottom already. I'd rather ride alone or even with a stranger than cut into my snowboarding time.

It felt so good at the end of the day, to take off my wet clothes and get into dry ones, and then we'd all pack into the van, heater blasting. It smelled terrible, like sweat and wet socks, but it never mattered too much because I was so tired, each of my muscles loose from use. I felt as passive and elastic as a rubber band. We'd listen to the radio until it cut out, a rock channel we didn't get way out in Redwood Trails, and sing along to the songs that we missed hearing, Sublime and Nirvana, even singing to Smash Mouth, not because we liked it but because it was fun to make our voices sound exaggerated and stupid like the singer's. As we drove farther and the other cars thinned out, people started to drop off to sleep. Sometimes by the time we arrived it was only me and the driver who were still awake, the radio turned over to fuzz, and the only thing left to pay attention to was the headlights of the van as they illuminated a tunnel across the twisting roads. Once we arrived, I ran to the shower to get in before all the others, turned the water scorching hot. As the water pelted me I felt clean and pure, my body something to use rather than destroy.

VOID

We had just gotten back from a day of snowboarding. Alyson and Adrian had stayed at the school, punished because they'd been caught making out again. I'd assumed she'd be there to greet me. But the lights were off, the entire school dead silent and still. For a moment I thought Stephen had come back and killed everyone.

A few minutes later, Rosie walked in, bundled in a coat and gloves and a scarf. "Oh thank God you're back," she said, and she and Carly and Vinnie, who had taken us snowboarding that day, went into the office, closing the door behind them without even addressing the rest of us.

"What the fuck is going on?" Kiran said.

We told Alex to go listen in the hall, but he didn't get the chance because right after, there was a knock. It was the cops.

"Holy shit," I said.

The adults headed outside to meet them. "Don't worry," Carly said, as she walked to the door. "Everything is fine."

"Where's Alyson?" I asked.

Carly stopped. "We don't know."

I searched the entire school for Alyson, figuring she had to be hiding somewhere. It was twenty degrees outside. She couldn't be out there in the cold. The whole time, this feeling built up in my stomach, a knot of nervousness, as I looked under beds, in the shower, the pantry—anywhere a person could hide. But I couldn't find her anywhere.

I didn't find her because she and Adrian had run away. I couldn't believe how stupid they were. They didn't have any supplies or money. There was nowhere to go. Rosie put us in the great room to watch cartoons, while she made phone calls in the office. I kept creeping in the hallway, hoping to hear the phone ring, hoping for news that they'd found her. When it was time for bed, I couldn't sleep, imagining Alyson dead in a snowbank somewhere, skin blue, eyes staring up at nothing.

After a couple hours of just lying there, I heard noise from the kitchen. Alyson and Adrian were in there with Rosie. Everyone else had left. The police had found them hiding in the barn to get warm. They'd made it to the main road, but turned around because it was too cold. There were blankets wrapped around them, their hands in bowls of water to prevent frostbite. They weren't even dressed warm, just coats over regular clothes.

"Hi," Alyson said. "Did you have fun snowboarding?"

I wanted to ask her what the fuck was wrong with her. I was so mad at her for being so stupid. I was even madder at Adrian, the idiot, the tough guy. If it wasn't for him, she never would have done something so dumb.

But I went to her, wrapped my arms around her, and was surprised to find myself crying. "I was so worried," I said.

Alyson took her hand out of the water, patted me wetly on the head. "It's OK," she said. "Everything is fine. Go back to bed. I'll be in there soon."

"Everything's fine, baby girl," Rosie said. "They're safe now."

Alyson came to bed a few minutes later. I pretended to be asleep because I still felt mad, like she had betrayed me for the stupidest guy. She was a snorer, which usually drove me crazy. But that night I was relieved to hear it, the scratchy ins and outs of her breathing. Just like normal.

But everything was not fine. The next day during school, Alyson and Adrian left. For good. They'd both been sent to stricter schools, not coed, more "discipline based." Besides that, we were told nothing. I wasn't even allowed to write her.

And just like that, my best friend was gone.

Just like that, I was alone.

Not long after, Stacy brought in her son CJ to work at the school. He was going to teach new classes, Philosophy and Drama. They were voluntary, held in the great room on the days that CJ worked as the boys' overnight counselor.

It seemed exciting, even if the excitement was only because it was new. We thought the staff finally realized that if we were treated better, we would act better. In Philosophy, we'd learn basic concepts and then discuss real-life issues. In Drama, we'd write and then put on our own play, complete with sets and costumes. It gave us something to look forward to.

Before he got there, all the girls were hoping CJ would be cute. He wasn't. Instead he was skinny and nerdy and pale, hair combed over preppy, which was confusing because he had a little hoop in one ear and a Buddhist tattoo on his wrist.

About the same time, a new boy named Jason came to the school. It was obvious he liked me but I couldn't tell if I liked him. He was good-looking, but not my type—he had very neat hair and wore boring clothes, Tommy Hilfiger and Nautica. He was funny and sweet, but he was from Alabama and talked with a Southern accent that made him sound like a yokel. Actually he was from Puyallup, in Washington, but he'd just moved there. He'd lived in Alabama for most of his life with his grandparents, but they'd recently died so he had to go back to living with his mom. He hated her. He said she was crazy.

Being from Alabama meant he had good stories. He told us about hunting armadillos, how they jump when you shoot them, except he didn't say it like that. This is what he said instead: *Dillers. They jump when you shoot 'em.*

I'd make him repeat this phrase, over and over again. No matter how many times he said it, it always made me laugh.

Jason had been diagnosed with ADHD. He said he didn't have it really, it's just when his mother sent him to a psychiatrist, he was so high he had a hard time paying attention to anything the doctor said, so she'd concluded that was what was wrong. He got put on Adderall, eighty milligrams, forty twice a day. That's a lot of Adderall.

I liked Adderall. Jason didn't; it made him feel nervous and sick. He said he'd give me his, but only if I traded him a kiss. I still didn't know if I liked him but I wanted the Adderall. I kissed him on the mouth, and there was something that felt good about it, light and innocent. The next time he kissed me, I let our lips linger longer, a real kiss that left a softness. A few days later, he asked me to be his girlfriend. I said yes.

Every day he gave me half his Adderall. Because I'd always had insomnia, nobody noticed. My room was still empty, Alyson's bare bed and shelves silently confronting me, so it was OK if I stayed up late reading because there was no one to bother. Soon, I'd read all my books. I moved on to the Harry Potters that were on the shelf in the great room. I didn't care about Harry Potter, it was just something to keep me occupied. Once I'd finished those, I went on to the psychological texts. There were a lot of them. I took notes. I learned all the disorders and all the symptoms and all the treatments and all the medications and their side effects. I became an expert on the human brain.

In Drama class, we read a lot of plays, Tennessee Williams and Arthur Miller and Chekhov. Once we'd read enough, CJ said we were allowed to begin our own. I was the only person who enjoyed writing, so I was put in charge of the script, which I liked because I could decide who said what and when. So in between reading about psychology and psychiatry (which I had learned were two separate things), I worked on the play. It was going to be an epic, about a school a lot like ours, except this one was set in the future. All the kids in the school had boxes installed, which regulated their mood and behavior, emotional cyborgs. Instead of doing farm chores, they learned to solder and to program, got put to work making more boxes. I wasn't sure what should happen next, but I'd figure it out.

But I didn't take well to the philosophy. It was Nietzsche's idea of Eternal Return that got to me. Back at home, sometimes when I couldn't sleep I'd go into the living room and watch PBS. They played space documentaries between 3:00 and 4:00 a.m. I'd learned about the distance of the earth to various planets, the distance between our solar system and other solar systems, and that the universe was infinite and always expanding. To think there was something larger than infinity, that there was something that not only went on forever, but this forever was always growing larger and more savage. It left me feeling untethered, like nothing I did mattered at all.

The thing that really did me in was thinking about my suicide attempts. According to Nietzsche, in some alternate universe, I'd died. The thought of this made me feel irrevocably doomed, locked in a bubble of impenetrable darkness, a black hole. In all of them, every universe and every path, I was a mistake, a suicide.

I started asking a lot of questions, hoping to prove both CJ and Nietzsche wrong. Hoping they had no idea what they were talking about, that these were ideas created just to fuck with us. Both Nietzsche and CJ seemed like sadists, their eyes intense and devoid of humor.

I could tell CJ didn't like my questions. At first he tried to answer them, speaking slowly like I was stupid, but eventually he gave up and just ignored me.

I also started to pretend to forget that CJ's name was CJ. Instead, I called him BJ, as in blow job, as in he was gay. I started a rumor, that he was hitting on all the boys. I wanted to hurt his feelings, to make him feel like he didn't belong here. He wasn't as smart or important as he thought. And it worked. Every time I called him BJ, the other students laughed and his eyes got all hard and hurt, just like Nietzsche's, and an ugly ball of pleasure rose in my chest.

The other thing I started doing was hallucinating again. All the Adderall had made me manic. Or maybe it was the lack of sleep and Depakote. At breakfast, I sat down with my bowl of oatmeal and suddenly the world froze into a snow globe, radiant circles of light around everyone's heads, the brightest around mine. At night, I saw shadows ducking in the holes. As I fell asleep, I heard the voice, whispering the same old thing: I was chosen. This time, though, I knew what I was chosen for. I was chosen to help rid the world of evil.

There were two evil things at Redwood Trails School: one of them was Stacy, and the other was CJ. I could see the shape of their auras, and they matched, both smoke gray, both narrow, reaching into the sky and down through the ground. I saw the birds in their faces, but they were less like birds and more like bats.

Between all of this, I started to become afraid.

I stopped taking the Adderall. I thought about what had happened with it and with the Ativan. I was done with drugs. I figured all I needed was some sleep, to take Depakote every night again. But on the third night of going back to regular, I was awake till dawn just crying in my room, exhausted.

The lack of sleep made me brittle. I began to yell at people, people I didn't want to yell at. Jason seemed afraid of me, was no longer seeking me out, left me alone in my room. One time I even yelled at

Vinnie. It was during breakfast. I was so tired and his voice was so loud that I couldn't stand him talking anymore, so I threw my bowl of cereal at him. I got in trouble, was sent to the office so Stacy could chew me out. In her office, I started to cry, which was embarrassing because Stacy was evil. I told her I hadn't been sleeping, I'd only thrown the cereal because I was so tired.

Stacy surprised me by being nice. She came out from behind her desk and hugged me and I let her but the hug made my bones cold, like being caught in a draft. She said she'd get the doctor to prescribe me something to sleep later that week.

I went to Philosophy class later that day, against my better judgment. I went because Jason wanted me to go, said he missed me. We sat next to each other and held hands.

CJ was telling us about Nietzsche's views on God. I don't know why it made me angry but it did. "These are only ideas, abstract and meaningless," I yelled at CJ. I told him he was stupid, that this was bullshit, that only a faggot would sit around learning this shit, and only a big gay faggot would not just learn this shit but try to pawn it off on others.

I watched his face turn red, and then he got up and left the room. The rest of us sat there, not sure what to do. He came back a few minutes later with Stacy. Under my breath I said, "Aw, he had to call his mommy."

I don't know if Stacy heard me, but she brought me to her office for the second time that day. She told me I was out of control, and dangerous, and that I was no longer allowed to participate in "extra-curriculars." This meant no more Philosophy, which I couldn't care less about. This meant no more Drama, no more play, which I was a bit sad about, but I mostly didn't care because I had hit a wall with my script anyway, hadn't been able to add anything new to it for a whole week now.

The thing I cared about was the no snowboarding. We were

supposed to go the next day. It was late in the year, and not unlikely that we wouldn't be able to go ever again. I told her this but she didn't care. "You're too unpredictable to be let off school grounds, anyway," she said. "Once you get on new medication, and get some sleep, we can reassess. For now: absolutely not."

I walked back across the parking lot. I entered the house through the door to the great room. They were still discussing Nietzsche like a bunch of idiots. They looked up when I walked in the room, surprised.

"You're just a big dumb asshole, BJ!" I yelled.

Then I went into my room. I closed the door. I left the light off.

I had a single razor blade hidden in the fold of a pair of socks. I got it out. I sliced into my arm. I never cut my arm because it was too noticeable, but this time I simply didn't care. I watched the blood ooze out, hot and bright red, but it wasn't enough, so I cut again, longer and deeper this time, and then again, a short little shallow cut, and then again, a fast slash.

The razor slipped on the last one, and I could tell I'd fucked up right away, I'd really fucked up, because it didn't bleed immediately. I'd cut so deep I could see fat. I looked at the paleness, a curiosity.

The bloodlessness didn't last long. I took the sock that had held the razor blade, pressed it against my arm to try to stop the blood, which was pulsing out of the gash to the beat of my heart. It didn't work. The blood soaked through. I pressed the other sock but the same thing happened again. I tried squeezing my other hand around my arm, a kind of tourniquet, but I couldn't get a tight enough grip because of all the blood. I started to feel woozy. I needed help.

I went back into the great room. I'd meant to leave one of the socks on the cut but I forgot, and the blood was dripping down my arm and onto the floor. Everyone's eyes bugged out when they saw me, especially CJ; he looked so scared and disturbed that I started laughing, laughing with blood dripping down my arm, onto the floor.

The maniac was back, laughing and covered with blood.

They got Vinnie and he handed me a towel and put me in the van. Somebody called the town doctor, who worked out of a trailer next to his house fifteen miles away. I started to get real sleepy in the van. The towel was all wet and red with blood. "Stay with me, honey," Vinnie yelled. I liked him calling me honey. It made me feel like everything was going to be OK, like I wasn't a maniac.

We got to the doctor's and his face paled, which made me realize once again that I'd really fucked up. The blood had slowed down some and it didn't hurt. It merely throbbed, a nice rhythm, predictable like a mechanical drum. I went into his office and he stuck a needle in my arm, which hurt a little, the only pain I'd felt yet, but then it went numb. He took out something like a staple gun, saying, "Stitches won't be quite enough." He went to work on my arm, applying the staples. I watched like it wasn't even my arm, it wasn't anybody's arm, it was just some piece of furniture. Vinnie didn't have the same reaction. "Oh God," I heard him mutter. "I'll be right back," he said and left the room. Soon my arm was all stapled up, nine staples, and then three on one of the deeper smaller cuts for good measure. He disinfected the whole thing, bandaged it up, told me to come back in two weeks, keep an eye on it.

I wasn't supposed to take the bandage off, but when I got back everyone wanted to see it so I took it off anyway. It was shocking to look at, crusted blood and bright silver staples, with a sickly smear of iodine. It reminded me of something. I was no longer a maniac. I had graduated. I was a Frankenstein.

MEMENTO

None of us could get the bloodstains out of the carpet. Now there was a permanent trail of rust dots trailing from my room to the great room, DNA evidence of my monstrosity. The socks and the towel had to be thrown away. The scar eventually softened from staples to scabs to a jagged mark, a lasting souvenir that ensured I would never forget: I am a maniac. I am a monster.

PATIENT LOG

PATIENT NAME: Juliet Escoria
AGE: 16 yrs 6 mo
SEX: F
DOB: 8/23/83

DATE: 03/21/00

HISTORY: Patient had severe incident of self-harm previous week requiring medical attention. Reported aggression, anxiety, sleeplessness, impulsivity.
Reported side effects of lethargy, muscle pain, upset stomach, hair loss (mild) (cont.).

PREVIOUS MEDICATIONS:
Zyprexa—discontinued 01/99 once stabilized
Wellbutrin—discontinued 03/99 (ineffective)
Tegretol—discontinued 07/99 (risk of overdose/replace w Depakote)
Paxil—discontinued 07/99 (replace w Remeron)
Remeron—discontinued 8/99 (weight gain/replace w Zoloft)
Buspar—discontinued 01/00 (somnolence)
Trazodone—discontinued 2/00 (replace w Ativan)
Ativan—discontinued 3/00 (replace w Trazodone)

TREATMENT:
Cont. Depakote 2000mg/nightly
Cont. Zoloft 50mg/nightly (for anxiety/depression)
Resume Trazodone 25mg/nightly (for insomnia)
Begin Risperdal at 0.5mg/nightly, increase to 2mg/nightly over course of 2 weeks (for manic symptoms)
Cont. group therapy, indiv. therapy

FUGUE STATE

Carly started doing something new with us called "relaxation therapy." Twice a week, we went into the great room before bedtime. She turned off the lights, and we'd lie on the floor on our backs like we were dead. She told us to clench each muscle, foot to head, and then relax them one by one, her voice low and smooth. When we were done I felt liquid, melting into the floor.

Sometimes she called us over to her office in the little house individually, to do personalized meditations. Her office was decorated exactly like you'd expect: a little fountain in the corner, crystals on the bookshelves, a bamboo plant on her desk. Gauzy curtain over the miniblinds, a sun catcher on the window that refracted soft rainbows onto the walls.

At first we did the same things in the individual appointments that we did with everybody else—the muscle clenching, and also "baths" in different colors of light. She did Reiki over my still-healing arm, a heaviness from her hovering hand, like magnets. But then one day she asked me if I was interested in investigating my past lives.

I didn't know if I believed in that kind of thing. It seemed too easy of an answer, how people were always Cleopatra or King Arthur, and never some poor serf or a chicken. Still, it sounded cool, to be someone else, even if it was only "real" like a dream. So I said yes.

We started with the relaxation of my body, foot to head. Then she told me she would count backwards from twenty. "Each number, you are going to be falling, falling, falling," she said. "By one, you will no longer be in this room. You will be falling into the earth."

The falling wasn't unpleasant. It was a sensation of surrender, like going to sleep. When I stopped, I found myself in a cave. I felt my way down, fingertips sliding on the walls, damp and cold. There was a door at the end, little and wooden. When I opened it, there was just more black. Carly told me to jump in. She said I would fall through time.

And it worked. My body changed, and I was still a young girl but this time I was paler and smaller, with darker hair. I ran in fields with my sister, endless green and clouds; Ireland or maybe England. I could feel what it felt like to have a sister, something I'd always wanted, but it wasn't like I would have thought—this weird knot of closeness but also repulsion, like smelling your own sweat. Time passed. When I was fifteen, my village deemed me a poet and a healer and treated me with reverence, while my sister was married off as soon as she was able to have children. In the mornings, we often sat together, not really talking, mostly just taking in the sky. I think we were both awkwardly trying to reestablish what we had together as children, running through the fields, but mostly all I felt in the air was resentment. Mine for her willingness to be reduced to such simplicity. Hers for me turning out special.

And then one day I saw our whole village getting sick. I saw my sister, what would happen to her, the nosebleeds and fever spots, and then I saw her getting buried in a shroud. I saw the population of our village halved. Stupidly, I told the people what I had seen. No one believed me until it was too late.

When it happened, of course they thought I'd caused it, that I'd summoned it from my hands as I treated people for headaches and cramps. They didn't believe me when I told them it had come from the water. I was not a healer; I was a witch, and so they sentenced me to drown. On the day that I died, I felt the water come over me, heavy as lead, and even though I was underwater I could still see sunlight poking through. I heard my mother crying. I felt a burn in my chest, no longer breathing. A quiet knowledge that I'd done this to myself.

I wasn't allowed to go on the school's first wilderness trip. Carly was taking only the boys. Up until then, we'd only done day trips, hikes around Mount Shasta, once an overnight camping trip at Lava Beds.

This time, they'd be gone for two weeks, hiking and rock climbing in Baja California.

It seemed unfair, especially since they planned to spend a night in San Diego before crossing the border. I tried not to think about it because it hurt, but I missed home, the warm sunshine, my parents, my friends. The things I missed most weren't the things I would have guessed: the velvet brown of the hills, the smell of the air. Sometimes I missed it so much I could barely stand talking to my parents on the phone, the pain of imagining them in the living room with that big ocean shining in through the window like it was nothing. But no, I had to stay in Redwood Trails, because Carly only wanted to take the boys.

It wouldn't have been so bad if the boys didn't seem so gleeful each time they received a new package from their parents, flashlights and quick-dry cargo shorts and bathing suits. When Jason spent evenings with me, instead of talking and laughing loudly with the rest of the boys while going over plans with Carly, I pretended not to care, only telling Jason to take lots of pictures.

The school was so quiet without them, lonely, especially because there was no longer an Alyson. I kept to myself the first couple days, writing lonely poems and reading books. Eventually they felt sorry for us, because Rosie said she would take us to an animal auction that weekend. We'd each get a lamb, feed them, take care of them, go into town for local 4H meetings. It would be an educational experience, an exercise in responsibility.

The auction was noisy and loud, held in a gigantic barn lined with bleachers, smelling of animal shit and hay. Animals were brought in, all types, cows and pigs, chickens, horses, and donkeys. The auctioneer spoke in the fast-paced garble that I hadn't thought auctioneers actually used, previously assuming this was something that only happened in movies. I couldn't even tell what was going on, couldn't understand anything except for when the auctioneer yelled SOLD. People went to retrieve the animals they'd purchased, real redneck types, in flannel and boots and cowboy hats. Rosie knew what to do, raised her hand at the right moments, bought the lambs for what she said was a bargain.

We wanted to hold the lambs in the van, but Rosie said we had to leave them in the back in their crate. We were going to house them in the empty chicken coop, which was inside a fenced-in pasture that had been cleared in the trees. We had to clean the chicken coop out first, though, scraping out old piles of shit and feathers, before finally putting down fresh hay, the baby sheep bleating in their crate the whole time, lonely and scared. I had wanted to let them out in the pasture while they waited, so they wouldn't be claustrophobic and so we could see them, but Rosie said they were fine and it was too cold.

Finally the coop was ready. Rosie pried the top of the crate open with a hammer, and the lambs spilled out, wobbly legs and downy ears. I picked out one as mine, pure white with a soft pink nose, and I was worried I wouldn't get her because she was obviously the cutest. But they let me have her. She was so soft and fuzzy and perfect as I held her in my arms, my baby, my little lamb. I decided to name her Fuzzy Navel.

We went back up to the house, boiled the bottles and long black nipples Rosie had bought at the feed store the day before. The lambs were still so little they needed formula every six hours, Rosie said, even at night—so we'd have to wake up to feed them, no matter how tired we were. Nobody minded.

I woke up bleary-eyed to Rosie flicking on the light and clapping her hands until I got out of bed. We put coats on over our pajamas, headed down there with flashlights, the baby lambs bleating and needing us as soon as we opened the door. I held Fuzzy in my arms, her heart beating against her chest as she suckled from her bottle. Christina was feeding her lamb next to me, which was gray and scrawny, the runt of the litter. We still hadn't spoken since I'd yelled at her about Luke. Her face looked so peaceful as she held her lamb in her lap. She caught me looking at her, smiled at me, a small, genuine smile, meaning nothing more than, *Aren't they just so cute?* Fuzzy finally finished sucking, rested her head against my chest, breathed in softly, and fell asleep. My heart swelled in my chest, a clanging sort of joy.

FORGIVENESS

We were put in pairs, alternating days where we'd clean out the pen, put down fresh hay, disinfect the bottles, and, later, clean out the troughs once we began phasing them to solid food.

Of course I was paired with Christina. The first day, we walked down to the pen, saying nothing, both of us looking at the ground. I planned on not saying anything the whole time, but it was necessary to speak, to decide who did what. I tried to keep it just to the tasks, telling her I'd go get fresh hay from the barn, but Christina stopped me. "Juliet," she said. "Hold on."

I thought she was going to tell me to get extra hay or something, but she didn't. She walked over to me, looked me in the eyes, her expression pained.

"I'm sorry," she said. "I just want you to know I'm still sorry."

Her face was sad and vulnerable, and I knew I could hurt her. But I was surprised to realize I wasn't mad anymore. She'd done a dumb thing that had broken my heart but without even trying I had forgiven her. "I'm sorry too," I said.

"Friends?"

"Friends."

She smiled, hugged me around my neck in a way that seemed spontaneous and genuine, and strangely I could feel my eyes tearing up, grateful to have her as my friend again.

THE BOYS ARE BACK

When the boys came back, they were tan and dirty, covered in cuts and bruises from their travels. The photos showed them high on cliffs, running on the beach, building a campfire. They had funny stories—Jason afraid to jump down, even though he was just a few feet above the ground and better at rock climbing than anybody, Beto translating in Spanish when they were stopped by the federales for no reason, getting them off without even paying the customary bribe, because he'd managed to make them laugh, a joke he refused to explain, saying it was untranslatable. They all had new nicknames and inside jokes, Big Hoopty and something about a jinglefeather.

They didn't know about the lambs until we told them. As soon as they heard, they wanted to go down to the pen and give them their bottles but we wouldn't let them. They were ours.

OOPS

The lambs' tails had to be removed, Rosie explained. It seemed cruel, but she said it wasn't really. If we left them on, they'd get crusted over with dingle berries, big ones, which could breed infection and actually be deadly. Cutting them off was easier and less painful than it sounded—we just had to tie rubber bands around the base and eventually they'd fall off all on their own, no pain.

A few days later, I was playing hide-and-go-seek with Fuzzy. I'd sneak behind the coop or a tree and she'd come running to find me, baaing in a way that sounded like laughter. She'd found me crouching behind the oak tree.

I don't know why I did it. I didn't even realize I'd done it until it was already over: tugged her tail, just a tiny bit, so lightly I was basically only holding on. But the tail came off in my hand. I yelped with surprise, and so did Fuzzy. There was a tiny bit of blood on the tail, a tiny bit of blood on the stump, but mostly the flesh was dead. I felt so guilty I left the pen right then, went back to the house, threw the tail in the trash. Later I went back down there, apologized, hugged her, rubbed her behind her ears the way she liked. Fuzzy didn't seem to care. There was a tiny scab on her stump, which I gently dabbed with Neosporin twice a day until it healed.

INTERROGATION

It was Carly who sat me down, calling me into the office. At first I thought I was in trouble. I tried to think about what I'd done wrong, but right away Carly said I wasn't in trouble. Then she said she needed to ask me some serious questions.

It turned out that Hank hadn't actually quit like they said. He'd been fired because somebody had reported him. Somebody said he'd inappropriately touched some of the girls. She wouldn't tell me who that somebody was. And Carly didn't use the word "inappropriately touched." She used the word "molested." As if we were children and Hank was some creepy uncle, rather than teenagers and a counselor we knew very well.

I tried to figure out which girls, and then I did.

Carly wanted to know if he'd ever done anything to me. She was looking straight at me, like she thought if she looked hard enough she wouldn't miss the truth. I looked straight back at her, at her brown eyes and the beginnings of wrinkles on her forehead.

"No," I said. "He never touched me."

"What about anything else?" she said. "Did he ever say anything, or do anything, to you that seemed inappropriate?"

I thought for a moment, weighing my choices. I considered the time Luke and I had sex in the van, which seemed so far away it was like it had never happened, a sort of fairy tale I'd told myself. I was no longer certain he'd stared at me, that we'd actually made eye contact in the rearview mirror.

It seemed too risky to tell her, and Luke was long gone anyway. I decided to pretend it hadn't happened.

"I'm thinking," I told Carly. I looked out the window so I wouldn't have to look at her. She was still staring at me. There was a hummingbird at the feeder hung from the eaves, the first one I'd seen in months. It wasn't a pretty bird, brown and white like a sparrow. Its beak was long and looked sharp. I made sure my expression was entirely neutral, flattened my eyes so Carly wouldn't be able to read anything.

"He swore around us," I finally decided to offer. "He sometimes let us smoke at the AA meetings, and also drink coffee." Minor offenses, I figured. Enough to get Carly off me, but not enough to get him in more trouble.

But that wasn't enough. "What else?" she said. She leaned forward in the chair, resting her elbows on her knees and her chin in her hands, like we were girlfriends telling secrets. It annoyed me, made me not want to tell her anything—but I also got the feeling that she wouldn't let me out of there until I fed her a few more stories. I told her about the chewing tobacco. I figured if nobody had told her about that already, then someone would soon—it had happened several times, over the period of a few months, to enough people that it was bound to come up anyway.

"OK," Carly said. "And what did you see him doing to other people? Or hear about him doing. It doesn't matter if you know it was true or not. Any little rumor."

It came out of my mouth before I even had time to think about what I was saying, in a voice that was too loud and didn't sound like mine at all. I told her what I'd seen that night we played Spy. I told her I had seen him with Christina in his car. I couldn't tell exactly what it was they were doing but it looked like they might have been kissing.

As soon as I finished talking I felt my face flush hot with guilt. "But I don't know," I said. "Maybe they were just talking. That was back when Christina was really depressed. He might have just been trying to help."

"OK," she said, in a voice that sounded like I'd finally pleased her. She stopped staring at me, turned to the desk where she had a binder out, and wrote something down. "Now would you be willing to testify about this, about what you think you might have seen. It doesn't matter if you know what you saw or not. You'd just say what you thought you maybe saw."

"What? What do you mean testify?"

"In court. We're trying to get a case together to prevent him from doing this kind of thing again."

I imagined myself in court, leaning into a microphone, Hank sitting across from me in a suit, watching me with a hurt look on his face. I knew I couldn't do it. "No way," I said.

Carly protested. She told me this was important, that he'd hurt people irrevocably, that if I testified I would be doing my part to ensure he didn't harm future victims.

"But you don't understand," I said. "He was our friend. He helped me. I don't think I would want to be sober if it wasn't for him. I can't do that, can't pretend he never did anything good, that the only thing he ever did that mattered was something I maybe or maybe didn't see."

She was silent for a long while, again staring at me, hoping to get me to do what she wanted. I must have sounded convincing enough because she finally told me I could go. As I was closing the door, she said, "I hope you change your mind."

A LETTER FROM THE FUTURE #5

It took years for me to realize Hank wasn't my friend.

It took years for me to realize this was just one more way I'd hurt Christina.

CULTIVATION

When the weather was finally beginning to get warm again, Rosie decided we would plant a vegetable garden. She had Bill and Kiran till a plot of land, right next to the lambs. That weekend, she brought in big pallets full of baby plants. We'd each be in charge of a certain vegetable. I told her I needed something easy because I was always killing things. She smiled, told me that Jason and I were in charge of the peas, that I'd be fine.

We were all given gloves and a brown paper bag to kneel on. We were quiet as we worked, the soil cool and moist between our fingers, the sunlight bright on our faces. I discovered I liked gardening, the stillness that came from collectively working with our hands, the exactness of digging holes just the right depth and width, the simple monotony of patting the soil into place.

Every day, Jason and I walked down there together after breakfast, making sure no birds or bugs had gotten to our little plants, and watering the soil when it was dry. We never spoke as we worked, because we didn't need to. Being with Luke had felt like a riptide, something barely perceptible between us that was strong enough to kill. With Jason there was none of this. When we were finished with the garden, we'd go feed and pet Fuzzy, and the constant tight feeling in my chest morphed into something different, something softer, lighter, more warm.

It happened so slowly it was hard to notice, but the little plants turned into bigger plants, the pale shoots deepening into a rich green as they widened and grew. We installed a trellis, helped the thin vines wrap around the rails, the new leaves reaching upward into the sunshine. Fuzzy grew larger too, her once high-pitched bleat finding its way into a bray, her knobby legs growing longer and stronger, less a lamb, more a sheep. I would leave soon, too soon to eat the peas or cry when Fuzzy left us to be sold for her wool or mutton (nobody knew which because we were all afraid to ask). But it was nice to know that for a while I'd have something growing, a good piece of me, in my absence.

BACKCOUNTRY

In April, we all went to Death Valley for ten days—the girls who weren't allowed to go to Mexico, and also Kiran and Beto because they were now on Phase Four and could do what they wanted.

The first five days, we would go backcountry camping, away from the road for a night or two, then returning to the van to drive to another area of the park and get more water. I had been back-packing with my parents many times as a child, and so the idea of carrying everything on my back wasn't a foreign concept. But this was more intense. We weren't staying at campsites, just along the trail, so that meant we had to carry all our water. When I'd gone camping with my parents, my dad carried a little stove and a set of dishes that nested inside each other, food that came in packets like oatmeal and rice. We had no such luxuries. For food, we were each given a giant bag of gorp, a hunk of cheese, a sausage, and several hard, tasteless disks called pilot crackers. The tents weren't like the tents I'd used with my parents; these were ultralight, didn't even have bottoms. And we had no pads to sleep on, just the ground, no pillows, just our bunched-up clothes.

The weather was hot and the sun was brutal. I got sunburned the first day, but by the fourth, my arms and face had turned golden, a color my skin hadn't seen since I spent my days playing on the beach as a child. The hikes were brutal too, winding up and down mountains, no trails because the land was so barren. There was nowhere to bathe, and each of us had brought as few clothes as possible, so we just stunk. Every night, I'd get in my sleeping bag, not even caring about the hardness of the ground, and in the moments before I fell asleep I felt like I was still hiking, my body moving up and down at the even pace we'd kept all day.

The scenery was dry and wasted and brown all around, everything looking the same, same, same—but only from a distance.

Once we were hiking, I saw life, the dusty puffs of green in the creosote and sagebrush, prickly outlines of cholla cactus and yucca. As we went deeper and farther from the roads, the land erupted upward, with caves and crevices, in reds and oranges and yellows. And the sunsets came in colors brighter than you could imagine, the brilliant blue scorched with neons. Even the most boring sunset I saw there was beautiful, an unusually cloudy evening, the clouds blotting out the rays of the sun, and everything streaked pastels.

There were, of course, no tissues, which might not have been that big of a deal if we were in normal weather. But we were in Death Valley, where the air was dry and dusty. So Carly showed us how to do snot rockets, by closing one nostril with our finger and blowing out as hard as we could, the snot and boogers shooting out of our noses, falling like a rocket to the desert floor.

There was something I loved in blowing snot rockets, as though I were a little boy, somebody innocent and dumb enough to take pleasure in snot.

The lack of bathrooms was even worse than the lack of tissues. If Carly was a normal person, she would have let us take a roll of toilet paper with us, bury our trash in the sand. But she was hardcore—bring nothing in, take nothing out. And there were no leaves or anything to wipe with either. The rule was: find a rock the size, shape, and texture of your elbow. So we all concluded we'd just hold our shit until we got back to civilization.

On the third day, all that poop started to become uncomfortable, so I decided to suck it up and take a shit. It was embarrassing, because when it really started to hit me, we were in the middle of hiking, which meant everyone knew what I was doing. "Carly," I said. "I need to find a rock."

Everyone started laughing, and we looked together as a group to find one. For the first time that trip I was glad Jason wasn't there, so he couldn't help find a rock for me to wipe my ass with. The rock selection was meager; the best we could do was a piece of sandstone. We were on a shallow ridge, and I found a small cave to do my business.

It felt so good.

It felt like I was ridding myself of something large and disgusting that had been building up for too long, because I was. The sandstone made my ass hurt, but I didn't have to wipe much because my shit was as hard as a rock.

When I came back, Christina said, "Did you do it?" and I nodded, and then everyone broke out in cheers. It was like I'd won something. It was like I'd done something incredible.

CIVILIZATION

We had to cut the backcountry trip a night short because we ran out of water. If I'd known that, maybe I could have held my poop another day.

That fifth night, we stayed in a hostel, dormitory style, on thin mattresses on cold metal bunks. Spartan. But that night, after four nights on the hard ground, those beds felt luxurious, like we were kings. Even better—the shower. I waited to take mine after all the others, long enough so the water would have a chance to get back to hot. I took off my dirty clothes, got in the water as it streamed over me, the rivulets dripping off my body a murky brown, stinging the rough patches on my shoulders and hips where the straps of my backpack had worn them raw, the blisters on my heels and toes. I saw my tanned limbs, the pale white that had been guarded by my shorts and tank top, the white scars on my thighs, the bright red of my still-healing Adderall war wound, and with the miracle of a little bit of soap and a little bit of water, I was clean again.

My hair was a different story. I'd given up on it by the second night, hiding it in a ponytail under the ball cap we were required to wear in the sun. No matter how much conditioner I used, I couldn't unknot this chunk at the back of my head, fat and long like a dreadlock. I decided to just keep it, a small part of myself still dirty and wild.

After we were clean and settled, we ate in a restaurant, a diner. Almost all of us ordered steak and eggs. It was the single best meal I'd ever eaten.

We went out for one more night of backcountry camping, this time feeling like we knew what we were doing and what to expect. In the morning, we hiked out to the Badwater Basin, the most famous part of Death Valley—the lowest point in North America, almost three hundred feet below sea level. Maybe it was because it was a Tuesday, or maybe we just hit some luck, but the basin was empty; we were seemingly the only living things in it.

There was a wooden plank path, and we walked over it solemnly, like we were on hallowed ground. The parched earth surrounded us, hexagons of dirt and salt, crystallized and almost sparkling in the blinding sunlight. The mountains yawned in the background, high and purple, and you could even see Mount Whitney, the highest peak in the forty-eight states, tip still shrouded in snow—the highest and the lowest visible at once, a metaphor.

We sat there for a while, drinking water and eating our gorp, before deciding we should race on the salt flats. We faced off in pairs, me beating all the girls. I remembered the days when I still cared about sports and was the fastest runner. Finally I had to race Kiran, who had beat Beto. I ran as fast as I could, ahead at first, but then Kiran caught me and I lost, the difference between childhood and adolescence. But it didn't matter, the sun was shining and my footsteps crunched and left clouds of dust, and I felt magical and wonderful, this sainted existence of my body.

Every day that I could, I sent Jason a postcard, telling him simple things, everything we'd done since the last postcard. The days were full and long—shorter day-hikes, soaking in a hot spring to soothe our sore muscles, a tour of Scotty's Castle, bonfires, scouting out the few wildflowers. But nothing compared to running across Badwater Basin.

SOLO

The last three days were spent on something we'd all been anticipating the whole trip, hanging unmentioned but always in our minds. The solo trip. Three days by ourselves. We drove out early morning, just after dawn, the sky a benevolent swirl of peach and pale blue, to the Harrisburg Flats. Each of us was given a tarp, some cord, more of the same food, two big jugs of water, a flashlight, our sleeping bag and clothes, and a whistle. We were allowed one book and a notebook.

The whistle was for emergencies only. "No joke," Carly said. "If you blow on these and there's not an emergency, that will be the end of the trip for you."

We weren't supposed to speak the entire three days. The silence was supposed to let us learn to live with the noise of our minds, then the noise was supposed to fade, and eventually we'd find peace. Three times a day, Carly would come check on us and give us our medicine when we needed it. We were also allowed to fast, for a "more intense spiritual experience," but Beto was the only person who took her up on it.

We were to find our own place in the basin, the only rule being that we had to be far enough apart so we couldn't see anyone else. The eight of us formed a circle, and then we were told to face outward holding hands. Christina squeezed mine, and I could feel her nervousness and excitement, could feel mine too, hoping it would work, afraid it would work. Three whole days with only myself, the maniac, the alien, the ghost. Three whole days of just me.

"I want you to close your eyes and think about what you want to accomplish during this time," Carly told us. "Set your intentions. Whatever you ask for will be given to you, if you have an open mind and an open heart."

It was the kind of thing I might normally find corny, but after all the time in that desert I was able to hear her. I didn't know what my intentions were at first and I stood there for a moment, the sun behind my closed eyes a radiating red, my mind blank and empty. But then I figured out what I wanted.

I want to know myself, my true self, whether it is maniac or ghost or something else.

"OK. Now go!"

And we all went with our packs, in eight directions.

Once I could no longer see anybody, I found what looked like a good spot, next to a couple creosote bushes and a dried out riverbed. I strung the rope from bush to bush, hung the tarp over it, making a tent, rolled out my sleeping bag. There. Camp made.

I didn't know what to do next. I felt like an explorer, wishing I knew edible plants so I could pick them and either poison myself or not. I figured I'd draw for a while.

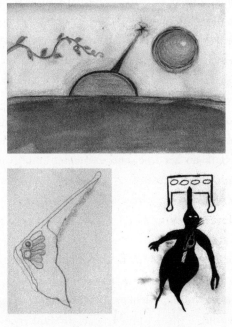

Solo drawings, April 2000.

The first part of Carly's promise about what would happen during the solo trip came true quickly—my mind would not shut up. It was like tuning into a radio at first, mostly static—bits of songs, random phrases. Then the voices, my mean self, got into the act, telling me what a piece of shit I was, how hopeless, how pathetic, how useless, how crazy. So finally I imagined all the bad thoughts were a game of Whac-A-Mole, and each time one came up it was my job to beat it back down, counter it with a positive thought. It felt corny, reminding myself I was smart and talented and not hopeless but hopeful.

At first, it felt like it wasn't working, but then it did. My brain shut up.

Near dark, I felt lonely. I pretended I was a little kid again, stuck a ball of feathery plants onto a short stick and it became a doll. I named it Jenna, the name of my best friend when I was six and we lived in Arizona. Then I thought about what I was doing. I threw the doll in the riverbed.

Carly came after dark. I didn't know what time it was because I had no clock, but I was guessing it was around nine. She was wearing a headlamp, filled up my water jugs and then gave me my medicine, her face solemn and betraying nothing.

The next day, time started to blur, the only thing to gauge it was the movement of the sun and Carly's visits. When she came at noon, there was warmth on her face, and excitement, and I felt I could read her thoughts like telepathy.

Her face: *How's it going? Are you feeling it yet?*

Mine: *Things are getting weird. I don't know if I like it.*

Hers: *But isn't it MAGIC?*

And as she left, I thought her face might actually be right.

A wind picked up, and I saw a jackrabbit, its ears big and black. It looked at me, unafraid, both of us silent, both breathing, alive and a part of the world.

I lay on my back as the stars came out, a handful multiplying into thousands. It seemed insane that they were just whirling balls of gas and dust, that in a way, we were the same, chaotic particles of matter that had somehow come together to make something that was similar to but not quite like anything else.

A LETTER FROM THE PAST

On the third day, we were supposed to write a letter to our future selves. Two years from when we left, whatever that date was, Carly would mail us the letter. I imagined the me of two years from now but the picture was fuzzy. I'd legally be an adult. When I was a child, I used to imagine myself at eighteen, looking something like Sandy at the end of *Grease*, a babe all in black. In my imagining, I was always next to an ice-blue Stingray. I don't know why that car, that color.

Now that version of an adult me seemed childish, ridiculous. Now I imagined myself mostly the same, just hopefully better at life, calmer, more sane, with longer or maybe shorter hair. I hoped that eighteen-year-old was clear-eyed and sober.

I thought a long time before I began to write. I sat there, cross-legged like a yogi, waiting for divine inspiration. The sun was setting, spreading gold across the basin, long shadows and cool air. I waited for quiet, for peace. It took a long time, but eventually I figured out what to say.

Dear Juliet,

Right now you're sixteen and very confused. You've changed so much in the last 9 months, yet you still feel so flawed. You feel selfish and bitter on the inside, and still you feel that deep sadness. Your thoughts are spacy and jumbled.

The future looks bright; you know this. There's graduating high school, getting your driver's liscence. Going home! meeting new, sober, friends. Going to college. Your life, as an artist, by the ocean. Your goals? ~~Send~~ *Leave RTS. Stay out of trouble, stay sober. Stay happy. Graduate high school and go to college. And overall, stay alive.*

— Juliet

I folded the letter in half, and then I folded it in half again. The wind picked up, pushing against my skin and hair, and I felt pieces of myself loosening to be carried along with it like dust. In that instant, I saw what was to come. The suffering. The grace. In the desert, the dots connected, the dots between me and her. Bowing my head, I gave up my spirit. It was finished.

AFTERWORD

REDWOOD TRAILS SCHOOL CLOSES DOORS
(CHARLOTTE ATKINS, *THE SISKIYOU TIMES*, MARCH 31, 2002)

Redwood Trails School, located in northern Siskiyou County, will close permanently next month due to a mounting array of legal problems, resulting from issues with licensing, regulation violations, prescription drug misuse, and a sexual abuse conviction of a staff member.

The school was termed a "therapeutic boarding school," and housed ten to twenty teens at any one time, who were being treated for various behavior issues and psychiatric disorders.

This is the second closure of a school for owner Donna Woods, a resident of Portland. In 1989, another property owned by Woods, a "wilderness therapy" boarding school located in Utah, was forced to close after the deaths of two students and a staff member in an electrical fire. It was discovered afterward that the building housing the students was not up to code in terms of fire exits and alarms.

Redwood Trails School had received a number of complaints from both town residents and parents since its opening in 1997, due to excessive discipline, numerous runaways, and uncertified staff.

Despite these issues, the school provided much-needed jobs for local residents of the nearby town of Redwood Trails, a former logging town that has been hit by hard times. Parents of former students also stated that the school "helped and healed" their troubled children.

Donna Woods was not available for comment.

A LETTER FROM THE NOW

Sometimes I will catch myself while driving, doing errands, sitting at this desk, and in those moments, I have been taken over by something. I know because I am suddenly thinner, slighter, less lined, less lived. I want to say: Farewell, homicidal teenage maniac. I want to say: May she rest in peace.

But I am still haunted by her.

ACKNOWLEDGMENTS

Thank you first and foremost to Scott McClanahan for all the love and support, and for tolerating me while I obsessed about the same things over and over.

Thank you to Monika Woods for being my fighter, advocate, and writing-related therapist. You are a true gift and I couldn't have done this without you.

Thank you to Taylor Sperry for helping me turn this book into a better version of itself, and for allowing me to keep the pictures and the wildness.

Thank you to the whole team at Melville, especially Michael Barron, Michael Seidlinger, and Sherry Virtz at PRH.

Thank you for the early reads, advice, support, and listening to me complain: Chris Oxley, Anna Prushinskaya, Elizabeth Ellen, Chelsea Martin, Elle Nash, Amanda McNeil, Bud Smith, Joseph Grantham, Megan Boyle, Mesha Maren, Randall O'Wain, Nico Walker, Katherine Faw, Carabella Sands, and Meghan Lamb.

Gigantic huge thank-yous to my wonderful parents, without whom I would likely not be alive and definitely not have written this book. I hope to write you a nice happy book someday.

And to so many other people who made this book happen. You know who you are. Thank you.

Also big ups forever to Nicorette Gum, Red Bull, and my tiny desk in the basement.

ABOUT THE AUTHOR

Juliet Escoria is a novelist, short story writer, and poet. In addition to the novel *Juliet the Maniac*, she is also also the author of the story collection *Black Cloud*, published in 2014. The collection has since been translated and published in German and Spanish editions. *Witch Hunt*, a collection of poems, was published in 2016.

Escoria was born in Australia, raised in San Diego, and currently lives in West Virginia with her husband, the writer Scott McClanahan. *Juliet the Maniac* is her first novel.

1. Juliet's voice is unrelenting, raw, and honest. How does the voice drive the narrative? Does her voice change over the course of the novel?

2. Despite the internal issues regarding the workings of Redwood Trail, do you think it genuinely aided the residents in recovery? Why? If not, do you think it helped them in other ways?

3. If you were Juliet's parents, what would you have done? Do you think she needed to be sent to an institution?

4. Discuss the effect of peer pressure on Juliet and other characters in the novel, and the harmful or helpful role(s) it played in their daily lives and in their recoveries.

5. Do you think Juliet's group of friends (especially Holly) before she left for Redwood Trail were good for her? If yes, how so?

6. How do you feel about the way the novel portrays mental illness? Were there any parts of Juliet's descriptions of her illness that particularly stood out to you?

7. Discuss Escoria's use of short chapters and images. How do you think they extend and balance the narrative?

8. Throughout Juliet's journey, was there ever a time where you weren't concerned? Was there ever a point where you thought things might be getting better?

9. What did you think of Juliet's relationship with Luke? Were you surprised that was allowed at Redwood Trail?

10. How does Juliet utilize confession and honesty: To express her grief, to deflect it, or for another purpose entirely?

11. What do you think the lambs and the garden represented at the end of the story?

12. Did the book change your perception of mental illness? If so, how?